One Warm Winter

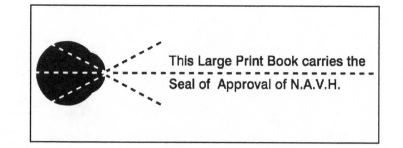

This Large Print Book carries the
Seal of Approval of N.A.V.H.

ONE WARM WINTER

JAMIE POPE

THORNDIKE PRESS
A part of Gale, a Cengage Company

Farmington Hills, Mich • San Francisco • New York • Waterville, Maine
Meriden, Conn • Mason, Ohio • Chicago

LIBRARY OF CONGRESS CIP DATA ON FILE.
CATALOGUING IN PUBLICATION FOR THIS BOOK
IS AVAILABLE FROM THE LIBRARY OF CONGRESS

ISBN-13: 978-1-4328-6635-8 (hardcover alk. paper)

Published in 2019 by arrangement with Dafina Books, an imprint of Kensington Publishing Corp.

Printed in the United States of America
1 2 3 4 5 6 7 23 22 21 20 19

To Mya and Ava —
the sweetest sisters I know.

CHAPTER 1

Wynter Bates closed the book she had been reading for the past two hours. It was about horse behavior. She had been studying horses for some time now. The types of breeds. How they thought. Where they came from. Studying them was fascinating. Of course, she was supposed to be learning how to ride horses, instead of studying them. But for the past three months the closest she got to ever riding a horse was standing beside her instructor while she brushed the horse.

Most ten-year-old girls would love it if their fathers surprised them with a beautiful thoroughbred horse. But Wynter was scared of hers. Terrified, actually. She kept imagining herself getting thrown off, slowly flying through the air, then crashing to the ground and breaking all the bones in her body. She had read about it happening to people. She knew that forty-three people had died in horse-related accidents in the past ten years. Most of them succumbing to head injuries. She did not want to be one of them.

Her mother had asked her why she always brought a book with her to lessons. Wynter didn't want to tell her that she had never once gotten on the horse after her instructor told her that everyone who rides falls. She didn't want to fall. So instead of riding, Wynter hung out at the stables. She helped feed the barn cats while she was there. Her instructor said Wynter was much more of a cat person than a horse person. The cats liked her. Especially the fat orange one. He would sit in her lap as she read, purring while she stroked his soft fur. She'd much rather have a cat than a thoroughbred horse.

But she had never told her parents that. Telling them that would have made her seem ungrateful. She wasn't ungrateful. She had a beautiful life. One that most people would dream of. One that she wouldn't have had if fate hadn't intervened.

Her parents had rescued her from an orphanage in South Africa. She was born what they called Colored during apartheid, when white and black people couldn't sit at the same table, much less create a life. So, she was given away. Born a crime, either unwanted or unable to be kept.

But her father had come along. A tech billionaire, touring the orphanage before he donated to it. The story was he took one look at Wynter and fell in love. She reminded him of a sister who he had lost when he was a boy. So, he adopted her.

He had taken her out of poverty, raised her with everything. She couldn't be ungrateful. Her mother told her that daily. She told her that she was lucky. Lucky to have dance lessons, French lessons, cello lessons, painting lessons, and community-service projects on Saturdays.

Her mother and father had both grown up poor. They had gotten none of that and because of that, they expected her to be a good girl.

Her father planned to run the country someday. He wanted to be the president.

He needed connections for that. He traveled all the time. Last week he was in Japan. Before that, he was in the United Arab Emirates. She had never heard of that place. But when her mother told her that's where her father was, Wynter looked it up in her book of maps.

Her mother had given it to her for her birthday. It was the best present she had ever received. It had a brown leather cover with a compass rose burned into it. The pages were gold-trimmed and on each of them was a map of a different part of the world.

Her mother had thought her odd for loving the present so much. So much more than the horse or the playhouse, or the beautiful clothes she got to wear. She loved the gift because her mother had thought about her before she ordered it. Thought about what she had liked. She had listened to her.

She claimed she bought it because she didn't want Wynter asking her any more questions about where places were. But Wynter knew better.

With the book of maps, her mother was telling her that she understood her.

That she understood that Wynter felt restless, like she didn't fit in, like she didn't belong anywhere.

They never spoke to her about her adoption. Never wanted to speak her about her culture or her homeland. She was told that she was their child now and there was no need to discuss anything else.

But she had wanted to go back to South Africa and visit, to learn more about herself and the place she had come from, but her parents — especially her father — had always brushed her off and she wasn't sure why.

She walked out of the stable toward the parking lot, where her driver was waiting. It was just about time to head to her music lessons. From there, she would go home and eat dinner with her mother. Her father was gone again. He was in New York this time. Not as far away, but still not close enough.

Wynter's eyes went to an old black car that she usually didn't see in the parking lot. The stable didn't get many visitors. At least not when she was there. A blond woman got out of the car. Her eyes focused on Wynter, causing her to stop for a second. The woman seemed to recognize her. Her face lit up. Wynter turned and looked behind her, because surely the woman couldn't be looking at her.

But when she turned back around, she saw the woman running toward her, and as she got closer, Wynter could see the look in her eyes was not right. They were huge and blue and filled with something that Wynter couldn't describe, but that something made her heart start to pound. Her feet stopped working. She knew she should move, but her brain was too slow to give that message to her body.

She tried to turn away, but the woman had grabbed her and wrapped her in a too-tight hug. Wynter was terrified, but the woman's smell struck her. Soft like sugar. There was something else there too. Some type of flower she couldn't identify.

"I've found you!" The woman kissed her

11

cheeks. "I've missed you so much, baby. They wouldn't let me see you."

"I — I —" Wynter's voice stopped working momentarily. "I don't know you."

"They took you away so I couldn't see you, but I knew I would find you." She grabbed Wynter's hand. "Come with me, baby. You'll never be without me again."

She tried to back away from the woman. "I don't want to go with you. I don't know you," Wynter managed to get out even though her fear was beginning to overwhelm her.

Her mother had warned her about this. She told her that her father was a very important man, that some people didn't like him. That they didn't want him to succeed. He had to travel with armed security. Men in black suits who barely said a word.

"You'll love your new home," the woman said. "I'll make it fun. You'll never want to leave." She tugged Wynter into motion. Wynter knew she couldn't allow herself to be taken someplace else. Her parents might never find her again.

"No!" she screamed. Wynter tried to break free of the woman, but her hold was too strong.

The woman looked hurt. "Are you mad at me? They kept me from you! I wanted you. I wanted you! Your father did this. It's not fair. I loved you so much."

"Hey! Get the hell away from her." Her driver came running out of the front office of the stable. He called over his shoulder for help as he ran toward Wyn. He scooped Wyn into his arms and shoved the woman away.

Wynter watched the woman fall to the ground as the staff from the stable started to appear. They converged on her, pinning her to the ground. She screamed out, but it wasn't in pain. It was hurt. It was a noise she didn't ever think she would forget.

There was something that wasn't right with the woman. She looked so wounded. Tears were streaming down her face.

"My baby," she sobbed. "Why won't he let me be with my baby?"

It was the last thing Wynter had heard before her driver had taken her away.

"Are you ready to go, ma'am?"

Wynter looked up at her bodyguard as he stood beside the counter. She hadn't heard him come in. She hadn't even sensed his presence. She wasn't sure if that was a good thing or a bad thing. She was at her kitchen table, so engrossed in a Russian document she was interpreting for the State Department.

She was a linguist by trade — a polyglot,

thanks to her years of private language lessons and a professor at a local university. In her free time she translated for the D.C. court system, but interpreting documents from foreign nations was the job she found most fascinating.

"Is it time already?"

"Yes, ma'am," her bodyguard, Cullen, responded in his soft Irish accent. He was dressed in all black: black turtleneck, black blazer, black pants, and black leather shoes. He looked deadly, like a trained assassin.

She wasn't sure if he was. She only knew that he had worked in British intelligence before he had come to work for her. Sometimes she wanted to ask him about his life before he came to her a year ago, but she didn't. She couldn't bring herself to.

The definition of the strong, silent type, Cullen never said more than he had to say. He was by far the quietest of her protectors and even though he had been with her for almost a year, she knew nothing about him.

"Your class starts in forty minutes."

She glanced at the clock, realizing that she had been sitting at her table for over an hour. Her toast had grown rubbery. Her tea was probably frigid; a slight film had formed on the surface. She had been so lost in what she was doing that she hadn't taken a single bite or sip.

Cullen seemed to know her well. Her travel mug had been removed from the cabinet, the string of a tea bag hanging over the rim. Her trench coat was in his hands.

"I would have been late if you weren't here." She stood up and tried to take her coat from him, but he wouldn't allow it. He held it out for her, helping her put it on. It was unnecessary, but she let him do this for her.

He must get so bored protecting her. She didn't lead a dangerous life. The only excitement she got was when she received a new book in the mail. But she still needed a guard, according to her father. One mentally ill woman tried to kidnap her when she was ten and she hadn't been allowed to be without protection ever since.

Cullen's hand briefly rested on her shoulder. It was warm and heavy. She often felt it on her back throughout the day as he was guiding her from place to place. He was close to her. She could smell his clean scent, feel his breath in her hair. She turned to face him, forcing herself to look him in the eye.

Her father had drilled in her that it was important to look people in the eye when you spoke to them. He said that it showed people you were honest. That you had nothing to hide. But still, she had a very hard time making eye contact with him. His eyes were very blue, almost piercing. It was like they could see through her. It unnerved her, along with the fact that she felt his eyes on her every day, all day. She would be teaching, going on about syntax or something else, when she would feel his eyes on her and she would look up. He would be sitting there, always in the back of the lecture hall, his gaze on her. Whenever she looked up, no matter when or how many times she did, he would be watching her.

He wasn't like her other bodyguards who were much more relaxed. They'd be on their phones or reading the newspaper. Their eyes wouldn't be glued to her in a way that would make her lose her train of thought. He took his job very seriously. He was a very serious man, one who she had never seen smile. It made her wonder about him.

It made her think about him more than she thought about any of the men her father had hired to protect her.

"Thank you, Cullen."

He frowned at her. "It's quite cold outside today. Would you like to get your heavier coat?"

"I'm just getting in and out of the car. I

have a light day planned. Class and then home. You'll get to leave early today."

He shook his head *no*. He never left early. And even when he went home, he was never far away. He lived in an apartment across the street. Far enough to give her privacy, but close enough not to give her space.

"One day you should surprise me and call out sick."

He shook his head. "Can I drive you today?"

"You won't take a sick day and I won't let you drive me. I don't want you to judge my taste in music."

"It's not my place to judge anything you do, ma'am," he said quietly.

"At least not aloud," she joked, but he didn't smile.

"We're going to be late."

She nodded, grabbed her keys, and headed to her car, which he had started for her.

He had made her uncomfortable, but he always did things for her with her comfort in mind. She wouldn't allow him to drive her because she needed this time away from him, to collect her thoughts to be relaxed before she had to put on her mask and be serious the entire day.

He followed closely behind in his own nondescript black sedan. There were times she thought about asking her father to get rid of Cullen, to hire a move jovial guard, but she could never make herself do so.

He did his job well. Her father hired the best and with his upcoming presidential run, she knew that he would demand top-of-the-line protection for her. That soon she would be rolled out on campaign-trail stops and featured in commercials.

The thought of it exhausted her. But as long as she could remember, her father had wanted to be president.

She turned up the radio and sang along to some pop song that had been dominating the top-40 stations this past month. Most people thought her so serious, mistaking her for someone who enjoyed classical or opera, because she had spent her youth taking lesson after lesson. But pop music was her guilty pleasure. Her music downloads were an eclectic mix of boy bands, pop princesses, and soul music. She couldn't sing to save her life, but she enjoyed belting out inane lyrics in her car on her way to work.

She wasn't joking when she told Cullen she didn't want him to judge her. He told her it wasn't his place to. But how could he not? She wondered what he thought of her. Was there any part of his job he enjoyed or was it just a paycheck for him?

But she knew the answer to that already. It was always just a paycheck. Her parents had hired many people to work with her over the years: housekeeper, nannies, tutors. Some of them she liked very much. Some of them she had even loved, but when they were no longer on her father's payroll the relationships ended.

The song had ended, a news report breaking through. She was about to change the station when she heard her father's name.

"Tech billionaire and future presidential candidate, Warren Bates, is embroiled in an explosive scandal. Letters have been leaked detailing a torrid affair with a mistress, accusing him of holding her captive and the mysterious disappearance of a love child, a girl who possibly died. That leads us to a thousand questions, including if his adoptive daughter, Wynter Bates, is actually his biological child. The handwritten letters aren't dated, but experts say they look legit. A couple are circulating around the internet right now, but our sources say there are dozens of them, all written by his cleaning-lady-turned-lover."

Wyn stopped listening as the story continued to go on. She blindly pulled her car over into the nearest spot. Her heart was pounding too hard, her head felt too clogged with information. She knew that this wasn't going to be something that dominated the news cycle for just one day.

For some reason, denial didn't come to mind. She couldn't be the one to say her father would never cheat on her mother. Of course, he could have. He was gone all the time. And while her parents cared deeply for each other, the union was more of a partnership than a relationship.

Her mother was the woman behind the man, the person always at his side, helping him to build his empire, cultivating their image as the perfect American family with humble beginnings.

Did she have any idea that their carefully crafted image was crumbling?

Wyn was still in her neighborhood, not far from her town house, but going home didn't seem to be the right thing either. She felt too choked to be inside, so she stepped out of her car and headed toward the park that she often walked in during the summer. It wasn't the summer right now.

Heavy winds ripped through her trench coat, but she didn't care. The wind burned her eyes, but it didn't matter because she couldn't see, anyway. She was blinded by the news. Her body was moving by instinct alone. She had walked the trails of this park so many times, she could find her way in her sleep. But there was a flash from a photographer. A shouted question. She froze in her tracks as the swarm grew. People were running toward her. How the hell did this happen so quickly?

Her chest grew tighter and she thought she was going to have a panic attack. She lived such a quiet life. She liked her peace, her solitude, after a lifetime of being over-scheduled.

She turned in an effort to escape them, the vultures who were screaming questions about a story that she desperately didn't want to be true.

She felt a large arm wrap around her, leading her in a different direction. "I've got you, ma'am."

It was Cullen, his scent familiar, his accented voice calming. She could barely see; The flash from the photographers and the wind was burning her eyes, so she allowed him to lead her. It was just a little while ago that she'd thought how uncomfortable his presence made her.

But he was there when she needed him; silent, unsmiling. Exactly what he was supposed to be.

He must have had a fit when she made

the unexpected detour. But she didn't care about how angry he would be that she broke protocol. She just wanted to get back home. She trusted him to get her there.

And soon they were there. She fished her keys out of her bag, her hand shaking so much that she couldn't open the door. Cullen placed his hand over hers and took the keys and opened the door to let them inside.

"Stupid arseholes," Cullen whispered.

Wyn paused and looked at him. She rarely heard him speak, much less curse. His accent seemed to have thickened when he did.

She had never seen him anything but calm, but right now he was seething as he glanced out of the window at the hordes of photographers waiting in front of her town house.

"I don't want to stay here," she managed to croak out. She still felt choked, like all the air had been sucked out of her body. "Not with them all out there."

"You *can't* stay here." He turned away from the window, removing his sunglasses as he did and faced her.

There was a scowl on his face. He was tall, muscular, but lean. His dark hair was cut ruthlessly short. He looked so damn dangerous in that moment. She knew he had been Special Forces. She knew that he had been shot multiple times fighting in Afghanistan and for a moment she wondered what he had looked like then, in his slightly younger days, all dressed in his uniform.

It was an odd thought for the moment.

She was focusing on him, him who she had seen hundreds of times. But it was taking her mind off the information she had just learned.

She knew it was true and that's what was bothering her at the moment. How could she, with no confirmation, believe such a thing about her father?

He was very good to her. She knew without a doubt that he loved her, but she believed the tale of the affair. What did that say about her feelings about her father?

"Sit down," he ordered as walked toward her. "You're trembling like a leaf." He shook his head. "Arseholes," he said to himself again. "The story must have broken overnight. It's the only way they could have found you so quickly."

"I need to call my mother." Her mother never had a bad thing to say about her father, even though he spent most of their marriage traveling the world in the search of more prestige, more power.

But now Wyn wondered if that were true. Maybe when he was gone he was in the beds of other women.

"Sit down first." He stripped off his gloves and led her to the couch, his hand on her back again. She felt the warmth permeate her coat. It was then she realized that she was frozen, so stiff she felt as if her limbs would crumble and blow away. "You can't go marching through the park like that. You don't want me to drive you, then you can't make any sudden moves like that. You could have frozen to death. Someone could have snatched you. You need to be careful." He softened his tone. "I'm sorry, ma'am. I didn't realize the media was trailing us until we were halfway down the street. I couldn't stop them."

"I didn't realize you could speak so much."

He frowned at her, his annoyance showing. She had never seen him annoyed before. Or happy or sad or anything in between.

It was refreshing and it had only taken a major scandal to reveal it.

Cullen Whelan had taken this assignment against his better judgment. The last thing he had wanted to do was protect some rich man's daughter. But he figured the job would be easier than his last assignment. There wouldn't be multiple attempts to end her life, as was the case of his last principal. No cars rigged with explosives. No snipers hiding in buildings hundreds of feet away.

Protecting a quiet woman with a peaceful life wouldn't leave him feeling like he had blood on his hands.

Wynter's father had been the bigger target. Billionaire-turned-politician. He wondered where the man was now. Probably tucked away in some secret place while his daughter was swarmed with reporters.

It wasn't his job to pass judgment on the people who employed him, but this arsehole had the nerve to announce his run for public office when he knew he had this skeleton in his closet. Cullen didn't know exactly what the scandal was, but he knew by the shouted questions from the reporters that another woman was involved. Not just an affair, but something much deeper. He'd never forget the look on Wynter's face as the reporters swarmed her. It was the first time he had seen any cracks in her serene mask.

He had been protecting her for nearly a year now. She was different from what he had expected. She was no party-girl heiress. There was no stumbling out of nightclubs.

No rubbing shoulders with celebrities. In fact, she rarely left the house unless it was out of necessity. Work consumed her, just as it had this morning when he walked in. She hadn't heard him enter. She hadn't noticed his presence with her in the kitchen, even though he was there for nearly fifteen minutes.

She was fascinated by whatever document she was reading, her forehead scrunched as she wrote furiously on a pad of paper. It wasn't the first time he had been in the room with her without her noticing. He wondered if it was due to the fact she had spent her entire life being guarded by someone. She must be used to large men in black hovering over her shoulder. It must be easier to block their presence out.

He would hate a life like that. There wasn't much freedom in it.

She could have spent her life on vacation. Traveling the world. Never working. But she volunteered in jails, community centers, and courthouses. She translated during interrogations. She taught English as a Second Language courses in the summer when her college classes were over. She worked with prisoners and poor people, without fear. She didn't treat them like she was better than them, even though anyone who looked at her could see she was.

There wasn't much excitement in his job, but it was one of the ones he took the most pride in after having served his country.

She was a good person. That was all. And he liked that, for once, he got to keep someone safe who was completely innocent.

"Sit down," he told her again. This time he physically moved her toward the couch. Her body felt frozen. He had almost had an aneurysm when she parked her car and headed toward the park. She was wearing a thin coat. Only good for getting in and out of warm cars. Not for mind-clearing walks on frigid days.

He hadn't noticed the news vans at first. They had been parked further down the street, but in D.C., where a scandal a week happens, he wasn't surprised to see them. He just never thought that she would be their target.

"You're frozen."

He removed her coat, before he gently pushed her down on the couch and dropped a throw blanket over her. He turned on her gas fireplace before heading to the kitchen to start a kettle and he cursed himself. He had gotten too comfortable, so used to her routine that he had become complacent. He had never thought she would take off on him, but then again, how could he blame her? She must have had the shock of her life.

He discreetly followed her in his car because she had wanted more freedom and he had never thought she would be in danger going to and from work, but now that was all going to change. He wouldn't be able to let her out of his sight until whatever just exploded had blown over.

He looked outside of her kitchen window to see the reporters back there too. They were on private property. They knew better. But the story must be too big, too juicy for them to care about something as minor as the law.

He swore again.

"Your accent gets thicker when you curse." He turned to see her standing in the doorway. Her voice was quiet and controlled, just like it had been every other time he had heard her speak, but he could tell she was still shell-shocked. Despite her professional clothing and sensible black heels, she looked much younger than her twenty-eight years. "They're in the back of the house, aren't they?"

He nodded.

Even though she was ruffled, she looked like a modern-day princess. She carried herself like one too. With grace. Her hair was long, jet-black and bone-straight. Most days she kept it tucked behind her ears or neatly pinned back. Today the wind had blown it, giving it a wild quality that softened her.

Her clothes were clearly well-made and her style classic American. No ostentatious brands. Nothing flashy. She wore a cream-colored sweater that looked like it was made to go with her brown skin.

She didn't wear much makeup, just a light touch, so as not to cover up, but to enhance. She was beautiful. Unobjectively beautiful, but in all the time he had been with her, he had never seen her with a man. There were no dates she had gone on. No men who called at her house. He had never known her to go anywhere. She was a private person, but when she came home at night she stayed there. He lived just across the street in a tiny apartment provided to him by her father. His job wasn't around the clock, but he kept an eye on her anyway. Her father might be dirty, but his daughter was the most important gift to him. And he paid Cullen a hell of a lot to keep her safe.

"I'm surprised they haven't started digging through the garbage."

"They will."

"All they'll find is takeout containers and tea bags."

"I know, ma'am."

"I'm incredibly boring."

Her serenity had slipped. He could see her trying to keep it there, but he could feel a change come over her. He had been with her for a year. He studied her closely. Sometimes he felt as if he knew her mannerisms better than he knew those of his closest friends.

She looked lost. Her eyes were wider than normal. Her body trembled slightly. There was an edge to her. It wasn't what he was used to from her, but he was glad to see she was having a reaction, because it seemed impossibly hard to go through life always being so perfect.

"You aren't going to ask me why they're here?"

"No, ma'am."

The kettle went off. Cullen turned around and fixed her a large mug. "Are we back to two-word answers? You know I study linguistics for a living and it drives me crazy that I spend most of my time with a man who barely speaks. I thought the only good part of this whole thing was being able to hear you speak more."

He wanted to ask her if hearing him talk

would give her any more insight into who she thought he was. But he didn't. It wasn't his place to ask.

"I don't get paid to chat, ma'am." He handed her the mug and motioned for her to sit.

"I know. I'm being ridiculous right now." She slid into the chair and looked up at him. "I apologize for how I spoke to you earlier. I was rude."

He almost laughed. She thought she had been rude.

"Did I say something amusing? I must be hallucinating, because I think you nearly smiled."

He shook his head. "You've had the shock of your life and yet you're apologizing to me. You don't have to apologize to me. I work for you."

"You work for my father, but even if you worked for me that doesn't mean I have the right to be rude to you."

He sat in the chair across from her. She had never been rude to him. She never ordered him about. It was within her rights to do so. But she had always been unfailingly polite; kind, even. It wasn't what he was used to.

His last principal, an arms dealer, lived like a spoiled king and treated the world like his servant. Screaming, cursing, ranting. Cullen hadn't been surprised that multiple people were trying to kill him. The only reason most of his staff had stayed on was because of the high pay. Cullen had planned to retire early after a few years with this man, but his death had brought him to Wynter and retirement no longer was at the forefront of his mind all the time. She was that easy.

"Drink your tea, ma'am."

"Please, don't call me *ma'am*. I hate it. Call me anything but that."

"Is *lass* better?"

"I quite like that. Do Irish people really say that?"

"Not as much as Americans think."

"The tea is very good. Did you put an entire cup of sugar or just a half?" She gave him a wobbly smile and he knew she was about to break. Her eyes were too bright and Cullen felt deep discomfort, which he wasn't used to.

"What are your plans, ma—"

"Wyn. Call me Wyn or *lass*. Just not *ma'am*." She shut her eyes for a moment. "I'm trying to focus on anything else, so I don't have to think about what just happened. Like if I ignore it, it will go away."

He knew how to whisk her away from a

horde of reporters, how to protect her from assassins, to keep her safe in a world that could be very dangerous, but he didn't know how to deal with emotions. He had never been trained to do that.

"You said you wanted to call your mum." He took out his phone and handed it to her. "I don't think you should be using your own phone right now. Just as a precaution."

She put her mug down and took the phone from his hand. Her fingers brushed his and he couldn't help but notice how icy they still were. Her hand trembled as she attempted to dial.

He took the phone from her. He knew her mother's number. He dialed for her and handed the phone back. The discomfort was growing stronger. He didn't like to see her in pain, knowing there was nothing he could do about it.

He had been in war zones. He had seen people's heads blown off in front of his face, but this woman was making him want to break out of this room.

"I'll leave you to your phone call." He started to get up and walk away, but she grabbed his wrist. Her icy fingers holding on to him.

"Stay," she whispered. The tremble in her voice made him freeze in his tracks. She didn't want to be alone right then. It wasn't a feeling he had often, but he understood it.

He nodded, but she didn't let go of him right away. She put the phone on speaker and waited while it rang. He could feel her anxiety. He could almost see her heart racing.

"Mother?"

"Oh, Wynter. You have to leave Washington. As soon as you can. They will not stop bothering you." The panic was evident in Mrs. Bates's breathless voice.

"Why would they be bothering me? I don't know anything."

"They are going to keep digging for answers until everything is revealed."

"But, Mother . . . Are you saying that there's truth to the reports? The letters are real?"

"I —" Her mother's voice broke. "I love you very much. I loved you from the moment I saw you."

Wynter shook her head, her bewilderment clear. "What are you saying?"

"I'll be going overseas this afternoon. I'm not sure when I'll be back or if I'll be back."

"What do you mean, *If you'll be back?* Where are you going?" Wyn's eyes filled with tears. "It can't be that bad. I'll come with you."

"No. You cannot. If the FBI comes to speak to you, tell them you know nothing."

"But I *don't* know anything. Why would the FBI be involved? Tell me what's going on!"

"Only your father can do that. It's not my story to tell. I love you, princess." The phone went dead and Wynter looked up at him, pure devastation mixed with confusion crossing her face.

She opened her mouth, but no words escaped. He felt as frozen as she was in that moment. He had never seen her this way and right now he'd rather be with the bloated blowhard who didn't know his name than the devastated woman before him. He knew how to deal with assholes. He couldn't begin to think of what to do with a hurt woman.

"She not denying it. She's not defending it." She shook her head. "I didn't want to believe it, but when I heard it on the radio this morning, I didn't disbelieve it. But I wanted her to say it wasn't true."

"I'm sorry." He didn't know what else to say to her, but he wasn't surprised. He had been around his share of rich men, the power seekers. Bates was the worst kind: sanctimonious, preaching to others about values and wanting to change the world for the better when he couldn't lead by example. It was almost disgusting.

She blinked up at him, looking almost childlike in that moment. "I don't know what to do now, Cullen."

He got this odd feeling deep in the pit of his stomach.

Both of her parents were fleeing the country, not offering a lifeline to their daughter. Not giving her even the simplest explanation, only confirming her worst fears. But the rawest part of it was that they left her alone.

There was no united-we-stand mentality in her family. There hadn't been one in his either, and it proved to him that sometimes the family you make as an adult is much more reliable than the one you were forced to have as a child.

"Wyn . . ." He said her name for the first time, realizing how odd it felt forming on his lips. She was looking to him for answers. Of course, she was. He was hired to take care of her, to protect her. He couldn't allow her to continue here, not feeling safe. "Go pack. I'm going to take you away from here."

CHAPTER 2

Wyn didn't know where they were going. She just did what he said and had gone to her room to pack, but as she stood in front of her closet, she once again felt at a loss.

She was running away from home. It felt so wrong to flee, especially when she didn't do anything wrong. In fact, it went against everything she stood for.

"You have to do it." She heard Cullen's voice from behind her.

"Get out of my head, Mr. Whelan," she responded without turning around.

"The reporters are still surrounding the house. I called the police and asked them to post a car in front. I've also asked them to arrest anyone they find around the back of the town house. They're trespassing."

"My neighbors must be loving me now."

"Don't worry about them."

"I'd rather worry about them than think about myself. Thinking about oneself for extended periods of time is exhausting."

"Then let me do the thinking about you."

That caused her to turn around to face him. It was something in the way he said those words that made her want to look at him. But there was no change to his face, no expression at all.

"What should I bring?"

"Light clothes. Nothing fancy. You'll need to blend in."

"So, don't bring my ball gown? Damn, I was hoping there would be a gala of the fugitives."

"You're funny when you're stressed."

"Funny? Is that a nice way of telling me that I'm being obnoxious?"

"I don't mince words, ma'am. I would never imply that you were obnoxious. You're handling this well."

"I don't know how else to respond."

"Pack. Then rest. I'll be downstairs making arrangements."

She had tried to rest all through that day, but she couldn't. Her mind was too wired. There was no escaping the news story that now had become part of her life. She had tried to call her father from her secured landline, the one her father had set up for her about a year ago, right before Cullen had come.

She wondered if her father had any idea then that this would be blowing up. She wanted to ask him, but her phone calls went unanswered. And the longer the silence from her father, the more her head spun.

There was nothing to take her mind off things. She tried to turn on the television, but that proved to be a huge mistake. She was bombarded by the story, by her father's image, by their family's. And then she saw the pictures of herself pop up on the television. She had lived such a private life that there weren't many. Her government ID photo, the pictures the photographers had snapped today, the one of the family holiday card that was sent out when she was still in college. But they had somehow managed to find pictures of her as a child. It had to have been nearly impossible, because her parents had kept her so sheltered, so busy with lessons, so hidden from the world.

There was one of her around twelve, posing with a trophy at some sort of academic competition she had won. But there was another photo, the one that made her pause the television screen and stare at it. It was of her when she was a baby, in her mother's arms. Her mother was smiling down at her, not one of those forced smiles you give in pictures, but a happy, unguarded smile. It was a photo Wynter had never seen before.

How the hell did the media get it?

She felt so violated. So raw. So gut-punched.

The media was comparing those pictures of her to ones of her father, searching for similarities in their faces. There weren't many. There never were. One of the things she used to lament as an adopted child was that she never looked like either of her parents.

She could believe that her father had an affair. She could believe that he had created a child as a product of that affair, but she couldn't wrap her head around that child being her. That he could take her from her birth mother. The reports stated that the child had mysteriously disappeared, that people were speculating that if it wasn't Wynter, the child might be dead.

Wynter's mind flashed back to that day at the stables. The pretty blond lady who ran up to her and grabbed her, trying to take her away. The woman who seemed so crushed when she was torn away from her.

Cullen walked into the room and grabbed the remote, pulling her out of her self-reflective tailspin. "No news, Wyn," he said softly. He turned the television to her Netflix account and put on some dumb comedy.

40

She obeyed him and remained there, watching movies that she couldn't remember the plot to, unable to focus on anything but the events of that day.

She never slept, even when darkness came and the reporters started to drift away, tired of waiting in the extreme cold waiting for her to appear. She knew they would be back. In the morning they would come refreshed and ready to stalk her.

But they wouldn't get their chance. Cullen came to collect her just past midnight. He had taken her to a small private airport, where there was a plane waiting.

It wasn't her father's private jet. She didn't know whose plane they took or how it was paid for, but Cullen seemed to know the pilot. He too had an Irish accent.

There was more warmth in their greeting than she had ever seen from Cullen. It made her wonder about him again, about his life outside of this job.

He was with her most of the time. She didn't know what he did when he left her for the night. If he explored D.C. or dated, or hung out with his friends and complained about his job like most people did.

She hoped he did. She hoped his life contained more than just her. It would be a truly boring life if it didn't.

She had thought that there had been no joy in him before, no personality. Out of all the guards she had had over her lifetime, she had known the least about him. Nothing about his home or family. There was no small talk between them. But today she saw a little more of who he was than he had ever revealed to her before. She learned things about him that she would keep stored away.

His accent thickened when he was angry. His hands were always warm. He liked his tea sweet.

He knew people. He had connections.

She was allowing him to whisk her off to some unknown destination. She shouldn't say *allow*. She had no other choice. She trusted him, not knowing why. Maybe it was because the bottom had dropped out of her world. Maybe it was because she could trust no one else. She had no close friends to confide in. No lover to run to. Not even her parents, who supposedly had loved her the most, would tell her the truth.

She found it ironic. She had lived her life doing exactly what her parents asked, being the good girl, never letting a whisper of scandal sully her name and in the end, it didn't matter. Her actions had nothing to do with her father's.

"This is a very nice plane, Cullen," she

said to him as she sat down.

"Aye. It is."

His back was to her as he placed their bags in the small overhead compartment. "Is it yours?"

"No, ma'am. I don't own a plane."

"That was my attempt at a bad joke. If you owned a plane like this, you wouldn't be spending your days bored out of your mind and looking after me. Hopefully, you would be someplace beautiful, surrounded by gorgeous people."

He turned around and looked at her. "Looking after you is no hardship, ma'am. I do not find it boring. D.C. is a beautiful city and you are by far the most beautiful person I have worked for."

She didn't know what to say to that. Heat started to creep up her neck. His compliment was so lavish and unexpected she didn't know how to handle it. "What did I tell you about calling me *ma'am*?"

"Sorry." He nodded.

Her phone vibrated, alerting her to a text message. She pulled it out of the pocket of her oversized sweater and glanced at the screen. It was from her father.

Cullen was suddenly beside her, his warm hand on her shoulder, the heat seeping through her seemingly permanently chilled body. "You look like you've seen a ghost."

"A message from my father. He says to do whatever you tell me."

"Anything else?"

"That he loves me."

She felt so damn hollow. That was it? She had called him half a dozen times and that was it. No explanation. No denial. Just do what Cullen says.

It made her so damn angry. How the hell could he control her life like this?

She had always done what he said, lived her life as quietly as he wished. For what?

She was an heiress, but she sure as hell didn't need his money. Her document-translating work alone paid for her town house. Her skills were valuable enough to get her work anywhere she went. She wasn't afraid of being cut off.

She had listened to him because he was her father and she loved him.

And all he could do was send her a text message. Not even a call.

He hadn't even attempted to lie.

"I want to get off this plane," she told Cullen.

"Why?"

"Because you told me to get on this plane and he told me to listen to whatever you say and right now I don't feel like being bossed

44

around by any man."

"I work for you. I would never order you about," he said, his voice low, his accent soothing her raw nerves. "You can get off this plane, but what then? They'll not leave you alone, Wyn. Your parents are out of the country. They only have you to go after. You'll not find peace in your own home. I believe that is one of the worst things a person can feel."

She felt choked then, her anger and frustration bubbling up inside of her, threatening to boil over and spill out, but then Cullen's warm hand slid up to her cheek. The backs of his fingers pressing into her skin.

"It's your choice, but I think we should leave D.C."

She was quiet for a moment, but then she nodded. It was all she could manage then.

"Try to get some sleep." He turned away, removing his hand from her skin, taking his warmth away in the process. He pulled a large chenille blanket out of one of the bags he brought with him and draped it over her.

More emotion bubbled up inside her. He looked like such a hard man, but he could be so incredibly gentle.

"This is my favorite blanket."

"I know. I thought you might want something from home, since you won't be back for a while."

"How did you know it was my favorite?"

"It's my job to know about you."

"And yet I know nothing about you."

"There is nothing to know."

"I don't believe that's true. Everyone has a story."

"Maybe I'll tell you over some good, strong ale one day."

"I would like that." She wanted to keep him talking. She liked his quiet voice. His accent. His strong presence. It was the only thing keeping her from crumbling at this point. But she couldn't think of another thing to say.

"I have some tea for you." He produced a thermos from the overhead compartment. "Drink it all and get some rest. We'll speak when we land."

She obeyed him and took a few sips of the tea. It was sweet, milky, and hot, but it didn't taste like the blend she was used to. She was just about to ask him what it was when her head felt heavy. Her body was sluggish, but warm. Her eyes started to droop and the last thing she remembered before she drifted off to sleep was his warm hand on her cheek and the words "Good night, lass," gently touching her ears.

She woke up when she felt the warmth of the sun hit her face through the small plane windows. Cullen was sitting across from her. He was slightly slouched in his seat. His legs spread wide. His short hair was mussed, as if he had been running his fingers through it.

She had never seen him so relaxed.

Or so sexy . . .

He must have felt her eyes on him, because he sat up straight, snapping to attention, his usual stonelike expression falling back into place.

His hair was still messy, a reminder of how he appeared in his unguarded moments. She would never forget that. He was suddenly more human to her.

"We're almost there. You're going to want to lose the coat when we de-board. It's eighty-one degrees where we're going."

"Where are we going?" She could see the ocean below them and she could already tell it wasn't the icy waters of the East Coast that she was used to. The water was clearer, and in the distance she could see palm trees.

"The US Virgin Islands. St. Thomas, to be exact."

"Oh." She sat up a little straighter. All of this seemed so surreal to her. "Why here?"

"You'll be safer here than anywhere else,

but we need to keep your identity a secret."

"You just said I would be safe."

"They won't betray you, but if they know who you really are, they'll feel like I betrayed them. I'm taking you to my people. My home."

She sat up straight. "Your family?"

"My family is pig-shit Northern Irish from Belfast. I wouldn't take my enemy there."

His accent had grown so thick then, she almost had a hard time understanding him. His family was a sore subject, apparently. One she could relate to. "Then who are your people?"

"We're all former military, black ops, Special Forces, CIA. Most of us have been in the intelligence field at some point in our careers. We own a large compound in the middle of the island. Half of it we rent out to tourists, but the other half is our home. It's a community. We each have our own cottages, but we take our meals together. We spend time together. We work together."

It sounded like a beautiful sentiment, but Wyn automatically felt uneasy. "So, what you are saying is that you are taking me to a compound filled with former spies?"

"Yes."

"And we are hiding my identity from them?"

"Yes. We made a pact to leave the world outside when we are there. No cable. No internet in the cottages. No talk of current events. Everyone there has had a hard existence. They only want peace. They'll go after anything that threatens that."

"Knowing that I'm probably the scandalous secret stolen love child of a presidential candidate won't do me any favors with them, huh?"

"No. They are fiercely protective of their privacy."

"I'll be an outsider no matter what my backstory is. Are you sure that they will be okay with that?"

"We're all outsiders. That's why we've come here. You'll be with me. They won't question why I brought you there."

"Who am I supposed to be to you?"

He was quiet for a moment. "You'll have to pretend to be my girlfriend."

"Your girlfriend?"

"Yes. I think this is the only way they won't question me bringing you here."

"Are we serious?"

"I think being as truthful as possible will work best for us. If they ask, you can say that we've known each other for a year. That very recently things have changed between us. Don't lie about your job or family, just don't reveal too much about them."

"You were a spy, weren't you? You create cover stories and all."

He nodded. "You'll have your own room in my house. I'll continue to respect you, but in front of them, we need to seem like we are a couple."

Wyn let that news sink in for a moment.

"I need to pretend to love you," she said.

"Can a person pretend to love?"

"Yes. It happens all the time. That's why people are blindsided by breakups."

"I wouldn't know. I'm not asking you to pretend like you're head-over-ass in love with me. I think it would be impossible for anyone to do."

"Why? Hasn't anyone ever been in love with you?"

"No."

"How do you know that for sure?"

"I never gave anyone the chance to." His answer was so matter-of-fact, she had no choice but to believe him.

"That's sad."

"It's sensible. I had the kind of career that doesn't allow for personal relationships. I took very dangerous assignments. I do private, round-the-clock security. There's no time for anyone else."

"Don't blame me for your lack of love life.

I was hoping you lived after you left me every night."

"You are supposed to be my number-one priority. You *are* my number-one priority. That's what I agreed to when I took on this job." He was so intense. She never felt like she was anyone's number-one priority. She never thought she would ever be and yet he was looking her in the eye and telling her she was. She knew she was his job, but still, his words did something to her.

"I would have quit if I were you."

"Why? It's the first time in my career I have gone a year without someone trying to kill me."

"Are you serious?"

There was no smile, no hint of humor on his face. "Yes."

"I'm like a paid vacation."

"Yes."

"Your friends are going to have to buy us as a couple. You wouldn't just bring a woman here you were casual with."

"No. It's one of our rules."

"I'm nervous," she admitted.

"I understand." He nodded. "Just don't mention too much about your posh up-bringing."

"So, don't mention my thoroughbred horse or the hundred-thousand-dollar shopping sprees I regularly partake in?" She shook her head. "You see where I work when I'm not teaching or with the government. You know I'm not a snob."

"No, ma'am. I didn't mean to imply that. It's just that most of us weren't raised — we were dragged up. They'll not understand the kind of privilege you've had."

"Or the loneliness it brings," she said quietly, not intending to be so honest. "You have people you can return to when you need them. Right now, it seems as if I just have you to depend on. And I'm sure you're only doing this because of how much my father is paying you."

He said nothing to that. But she knew it was true. She had been told she had been saved from a life of poverty. She was raised to be grateful for the massive amounts of wealth at her disposal, but right now she would have given all of it just to have a normal family, a normal life.

"Your last name is now Anderson, if anyone asks."

"So, no one knows that you work for my father?"

"Just some very rich man."

"I don't know anything about you. How are they supposed to believe we're a couple?"

"I'll tell you the basics in the car on the ride over."

"There's one major thing I think will give us away."

"What's that?"

"Ma'am. No one calls their girlfriend *ma'am.*"

Cullen was uneasy about his choice to take her to his home. But it was the only place that made sense to him. She needed to be where no one could find her. And no one would find her here, because no one would look for her here. Whenever he was here he felt like he was on another planet, because this place was too calm, too peaceful to be on the earth as he knew it.

"When's your birthday?" she asked him, and he almost didn't hear her because he was getting lost in his thoughts. That happened to him when he was here. The ocean air, the warm sun, the scent of salt water, did something to him.

But unlike his other visits here, he wasn't here on vacation. He was still at work. He couldn't relax completely. He couldn't allow himself to let down his guard.

He had never brought anyone to this place. Never even told another person about it. It was that private to him.

But his first thought was to bring her here. He had gone through the other options where he had contacts. New Zealand. Thailand. Denmark. None of those places seemed right, because of logistics. He kept circling back to here. And if he were truthful with himself, his soul was pulling him here. He had been gone too long.

All the important people in his life were here and he wanted to see them again.

Yet, he couldn't help but wonder: How would they respond to her? She was so damn different from them. Not stuck-up, just bred to be better than they were.

"It's February twenty-fifth," he answered.

"It's coming up. I'll have to get you a present."

"You don't need to." He almost said *ma'am,* but then he remembered himself. He was going to have to pass her off as his girlfriend. It was the only part of the plan he didn't think out. The only part of the plan he hadn't allowed himself to think out.

"That's what you said when I gave you your Christmas present. I know I didn't need to. I wanted to. You're supposed to say *thank you.* It's polite."

"I wasn't raised with good manners like you. Besides, none of my principals had ever given me an actual gift before. I was surprised."

"I always give my security gifts. I like to give them something personal. I knew Bobby loved jazz, so I got him tickets to a show, but I don't know anything about you, so I just got you leather gloves."

"You miss Bobby, don't you?"

"I do. Very much so. He was my friend."

He had never heard of anybody describing their personal bodyguard as their friend, but he remembered Wyn's life. She worked and she went home. That was it. There didn't seem to be much more to it.

"What happened to Bobby?"

"He got old. My bag got snatched when I was in Barcelona as I was coming out of a guest lecture. Bobby ran after the guy, but couldn't catch him. There wasn't even anything important in it. I keep my phone and my wallet on my body when I'm overseas, but my father heard about it and had a fit. He fired Bobby. He was with me for twelve years and he just let him go. He told me he had been slowing down for years and that since he was running for office he needed someone younger and faster. I told him I didn't need a bodyguard anymore. The next thing I knew, you were hired."

"That's enough to make you resent a man."

"Not really. I made sure that Bobby was taken care of. And I learned from an early age that to my father, most people are disposable. Including the women who love him."

He heard bitterness in her voice. He had always wondered how she had felt about her father. He seemed content to spoil her. The way Wyn lived her life seemed to be in direct opposition to what her father wanted. She never attended his events. She rarely visited his office. Her mother was clearly the parent she was closer to. It made Cullen's job a hell of a lot easier, but it also sent a firm message to her father. She wanted no part of his political life.

"How old are you, Cullen?"

"I'll be thirty-six."

"When did you join the military?"

"When I was seventeen. I had left Northern Ireland for London when I was fifteen."

"I love London. In which part did you live?"

"On the streets," he said, keeping his eyes on the road. "Until me mum's cousin found me and took me in. He got me enlisted."

"What happened to your parents?"

"Mum's dead. Bomb killed her during the

Troubles when I was a boy. My father is a drunk. I was on my way to becoming a low-level criminal. The army changed my life. I went right into the infantry and saw action even before I was old enough to drink."

"But you became Special Forces? Isn't that rare for someone so young?"

"Aye." He nodded. "I was good at what I did."

"Why aren't you in the military anymore?"

"Got shot. Three times. Still got half a bullet in my shoulder."

"Oh. I broke my arm in three places when I slipped by the pool. I had to get surgery to repair the damage. Left a nasty scar. We'll have to compare battle wounds one day."

He glanced over at her to see if she was serious. But a little smile crept across her face. "Aye, Wyn. We will."

He wondered what was going through her head. She seemed to be taking everything in stride, but he knew she must be a mess. She had slipped back on her calm and collected mask. She made little jokes. Her quiet gracefulness had returned, but he could see it in her eyes. She was still bewildered. Her father would not speak to her. He offered her no answers. But he had spoken to Cullen. He was ordered to stay with Wynter round the clock until further notice and to keep her from finding out anything else. He wanted her shielded from this. Cullen didn't know how he was expected to do that. She would want answers. She wasn't a child who could continuously have the wool pulled over eyes. And yet he agreed. His salary instantly tripled as a reward.

Cullen had already been paid very well, but this money was enough to set him up for life. Wynter was his last principal. He knew that going in. As soon as he was done with this job, he would retire from everything and spend the rest of his days living his life on this island.

He pulled up to the compound where he and his friends lived. It was gated. Separated into two sections. One they rented out and the part they all called home. Most of the property was hidden away in the lush rain forest.

They had agreed to make it nice. Their dream home. Hardworking people who had saved their entire paychecks for years spent their money on this. It was the only thing they had.

"We built this place ourselves with the help of the locals," he told Wyn. "In the center is the community house. That's where we prepare and take most of our meals. When we go shopping, the rule is half of what you buy must go into the community kitchen. We take turns cooking as well. Most of us aren't good at it, so you'll be having a lot of grilled meat."

"I can cook. I like to." She turned to face him. "Where do you shop?"

"There's a village not far from here. We get packaged things from there, but you can pick bananas, mangoes, limes, and a bunch of other fruits right on the property. We fish from time to time. There's a couple of good restaurants that the locals go to that we like."

"What else should I know?"

"You'll meet most of the crew soon. Some of us spend most of the year someplace else working. We come here to play. To relax." He almost said "to heal," but he left that part out even though it was probably their number-one reason for coming. "Some of us stay here full-time to run the business."

She nodded and looked at him in the same way she did when she attended a conference — with curious interest. He was surprised she didn't pull out a pen and paper and take notes. "Anything else I should know?"

"Probably, but it's not that important at the moment."

"I think I'll like it here."

He wasn't so sure that she would, but he wanted her to. It was a daft thought. She was here, not because she wanted to be, but because her serenity had been blown up stateside. Maybe he wanted her to love it because he loved it here. This was his home. This is where he wanted to spend the rest of his days. In peace. In quiet. In relative solitude.

He pulled up to his cottage, which was the furthest out on the compound. It was green with white shutters and had a porch wrapped all the way around. There were wildflowers everywhere and the sounds of birds and wind and peace.

This was his paradise.

"It's lovely," she said.

"Thank you," he said with some pride. He had designed every inch of his home. He had been awarded for bravery by his government, but he was prouder of this, because for so many years he never thought he would have a place to call his own. "Let me show you inside."

He led her into the house. It was open, the living room and kitchen one big space with tall ceilings that made it feel airy even when the climate was so humid. The decor was simple; sparse, even. He thought he should put something up on the walls: a painting, photographs . . . something, but he hadn't been here in a year and he would have all the time in the world to make this place feel more like home after he was done with Wyn.

"You can take the master. There's a bathroom in there, so you'll have more privacy."

She glanced into his bedroom and then walked past it and into the room next door. "I'm not sleeping in your bedroom."

"But, ma'am. . . ."

She shook her head and walked over to the window, looking out at the view. "It's so beautiful here."

He could no longer see her face, but her shoulders had sagged a bit. He walked up behind her. "What am I going to do now?" she asked herself, more than to him.

It was a good question. One he didn't know the answer to.

"Ayo, Cullen!" he heard a booming voice behind him yell.

He'd know Kingsley Clark's voice anywhere. He was a massive man with a huge smile and a huge personality to match. He was Nigerian by birth, British by citizenship. They had met in the army when they had both been deployed to Afghanistan. Kingsley was his first friend when Cullen was a skinny pale boy who was scared shit-less.

"King!" He hugged his friend, who he hadn't seen in over a year. He was away the last time Cullen had been here. Over Kingsley's shoulder he saw Jazz. She was the kind of gorgeous a man rarely got to experience. She disarmed people with her looks, which had made her the perfect agent.

"Jazz." He grinned at her. "Get over here, you minx."

He hugged her too. She still smelled and felt the same. He was happy to see her again.

She didn't miss a thing. Her eyes zeroed in on Wynter, who was standing slightly behind him, looking like the proper intellectual she was. Automatically, he knew she wasn't going to fit in. But he knew that she wouldn't the moment he decided to bring her here.

He took her arm and brought her closer to him, feeling the need to protect her from them. "This is Wynter. She's special to me."

"I'm so pleased to meet you," she said, sounding every bit the like American heiress she was raised to be. "Call me Wyn."

Kingsley grinned widely. "Little sis!" He scooped her into a bear hug and spun her around. "Welcome to the fam."

Cullen was afraid of how she was going to

respond, but he saw that she was genuinely smiling, her cheeks slightly flushed.

"Thank you." She grinned at Kingsley. "I think everyone should be greeted like that every day."

Jazz's greeting was less warm. "I'm Jazz. It's nice to meet you. Cullen didn't tell us he was bringing you along." Jazz's eyes took every inch of Wynter in, no doubt making judgments about who she was just based on her body language. Unlike most people's snap judgments, Jazz's were always right. It was why she had been so excellent at her job.

"I didn't know I was coming here either. He surprised me with this trip."

"Where did you meet?"

"In D.C.," she said without hesitation.

"How?"

"I'm a linguist. I often work for the government and act as a translator in high-level meetings. I met Cullen while he was working."

Jazz nodded. Cullen was impressed with how smoothly she handled that interrogation.

It wasn't exactly a lie. He had been hired to work for her when they had met and the very first thing he accompanied her to was a meeting at the Pentagon.

"How many languages do you speak?"

"Eight fluently."

Jazz said something to her that sounded like Russian.

Wyn replied in the same language and then switched to Spanish with lightning speed. Cullen could see it took Jazz a moment to catch up to what she was saying. He knew Jazz hated that. She liked to think she was the smartest person in the room at all times.

"You don't speak Castilian Spanish?" Jazz probed.

"I do, but I find it useless when most of the people I translate for are from Latin America. Have you been to Mexico City? It's my favorite place in the world."

"I haven't. I spent most of my traveling time in Europe."

"Really? We'll have to compare travel stories sometime," Wyn said with a smile.

Cullen was shocked that Wyn was holding her own with Jazz. She intimidated most mortals. But quiet, bookish Wyn was made of sterner stuff, apparently. "I was just showing Wyn around the house. It's been a long journey for us. Give us a few minutes to get settled and I'll meet the rest of you at the community house."

Jazz and Kingsley left them alone.

Wyn let out a deep breath. "Kingsley is lovely. Jazz hates me. She's clearly in love with you."

"What?" Her comment knocked him off guard. "No. She's like a sister to me. That's what you're seeing."

There was a brief time, maybe five years ago, when he thought there could be something between him and Jazz, but it didn't work out because it couldn't work out. There was nothing left between them except a decades-long friendship.

"I want to tell her that I'm no threat to her, but I'm here as your girlfriend. To her, I *am* a threat." She shook her head. "I'm not sure how we're going to do this. Or if I can do this."

"It's too late. We don't have a choice. This is the safest place you can be. If I vouch for you, they'll die for you."

"They'll die for *you*. I'm just some girl you brought along." She turned away from him. "I think I need to be alone for a little while." She walked out of the cottage. Cullen was right at her heels, prepared to follow her, but he stopped himself.

She wasn't in D.C. She was at his home. And here he wasn't supposed to be her bodyguard. He needed to give her some freedom, but it was harder than he expected to let her go.

CHAPTER 3

Wyn had no idea where she was going as she left Cullen's cottage. She knew she just needed to get out. She had been trying to hold it together since she heard the news that had rocked her entire being. She hated crying. She hated feeling sorry for herself, so she refused to do it, but she couldn't be inside anymore.

It was one thing when they were in D.C. in the little protective bubble that Cullen had created, but he had taken her away from there. She had never been to the Virgin Islands before, and on the car ride over here she had been too preoccupied by learning all she could about the man who was supposed to be her lover that she barely paid attention to her lush surroundings, but she was here. In paradise. With the heat on her face and the humidity pulling at her straightened hair. A few minutes here and she already didn't feel like herself.

She hadn't spoken to anyone else but Cullen since yesterday, but his friends had come to greet them and suddenly the past two days caught up with her. She was supposed to pretend that her life hadn't been rocked. She was supposed to pretend that she was in love with a man who before yesterday she'd barely had a conversation with.

It all seemed like too much. Especially when one of the people she was trying to fool had been suspicious of her before she said one word.

Maybe she should have stayed in D.C., let the reporters hound her, let them dig. They might have found something. Just like they had found the pictures of her as a child. There were just letters now. Speculation, even though she knew the tale was true due to her father's silence alone, but she wanted proof. She needed it. It would claw at her soul if she didn't have it. But she didn't know how to go about getting it. She didn't know where to start, or even how to go about looking. But she knew it would be nearly impossible for her to stay here for any length of time and just be idle.

She worked. She always had. It was tied to her identity.

Wynter sat on a rock to the side of the

hiking trail she was on. She wasn't sure how far she had gone or how long she had been walking. Her feet ached a little. Her simple designer flats were not right for this setting. She had been too shell-shocked yesterday to ask Cullen where they were going.

He had told her to bring casual clothing and she did, but nothing she owned was appropriate for here. For the middle of a rain forest. The sound of a bird made her look up, take in her surroundings. She was assaulted with color. With vibrant greens and clear blues. And noises too. She shut her eyes for a moment and listened to chirping and buzzing and the unmistakable sound of rushing water in the distance.

She considered herself well-traveled, but she had mostly been to big metropolitan cities. Beach trips included summers in Maine and Nantucket. As an adult, it had been business trips, educational summits, and conferences.

She had never been anywhere like this before. She could see why Cullen had made this place his home. Never in a million years did she suspect her silent, black-garbed bodyguard would return to such a lush place like this.

There was so much she had learned about him in the past few hours. More than she had learned in the year that he had been with her.

"Excuse me, ma'am. I'm not sure if you realize this, but this is private property. No tourists are allowed over here. We are not renting out bungalows at the moment."

A large barrel-chested man appeared from the forest. He was sweaty, with a streak of dirt on one cheek and a short, thick scar on the other. He also had an accent, one that she couldn't quite place. But he was handsome, with silver hair and very green eyes. Some might even call him dashing.

She knew immediately that this was another one of Cullen's family.

"Hello, I'm not trespassing. Cullen brought me here." She stood up and extended her hand. "I'm Wyn."

"Cullen brought you here?"

"This morning. We arrived about a half hour ago."

The man's face bloomed into a smile and suddenly he turned from scary to friendly. "I'm Darby." He grabbed her hand and shook it enthusiastically. "It's good to meet you. Cullen didn't tell us he was bringing a girl."

"It was a surprise."

"What are you doing out here by yourself? Cullen's back. We've got to celebrate."

"Celebrate? Right now?" The last thing she felt like doing was celebrating. There was no reason for her to be happy. "I'm sure Cullen will be very glad to see you. I need to take a walk and get some air. It's very cold in D.C. and I've been cooped up inside for days. I just need to be outside for a little while."

Darby nodded. "I understand what it's like to be stuck inside somewhere when you're itching to get out." The way he said those words, the way he looked at her, told her that he understood, maybe in a deeper way than most. "Take your time, Miss Wyn. I'm sure I'll see you later."

"Thank you, Darby. It was nice to meet you."

He left her alone and she took a deep breath. She told herself to just keep breathing.

Cullen sat at the counter in the kitchen of the community house. Most of the crew had assembled around him. They were all talking over each other, catching up, joking around as if no time had passed. He wanted to enjoy himself like he always did when he was here, sink into the comfort of his friends, but he couldn't totally focus. His mind was elsewhere. On Wyn, specifically.

71

He wondered if he should go looking for her. He knew she would be safe here, but in all the time he had known her, he had never not known where she was. It was unsettling in a way he didn't want to examine. His principal was always supposed to be his number-one priority, but he didn't think about his last principal the way he thought about Wyn. He took time off. He relished his free hours. But with Wyn, his free hours were spent wondering what she was up to and if she might need him.

"Cullen!"

"Huh?" He snapped to attention.

"Your head was up your ass," Kingsley said. "You didn't hear a damn word that anyone said for the last five minutes."

"He was thinking about that pretty little girl he brought with him," Darby said.

"Yeah," Jazz said, zeroing in on him with her feline eyes. "What is with you and little Miss Prim and Proper? You don't seem like a couple."

"And what do couples seem like, Jazz?" Damn Jazz. He should have known she would be the hardest sell. She never took anything at face value. She never trusted anyone. Occupational hazard that all of them had at one point, but there were some people he had to learn to trust and it was important for him that some people trusted him.

"Like they suit each other," Jazz started. "Summer —"

"Wynter," he corrected.

"— doesn't seem like she fits you."

"I can see why he likes her," Kingsley said. "She's one of those posh types, keeps him from dragging his knuckles on the ground. Classes our boy up a bit. Cullen ain't lying when he says he's from pig shit. You should have seen him when I first met him. He wasn't even toilet-trained."

"I wasn't as bad as all that, you arsehole," he said with a grin. "Wyn's a good girl."

"She's a snob." Jazz rolled her eyes.

"I don't think so," Darby disagreed. "She seems like she's going through something, though." He looked at Cullen for confirmation.

"She got too close to an investigation in D.C. and she needed to get away. Plus, she's had a falling-out with her parents."

"She said she was a linguist," King said. "Heard her speaking Russian. I bet she knows some stuff."

He nodded. "She was translating the same document for the past week when I pulled her away. I don't think she's very happy with me at the moment."

"So, you've had a big fight?" Jazz perked up. "About what? Did you use the wrong fork at dinner?"

"No, we haven't had a fight. She's upset that I pulled her away from her work. But she needed to get away. And what the hell was that back at my cottage? Why did you have to go and try to make her prove herself? I've never brought anyone here and the fact that I brought her should tell you something. You accused her of being a snob, but the fact of the matter is that you're the one who came off like you thought you were better."

"Jazz is threatened." Kingsley wrapped his massive arm around Jazz and pulled her into his side. "She doesn't know how to play well with other girls. Especially pretty, dainty ones. Don't worry, Jazz." Kingsley gave her a loud smacking kiss on her cheek. "We'll always love you the best. It doesn't matter how many nicer, sweeter, more ladylike girls we bring around."

"Shut up, King. No one asked you." She focused back on Cullen. "So, she's well-traveled and well-educated and judging by those expensive flats, she has money. Not new money either. I'd bet she's never worn underwear from a pack in her life."

"She makes her own money," he told her.

"Government contractors get paid very well."

Jazz was too damn smart for her own good. He wouldn't be surprised if she already knew Wyn's whole story. "She's also a full-time college professor. She doesn't depend on anyone else for her survival." It was true. Her lifestyle wouldn't change at all if her trust fund disappeared. Except for him. She wouldn't have private security round the clock.

Jazz rolled her eyes. "You're with her because she elevates you. But the question is, Why is she with you?"

It was a fair question. He hadn't been with anyone like her in his entire life. And if they were together, it would be a question he would ask himself. "You don't think I'm good enough for her?"

"No," they all answered at once, causing him to grin.

"I'm a prize and you know it."

"Of course you are," Jazz said. "I just don't see you with her, that's all."

"Start seeing it, Jazz. I brought her here to meet all of you."

"She must be special," Darby said.

"What did you tell her about us?" King asked him.

"Not much. Just that we all are former

military or agents for our respective govern-
ments."

"So, you didn't tell her you brought her
to the island of misfit toys, then?" Jazz
asked.

"That's a stupid name for this place."

"Why?" Kingsley frowned at him. "It's the
truth. We've all got our shit."

"Does she know everything about you,
Cull? Does she know about your shit?" Jazz
questioned.

Wyn didn't, of course. No one knew all of
it. Just bits and pieces that he chose to
reveal at sporadic times. "She knows about
my past." It was a non-answer. Not exactly
a lie. She knew the few things that he had
told her on the ride up. He knew so much
more about her. But he knew things that
she never told him. Chinese was her favorite
takeout. She loved children and going to
the park when it was warm so she could
people-watch. He knew that her favorite
color was buttercream yellow and that she
always checked twice to make sure she had
her keys. He knew that she was quietly
generous. That the only thing she had ever
asked him to do for her was deliver things
to some of the people she translated for.
She paid legal fees and mortgages and once
she covered the tuition for one of her

students who was going to get kicked out of school because they could no longer pay. And she never said a damn thing about it.

He had never asked her about it, but one time his expression — a raised eyebrow, a twitch of his lip when she handed him a large stack of cash — gave him away.

"I was saved once," she said simply. And then she smiled at him. One of those sweet, kind of saucy smiles that had knocked him off guard. "My father gives it to me. He can't tell me how to spend it."

He tried not to have much of an opinion about his principals. But he decided that he liked her then. It must have been the nature of this assignment. She wasn't like his last boss who sold weapons to bad people, who had meetings in the most dangerous parts of the world, and attended lavish parties. Then there was so much to focus on. There was so much that could and did go wrong. But Wyn's life was simple and quiet. It was routine. He only had her to focus on. To worry about. He could anticipate her moves. He could read her emotions.

He had an advantage and all she knew about him was next to nothing.

It wasn't fair. But he was still working. He was still protecting her.

And then she walked in. All eyes turned

to her. She walked over to Jazz and looked her directly in the eye. "Can you take me shopping? I don't have the right clothes."

The request shocked the hell out of him.

"I'll take you shopping, Wyn." He stood up and touched her arm.

"Thank you," she said politely, not taking her eyes off Jazz. "But I didn't ask you. I asked Jazz. Will you take me?"

Cullen was at a complete loss. Jazz had in-your-face sex appeal. She wore a crop top and little khaki shorts. Her long hair was loose and wild, showing off every inch its luscious texture. Jazz was the kind of woman you'd want to spend hours with — locked in a room. Wyn was the kind of girl you'd ask to help you with your homework.

He wanted to step in, but he knew better. The urge to keep them separate was overwhelming, but they were going to be here together for what could be months. He had to trust Wyn to hold her own, to keep their secret, to keep her head up. And he had to trust Jazz. She was a hard-ass, but she was his friend and she had a good soul beneath all the hard surface.

"Yeah." Jazz looked Wyn up and down. "Your dumb-ass boyfriend should have told you where exactly you were going before you packed."

"Thank you." Wyn nodded. "I'll go get my handbag."

She turned away, but Cullen grabbed her hand. "Are you sure you don't want me to come with you?"

"Yes. You go everywhere with me." She went onto her tiptoes and gently kissed his cheek. Her lips lingered. They were smooth and warm. It was just how he imagined a kiss to be from her — if he had ever imagined what it would be like to be kissed by her. It was a shock to his system. Wholly unexpected. He had never been touched by a principal before, much less kissed by one. But then he remembered he wasn't supposed to be her bodyguard. He was supposed to be her boyfriend here. It was a role he was going to have a hard time getting used to. "I won't be gone too long."

"Okay," he said, still knocked off guard. "I'll see you when you get back."

CHAPTER 4

If Wyn was being honest with herself — and she always tried to be honest with herself — she would admit that Jazz intimidated the hell out of her. Jazz was one of those tall, ethnically ambiguous gorgeous people who other people liked to stare at. Even on the island, where she must be known to the locals by now, she didn't escape the looks. She didn't seem to notice people staring at her either.

It was the direct opposite of Wyn's experience. She had never stood out in any way — not that she wanted to, of course, but no one had ever paid her much attention. She wasn't short or tall. None of her features were particularly beautiful. She wasn't popular in school. She wasn't very good at anything except learning foreign languages, but that didn't gain her any notice, just a career that she loved.

A career she wasn't going to be able to

have for a little while. She felt a pang of sadness strike her deep in her chest. She wondered what her students must be thinking. Not the ones at Georgetown, but the ones she taught at the community center. The ones who didn't call her Dr. Bates, but simply just Miss. She had seen them through so much. They had two more weeks left in the course and then they were going to have a little ceremony and a party afterward and she had just disappeared on them. Without a word or explanation. But maybe she hadn't needed to give an explanation. The story of her father's scandal had been splashed all over the television. They may not have known she was the daughter of a presidential candidate then, but they would know now.

It would be hard to step back into that life after all of this died down. Could she ever get her privacy back? Her anonymity back? It was hard to imagine that she could. It was hard to think that people could look at her and not think she was the possible love child of her father, that her whole life up until then had been a lie.

"Here." Jazz tossed another sundress at her. She kept doing that during their shopping trip, not seeming to want or care about Wyn's input. Wyn wanted to protest, but so far she had liked everything that Jazz had given her. They weren't the understated neutrals she would have picked. They were bold colors, tighter fits, lower necklines. Things that would have shown off her body instead of covering it.

"So how long have you been with my boy?"

Her boy. Cullen didn't think Jazz had a thing for him, but he was wrong. "We met a year ago. Things changed between us fairly recently, though."

"Must be serious. He brought you here to meet the family." She nodded her head toward the dressing room. "You should try those on. They're on clearance and you can't return them."

"That's a good idea." She walked into the dressing room, Jazz on her heels. Jazz entered with her.

"Go ahead. You don't have anything I've never seen before."

She held up her head and undressed, not showing Jazz any emotion at all. "How long have you known Cullen?"

"He was still in the British Special Forces. Not long before he was shot."

"You knew him then? Was he different?"

"You mean was he less damaged?" She shrugged. "Probably not, but he is a highly trained solider. He's not the type to go wearing his heart on his sleeve."

"He doesn't give anything away."

She said he was damaged. There was nothing about him that would make anyone think that. But Wyn knew that he had been through a lot, that they all must have been through a lot.

"I can see why he's attracted to you now," Jazz said, passing a critical eye over her underwear-clad form. "You've got a body."

"All humans have a body."

"Yours is hot." The way Jazz said it, it wasn't a compliment.

"Mine is nothing compared to yours," she said truthfully. "I wish I was as beautiful as you." Wyn didn't often look at herself in the mirror. She quickly got dressed and just checked to make sure she was neat and presentable. She had never felt very comfortable in her own skin. She had been chubby all her life. Her body never seemed to fit into the designer clothes that her mother always wanted to put her in. She wasn't like her schoolmates. She had never been stylishly thin. Her skin wasn't pale. Her hair wasn't straight. She had never fit in.

"My body was used like currency to gain secrets from powerful men. Don't wish for shit you know nothing about."

Wyn stared at Jazz for a moment, surprised she had revealed so much of herself to a stranger. There was a reason that Cullen's friends had escaped to this island. Perhaps it was to escape it all. Perhaps it was to heal. But this was more than just a vacation spot for them. "Cullen said I'm not allowed to ask you about your jobs."

"You're not."

"I was mildly curious before, but now I really want to know who you people are."

"Suffer," Jazz said, flashing her the most gorgeous grin. "Try the dresses on. I don't have all day to stand here and look at you in your ugly underwear."

"Is my underwear ugly?" She forced herself to look at herself in the full-length mirror. She wore beige undergarments. Well made. Supportive. Plain. But she looked past them at her body. Her thighs were full. Her hips were full. Her breasts were always just a little bigger than she would like. Her belly ever so slightly rounded. It was far from a perfect body. It was far from Jazz's body, but she didn't hate what she saw.

She did know why she had asked Jazz to come shopping with her. Maybe it was because she was beautiful. Maybe it was because she was a woman. Maybe it was because being with someone she knew didn't like her was a distraction from her own life, from the mess that she had run away from when she came here.

"It's terrible. I'm surprised Cullen can even get it up, seeing you in those."

"I don't wear them to bed." The topic was making her uncomfortable. She had no idea what Cullen found sexy. She hadn't been with anyone in years. Her last relationship was when she was a doctoral student. Her boyfriend was in her program. He was quiet and studious. They had always made love in the dark, under the covers. There was no sweaty sex. No grand passion like one would see in the movies. It was sweet. And then he moved away, halfway across the world when he took a job in Egypt.

"You're different from every other girl he's been with."

"Really? What's his type?"

"You've never notice him glance at other women?"

"No," she said truthfully as she slipped on a dress over her head. "When he is with me, he is completely focused on me or at least he's really good at pretending like he is."

His stare was so intense. She chalked it up to him being different from Bobby, who had been a D.C. cop before he worked for her father. His training was different, more intensive.

It was something that she thought she would get used to over time, but she hadn't. And right now, she was away from him, away from his protection and gaze. It felt like something was missing. Maybe she had become accustomed to it.

"He usually goes for those model types. Those girls that wear too much makeup and document every moment of their day for Instagram."

"Really? But he's so private and so serious. I can't imagine him with someone like that."

"He was with women like that because they were beautiful and completely self-absorbed. None of them really wanted to get to know him. It was perfect for him. No one got too attached."

"You know so much about him."

"I do." She nodded approvingly. "You're buying this dress. Why are you with him? I'd bet anything he's not like the typical guy you date."

"There is no typical guy. People capture your heart for different reasons."

"What did he do to get yours?"

Nothing. They weren't a couple. This was all a lie, but Jazz wasn't going to let up. She saw now why he told her to lie. They wouldn't have accepted her at all as some stranger, the daughter of a politician who could ruin their peace and quiet with an invasion of reporters. "His hands are always warm."

"Excuse me?"

"He puts his hand on my lower back and I can feel the warmth travel through my entire body. I feel safe with him. He's always there."

Jazz blinked at her. "I wasn't expecting you to say that."

"I didn't realize how important it is to me that he's always there. I take him for granted."

"He's sexy too. Don't forget that. That is also important."

"Some things go without saying." She wanted to think that she had first noticed how appealing he was that morning on the plane when she saw him with his guard down, but that wouldn't be the truth.

She remembered the day she had met him. It was right after New Year's, one of the rare times her father had been in town. He had summoned her to his office and when she arrived she spotted Cullen there. He rose as soon as her feet crossed the threshold and she was immediately struck by his appearance. The angles of his features. The richness of his brown hair. The color of his eyes paired with the intensity of his gaze.

And then he spoke.

"How are you, ma'am?" The deep Irish brogue. She should have realized that this black-clad figure was there to be her new security guard, but she had gone a little dumb when she had met him, because he was beautiful.

And when he shook her hand, his fingers engulfed hers. His hand was hot and completely warmed her up. She had a reaction to him then. It was a memory she had repressed. It was something she thought would never happen to her, but it had.

She didn't want him for a bodyguard, but her father didn't care. And now here they were, on an island together, pretending to be lovers when they were very far from it.

"I need a bathing suit," she told Jazz. "And new underwear."

Jazz grinned at her. "I know just the place we can go."

The house was so damn quiet without Mum there. It was just after five. Normally there would be the sounds of her rummaging around in the kitchen for dinner. Pots clanging, Mum's voice yelling like a fishwife at the little ones who were always running through the kitchen. But it was quiet now. Even the little ones were gone. His brother and sister taken by some relatives that were better off than they were. They didn't want to leave them with Pop. Pop never held a steady job. Pop who had always drank a little too much. Pop whose mouth and temper always got him in trouble.

He hadn't been to work since Mum had died. He had barely come out of his room. His father was shit, but he was a man who loved his wife. Her death had devastated him. The whole neighborhood was heavy with grief. His mum was innocent, caught in a battle between the IRA and the UVF. Five other people had died, civilians, just regular people going about their business.

It was senseless. Mindless. Never-ending bloodshed. And for what? Cullen wasn't even sure anymore.

"Boy!" his father yelled and by the tone of his voice Cullen knew he was in one of his moods. He went back to the room. It stunk like booze and sweat and sadness. He was fifteen and he knew what sadness smelled like because he had been a witness to it for so much of his life. He never remembered a time when it was peaceful, when people weren't always clenched with worry. But there had been happy times. Mum had made things happy. She was always smiling and singing, even when Cullen had thought she had nothing to smile or sing about.

His father was sitting on the edge of the bed. He looked like death. His eyes had circles so dark beneath them, it looked like he had been punched a dozen times. His undershirt was filthy. He probably hadn't changed it for a week. He stunk to high hell. Cullen wanted to cover his nose as he walked further into the room, but he knew that would only make the bugger angry.

"Yes, sir?"

"Bring me food," he demanded.

"We've got no food."

"Bullshit. The neighbors brought some over after she died. The freezer was full."

"That was two months ago. Food is gone."

"Then what the fuck have you been eating?"

The neighbors were feeding him. They'd see him pass on his way to school and give him whatever they had. Sometimes, it was sausage roll or a bit of potato bread. If he was lucky, he got stew. All the neighbors gave them what they had, knowing he could no longer depend on his father to provide a thing. "I ate at school today."

"You're lying. You're a no-good lying little shit."

"I'm not lying. There's nothing in the house. If you don't believe me, you can bloody well go look your damn self." He had known he had said the wrong thing as soon as he said it. His father looked for any excuse to go into a rage and lately it took next to nothing to set him off.

The first smack came quickly and was delivered with so much force that Cullen's head snapped back. His felt his lip split open again. It had just healed. Just stopped stinging when he ate something or brushed his teeth.

His father's hand raised again, but Cullen couldn't take it anymore. He couldn't be beaten anymore. He was just as tall his father. He was just as angry. He grabbed his wrist and bent it back.

The cry of pain awoke Cullen from his sleep. He opened his eyes to see Wyn standing over him as he lay on the couch. He had her tiny wrist in his hand. He let go immediately and jumped up.

"Wyn!" He had hurt her. "I didn't mean it. I'm sorry." He could see that it was already red and swollen. "Is it broken? Let's get you to the hospital. I'm sorry. I would never hurt you on purpose."

"It's fine." She stepped back from him,

looking as wary of him as she would of a wild animal. "It was my fault. I should know better than to stand over someone when they are sleeping, especially someone trained in hand-to-hand combat. I can move it." She twisted it from side to side and he could see that she was in pain. "See?"

"Let me get you some ice." He ran to the freezer, only to find there was nothing there except some old pizza pockets. He still grabbed one, wrapped it in a paper towel, and returned to her. "I'm sorry."

"Stop apologizing. I'm not upset with you. I heard you say something. I came over to check on you."

"I hurt you . . ." He felt helpless. He had dreams all the time. It was why he didn't do sleepovers with the women he was seeing. He didn't want anyone to know the depth of them. They had gotten better in the past six months. He rarely had any dreams now, but today they had returned. "Can I see your wrist?"

She held it out to him. He took it as gently as possible. He could clearly see the marks left by his fingers. He pressed the frozen pizza pocket to it, knowing it was inadequate. "It's fine. It's fine," she assured him. "It was my fault."

"I'm not used to anyone being around. I

had forgotten where I was."

She looked up at him, her eyes huge. "You don't have to explain yourself to me."

"I don't want you to be afraid of me," he admitted. "I'm supposed to be keeping you safe, not be the one that hurts you."

"I'm not afraid of you, Cullen. What can I say to put your mind at ease?"

"Nothing. Just do me a favor. If you ever hear me having one of those dreams again, don't try to wake me." He walked away from her and went to his room, locking the door behind him. He felt too damn guilty to even look at her.

Cullen avoided Wyn for the rest of the day. She felt terrible. Almost sick to her stomach. It had been completely her fault. She had heard him cry out in his sleep. He had been napping on the couch when she got back from shopping. Not just dozing, but in a deep sleep. She had known he was tired when she had left him earlier. He probably hadn't gotten any sleep the night before. Knowing him, he probably hadn't meant to fall asleep there. He had probably been waiting for her to get back to make sure she was safe.

But she had been fine with Jazz. Jazz had taken her to a little town that had been set up by expats and retirees from all over the world. It wasn't the touristy part of the island, she was relieved to find. There were no American papers with her father's face and sordid story splashed all over them. She had come back feeling better than when she left and then she had heard him cry out.

She had gone over to check on him and saw that he looked distressed. His face was twisted in agony. He was mumbling words she couldn't understand. She had absently reached down to touch his cheek and that's when he grabbed her, his fingers like a vise around her wrist. He had bent it back and that's when she cried out. His eyes opened immediately. Cullen had always been so cool and calm, but she had seen panic there, then deep regret, then self-loathing.

She understood that he could have broken her wrist. But she should have known better than to touch him. She knew a little about PTSD dreams and that she shouldn't have interfered. But the sound that escaped from him wasn't just one of pain. It was one of anguish and now he would barely look at her.

They had gone to the community house for dinner. It was Kingsley's turn to cook. He was standing at the grill in a chef's hat and apron. His heavily muscled arms were bare and bulging as he flipped the meat that he was cooking. She had stuck close to him, because out of all of them, he was the most welcoming to her. She helped him cook, making mango salsa to go over the chicken, putting together a salad and making a pot of rice.

King had tried to send her away to relax by the pool with the rest of the crew, but she couldn't relax. She needed to keep busy. There were times during the evening that she would catch Cullen looking at her. Before, she could never tell what he was thinking, or if he had any feelings at all, but she could see how he felt when he looked at her today.

There was tremendous guilt there. She didn't know how to reassure him.

"Jazz," King called. "Get off your ass and help Wyn set the table."

Jazz rose and frowned at him. "Set the table? We don't set the table."

"We do tonight. Our boy is home. Get the good wine and the glasses."

"He's been here before. Why are we going all out for him?"

"Because it's been a long time. And he brought this lovely girl back with him and we are trying to make her think we're not a bunch of hooligans. Now please, love, go help."

"Hooligans? Who says hooligans?"

Wyn was surprised to see Jazz follow Kingsley's directions without much more of a fight.

"Are you happy, your royal highness?" Jazz said after she completed her tasks. "Good wine. Actual plates."

Kingsley put down his tongs and wrapped Jazz up in a tight hug. "Good girl." He kissed her cheek. "You're almost on your way to becoming a kind and reasonable person."

"Shut up, King."

"It's a good thing you listened. I was going to have to punish you if you didn't. Throw you over my shoulder and take you back to your house with no supper."

"It took her two times before she realized he wasn't playing around." A tall, Adonis-like man appeared from somewhere in the house. He was clearly American. Blond, blue-eyed, dark-tanned skin, straight white teeth. He looked like he had stepped from an ad.

"Hello." He gave Wyn a friendly smile. "I'm Jack. I haven't seen you in these parts before. Are you Jazz's sister?"

"No. Unfortunately, Jazz and I don't share

any DNA. I'm Wyn."

"She's mine, Jack," Cullen said, leaving his spot outside. "Touch and I'll break your goddamn nose."

"Cullen!" Wyn was surprised at him and she surprised herself by liking the possessiveness in his voice.

"Jack nearly got King's mother in bed," Jazz informed her. "Cullen needs to stake his claim hard. Women fall for Jack. And Jack falls real hard for women."

"King's mother looks damn good for sixty. She's still got those legs of a dancer."

"You had better be glad Jazz and Darby were there to hold me back. I would have murdered you."

Jack grinned. "I regret nothing." He faced Cullen. "How the hell are you, man?" He gave him one of those macho hugs that men give each other.

"I'm good. How's business?"

"Great." He turned back to Wyn. "Let me know when you're free. I'll take you up in my helicopter and give you a tour of the island. Or if you're really adventurous, I'll take you up in one of my planes."

"Jack was a fighter pilot in the Air Force. He can also do all those stunts you see in air shows," Cullen said, speaking to her for the first time in hours.

"That's amazing. Will you come with me on the helicopter tour?" she asked to keep him talking.

"You think I would leave you alone with this bugger?"

"Do you think a pretty boy with a nice smile could turn my head? Give me more credit than that. Moody Irishmen are the only ones for me."

He flashed her a brief smile. She had never seen him smile before, at least not at her, but it was there, right under the surface of his usually expressionless face. But his smile had faded as quickly as it appeared.

The guilt returned quickly and she hated that it was still there, even hours later. She didn't have to forgive him. He had to forgive himself and she knew it wasn't going to be easy.

"Jack is just in time. I think dinner is ready."

They sat down at the large table on the patio. The sun had started to set and colorful lanterns had been lit to illuminate the area. Wyn had been a lot of places in her life, but this was one of the most beautiful. The rain forest around them, the orangy-purple of the sky, the light glistening off the pool water. But it wasn't just what they could see. It felt warm there. These were old friends gathered around the table. They were laughing and enjoying each other's company. And they did this every night when they were there. It was so different from how her nights were spent. Dinner for her was nearly always alone. Eating something simple. Catching up on emails or work.

She looked at Cullen, who sat across from her, rather than next to her. Did he still feel like he was at work even though he was here?

Time had seemed to fly by. She was mostly quiet during dinner, just watching the old friends interact. Even when the food was gone and the plates were clear, the friends didn't seem to want to separate from each other. They had congregated around the pool, drinks in hand. She could tell it was something they did a lot. She had helped Darby clean up, even though he had tried to send her away to relax. She felt like an outsider there and she didn't want to interfere with their time together.

But soon there was nothing left to clean up and it would feel wrong to leave them and return to Cullen's cottage. She spotted him sitting on the glider, a space next to him, waiting for her. She went over to him, slid into the seat beside him and wrapped her arm around him. He stiffened immediately, uncomfortable with her touch.

"You're supposed to be my boyfriend," she whispered in his ear.

He relaxed and, looking her in the eye, gave her a little nod. He picked up her wrist and studied it and then he surprised her by kissing it, letting his lips linger there. Every nerve ending came alive.

His body was hard and warm. He was always so warm. Not in his mood or attitude, but his hands, his body. She had always liked it and if she was being honest with herself, she realized it was something that she had looked forward to on those cold D.C. days. Now she was cuddled into his warmth on this breezy night. A week ago she would have never imagined this.

This was supposed to be a charade, a show they put on for others, but she enjoyed this feeling. The safety of it. Of not feeling alone. Of being able to lean against someone.

It was something she would never tell anyone.

CHAPTER 5

The next morning Cullen wasn't sure what to do with himself. Wyn wasn't there when he woke up. He threw on his clothes and rushed out of the cottage to look for her, but then he remembered himself. She would be safe here. It was the reason he had brought her here. He wasn't supposed to act like her bodyguard and if he tore up the compound looking for her, it would sure as hell give them away.

He needed to remember that here he was her boyfriend.

But the fact that he was getting paid a very large sum of money to keep her safe was never far from his mind.

He was finding it difficult balancing the two roles. He was having a hard time remembering what a couple should look like. His parents didn't have a model marriage. His father was a drunk. His mother was always scrounging around, trying to make ends meet. They claimed they loved each other, but even as a boy he knew that that's not what love should be.

As an adult, he stayed away from long-term romantic entanglements. There were a few women he would visit while he was on leave. Some women he had just dated for one night. He had never been someone's partner as an adult. He hadn't spent any time around loving couples.

He was assuming a role he had done no research for.

He knew there should be simple affection between two people who were seriously involved. Hugging. Kissing. Touching. It wasn't something he was used to.

He had been physical with the women he had kept company with. At night. In bed. There was never time or need to do anything else.

Wyn was different from him. She seemed to know what to do. He had been a leader, a decision-maker for a very long time now, the one who was always in control, but he had to defer to her on this. He brought her to his adopted family and he was going to need her to pull this thing off.

When she snuggled up to him last night at first, it was a shock. Not the act itself, but the way it felt. She was so incredibly soft. Her skin. Her curves. Her scent.

Her heart.

He had nearly broken her wrist yesterday. He wasn't a spiritual man, but he thanked God that he had woken up before he did. He could barely look at her, he was so consumed with guilt, but she had forgiven him. She snuggled close to him and rested her head on his chest. She had even fallen asleep there. That was trust. That was her feeling safe, when part of him felt like a monster.

He would be fooling himself if he said he didn't like the way she felt. He went to bed that night with her scent lingering on his clothes and the heat of her body still warming him. He missed the softness as he lay in bed alone. It had been far too long since he had had a woman. He shouldn't be this affected by her.

"Cullen?" she called to him. He was in the back of the house in the little sitting area he created so he could look out into the rain forest.

He stood up. "Yes, ma'am?"

"Stop that." She sat down. "I hate it when you call me *ma'am.*"

"Yes, lass," he said softly, correcting himself.

She smiled at him and stepped forward,

handing him a mug and small bowl. "I brought you some coffee and some fruit. There's a big pot of oatmeal at the community house if you're hungry. I set out nuts, berries, and brown sugar if you want to make it more special."

"Is that where you were this morning when I woke up?"

She nodded.

"You damn near gave me an apoplectic fit."

"No one is going to kidnap me here. Hell, no one was going to kidnap me in D.C. You can relax."

"We both know I can't." Not around her. It was impossible. She made every part of him feel like he was about to fall off a cliff.

"Try," she urged. "Sit back down. Your friends are going to think I'm a horrible girlfriend if you continue to be so uncomfortable around me."

He sank back down in his seat and she sat beside him, not as close as yesterday. Not snuggled up and pressed into him. "I'm not supposed to be touching you."

"This was your idea."

He placed the coffee mug and the fruit on the table beside him. "Don't remind me."

"I'm sorry this has been such a hardship for you."

"It's not a damn hardship. I'm just not supposed to touch you." He would get used to it. He would like it. He would be in trouble. "I get paid to protect you. Not paw you."

"You shouldn't flinch every time either."

"Do I flinch? I don't mean to. I've never had a principal kiss me."

"Who was your last principal?"

"An arms dealer. He was hairy as a goat and had a gut the size of a keg."

"Why don't you work for him anymore?"

"He's dead," he said emotionlessly, even though he sometimes dreamed about that night. "Assassinated by a sniper using one of the guns my principal sold."

"Were you there when it happened?"

He nodded, not wanting to go into any of the details with her. It was weeks before he stopped feeling the spray of blood that hit his cheek when the bullet went through the man's head.

"I'm not important enough to be assassinated."

"But you *are* important. You are your father's world. He doesn't want me to let you out of my sight."

"I find it hard to reconcile that with the fact that he rarely saw me while I was growing up and now he refuses to speak to me at all. It's a very funny way of showing someone that they are your world."

The hurt in her voice was clear. It was uncomfortable for him. He didn't know how to deal with it. He took her hand in his. It was small, her skin smooth. He ran his fingertips over her palm. "I'll be better," he told her. "I'll just need to get used to this." He looked at her. He hadn't failed to notice how she looked when she walked up. He had just tried to ignore it. But it was hard. Instead of her subdued neutral colors, she wore a pink sundress. If any color was made for a woman, soft baby pink was made for her.

Her hair was loose. Her arms and shoulders were bare, all her rich brown skin on display. He had been with this woman every single day for the past year, but it was like it was sitting next to someone he had just met and now he was touching her. He wasn't at all sure he made the right decision to bring her here.

"Kingsley is in love with Jazz, isn't he?"

He looked up at her. "Aye. Very much so. How could you tell?"

"It was something small. At dinner last night she was asking him to help her fix something and King nodded and leaned over to kiss the side of her face. It was like he couldn't help but to kiss her in that moment. And the way he looks at her . . . Every woman wants to be looked at like that."

"Jazz doesn't know, or rather she doesn't want to admit it. She just thinks he's her best mate."

"Is that why you and Jazz were never an item?"

"Yes." He was surprised at how perceptive she was. She had only been there twenty-four hours and yet she knew what even the other members of their little community never figured out. "You don't date the woman your friend is in love with."

"She loves him too. She just doesn't know it yet."

"He saved her. Five years ago, someone was hurting her and he saved her. She's loyal to him."

"It's more than loyal. She loves him too."

She sounded so sure. But he had known these people for years. He knew things about King that she would never know. "How can you tell? You just said that she was in love with me."

"She's attracted to you. And she does love you, but not in the same way she loves King. She let herself be kissed last night. Her guard was down and she leaned into it. Her eyes closed just for a fraction of a second and she relished it. It was beautiful."

"You're a linguist. How do you know so much about behavior?"

"I like to watch people. My father is such a public figure, but he has made sure that my life was lived in private. I had private dance lessons and private horseback riding lessons and private language lessons. I went to school with kids my own age, but I never got to just hang out with them. I spent a lot of time with adults, with the people who worked for my parents. Our housekeeper, Marta, used to take me home with her when both of my parents were out of town. They still don't know about it. My bodyguard never told them. I'm not sure why."

"He seemed more loyal to you than the man who was paying him."

"I think he could see that I needed some normal in my life." She smiled softly at the memory. "Marta had a huge family and I used to just watch them. Watch how they interacted with each other. Watch how they would hold hands and hug and kiss each other. It was so different from my family. It made me want to watch anybody I came in contact with and when I began to study languages, I studied the people and the cultures associated with them. The ways people say *I love you.* The words they use when they are happy. How they react when they are mad."

"Is that why you like to translate during interrogations? I heard you say that a few of them were innocent. I wasn't sure how you could tell."

"I didn't know for sure. It was a feeling."

They were quiet for a moment, the only noise coming from the nature around them and their soft breathing.

"How are you feeling today?"

He touched her wrist, where he had grabbed her yesterday. He still felt guilty about it. He had slept with his door locked for the first time, afraid he would get up or she would come in. "I'm in paradise. But all I can think about is what is going on at home. I haven't missed a day of work in the last four years. I don't know what to do with myself."

"So, you make oatmeal for my friends?"

She nodded. "They've all got to eat and I need something to do."

"You should enjoy yourself."

"How do I do that? I'm not sure how."

"We're on an island. Let's go to the beach."

Wynter hadn't realized how much land Cullen and his crew owned, but it stretched all the way to the ocean and a little private beach that was just theirs to enjoy. She thought they were going to a public beach with everyone else, and even though it was on a small, usually quiet island, she had been filled with anxiety about being around people, mainly American tourists who might recognize her.

Cullen told her that she needed to relax, but she was finding it hard to. Her thoughts of what was happening at home were never far from her mind.

"You okay, sis?" Kingsley asked her as she stood beside him at the back of the jeep. The men were unloading their supplies. Blankets, chairs, the coolers full of food and drinks she and King had prepared before they left. Their homes weren't far from the beach. It would have been easy for them to go back for food, but Cullen told them they were going to spend the day by the water. They all agreed. Even Jack came. He had brought a boat with him and some Jet Skis. They were supposed to have fun today. Wyn tried to think back to the last time she had this kind of fun, but her mind was blank.

She couldn't remember her last vacation.

"I'm fine, King. I'm just a little nervous about the Jet Ski."

"You don't have to ride." He wrapped his

arm around her in a brotherly way. "I won't get on one of those damn things either."

"I've seen you jump out of an exploding building," Cullen said to him with a frown. "But the Jet Ski is the thing that causes you to tap out? For fuck's sake, man."

"He's three hundred pounds of muscle," Wyn said, defending him. "I think he would sink like a rock in the water."

"Yeah." Kingsley nodded. "My body was made for fighting. Not for floating."

"When's the last time you trained?" Cullen asked.

King shrugged. "I don't need to train. I'm done with that life."

"You never know what can go down," Cullen said cryptically.

"I can still kick your skinny Irish ass with one leg and both hands tied behind my back." King shook his head. "You should have gotten out sooner. You're still in that mind-set. That's why we have this place. So you don't have to be on watch anymore."

Cullen nodded, but Wyn knew that he couldn't let his guard down because he was *her* guard. He had brought his work home with him and it would be hard for him to relax. She felt bad for him, but at the same time she didn't. He didn't have to bring her here, to his friends. She was supposed to be pretending that they were lovers. And yet he flinched whenever they touched. Like her contact was unwanted.

This morning he had to practice holding her hand. He was impossibly gentle with her, lightly trailing his fingers up and down her skin.

When she first met him, she would have never described him as gentle. But he had surprised her. He always was gentle with her. She couldn't count when he had grabbed her wrist, because that wasn't fair. He didn't know it was her and when he did know, he cradled her wrist. He held it lightly in his large hands; he had even kissed it that night.

Who could think that a kiss to the wrist could feel so good?

She couldn't help but to wonder how he was with his lovers. He was dark and quiet and intense.

He always was so in control, of his emotions, of his reactions.

But was he passionate? Did he ever lose himself?

Did he ever push women against walls and kiss them until they dissolved into goop? Did he rip at their clothes?

Or was his more controlled?

Stripping away each item.

One by one.

Not breaking eye contact until they were nude and she was quivering for his touch.

Wyn's body heated up, but it had nothing to do with the sun. "Are you sure you're okay, Wynter?" Cullen asked her and she couldn't miss the touch of concern in his voice.

No, she wasn't okay. She was thinking about him in ways she shouldn't. "I'm just feeling a little warm. I think I'll head for the water."

She stepped slightly away from the men and took off her cover-up. She had never felt comfortable in a bathing suit, but today she felt extra-exposed. She wore a bikini for the first time. Jazz had picked it out. It wasn't horribly revealing. Her bottom was covered for the most part. But the top was held together with a bow tied in the center of her breasts. Just one pull and she would be exposed. When she mentioned her fear to Jazz, Jazz just smiled and told her that was the fun part of it.

And for the first time she felt like being a little adventurous, mischievous. But now she was wondering if she had made a mistake.

"Wait for me," Cullen ordered. His eyes took her in, but his face was completely unreadable. She wondered what he thought.

She told herself it didn't matter what he thought of her in it, but she still wondered.

He turned slightly away and stripped off his shirt, revealing his hard shoulders and chest. It was her turn to stare. As his girlfriend, she was supposed to have seen his body before. But that was pretend. She had never seen him before. She had never seen the trails of scars that lined his back.

She tried to keep her face neutral, but she wasn't sure she could manage it. Those were no run-of-the-mill scars. She could see where he had been shot, but it was the long, band-like scars that snaked up his back that made her chest ache.

He had been tortured.

She knew so little of his time before he came to her. But it must have been brutal. It made her problems seem so damn small.

"Come." She reached for his hand. He took it, sliding his fingers into hers without a flinch this time. They walked down to the water silently. Her heart was pounding. She wouldn't look into his eyes, too afraid that her own might betray her feelings.

He would hate her feeling bad for him. But the thought of anyone in pain made her feel sick.

The water was warm. There was no brief

shock of cold. It felt like a bath waiting to welcome her. He led her deeper and deeper into the water, away from the shore, away from his friends, away from where her feet could touch the bottom. "I can't stand."

"Grab onto me." He wrapped her legs around his waist. Her arms looped around his neck and her breasts pressed to his chest. "Did Jazz pick out your bathing suit?"

"Yes. How did you know?"

"It's not something you would pick out for yourself."

"You don't like it?"

"I like it just fine," he said gruffly. "I was counting on you coming out here in a tan one-piece. Not this."

"Why does it matter what kind of bathing suit I wear?"

"It took me by surprise, is all."

"Why?"

"Your body . . . It's unexpected."

"I didn't think I looked so bad, but the fact that you dragged me out here where no one can see me has me rethinking that."

"I didn't drag you out here because you look bad. For fuck's sake. I dragged you out here because I didn't want my friends staring at you. You look like one of those girls in the magazines that I used to keep hidden under my mattress as a boy."

His accent grew thicker and she smiled and buried her face in his shoulder. Her nose brushed against one of his scars. Her smile faded as she thought about how he had acquired it.

"Jack's head swung around so fast, I thought his neck would break," he said, sounding annoyed. "He's one of my best mates, but don't spend too much time with him."

"Do you really think he would try to seduce your girlfriend?"

"If he thinks there's no love between us, he will."

"I would never cheat. It's such a violation."

"But we're not really a couple. You wouldn't be cheating."

"If I violated your trust I would be cheating. Even if we aren't sleeping together, there's a relationship there. You're the only person I can trust right now and I want you to trust me."

He made a low noise in his throat. "You're a good woman, Wyn."

They stood there for a little while in quiet. Wyn felt guilty for enjoying his closeness. It was fake. A show for his friends, but she liked the way his body felt against hers. Hard against soft.

And the way his hands felt on her waist: clamped on. Possessive. She liked it more than she wanted to admit.

She liked the way he smelled too, like soap and salt water and sunscreen.

The ocean was warm. The sun was gently beating down on them and for a moment she had forgotten who they were and why they were here. It just felt nice to be the center of one person's attention.

She moved her hand so she could feel the scars on his back. He stiffened slightly, almost as if he were in pain, but she wasn't hurting him. The scars were nasty, but they were old. He was still a young man. He must have seen so much in his short life. "Who hurt you?" she whispered, her lips grazing his ear.

"Don't ask me that." He looked her in the eye and she could see hardness there. "You don't want or need to know."

CHAPTER 6

Cullen lay in his bed later that night, unable
to sleep. He should be passed out. Wyn was.
She had fallen asleep right after they came
back from dinner. A day in the sun and
water had a way of draining the energy out
of a person and lulled them into a good,
deep sleep. It was what Wyn needed. She
looked so sweet when he went to check on
her and so vulnerable, her body curled up
in her bed.

He had the urge to kiss her face and pull
the blankets more tightly around her, but
he didn't, because he knew he could touch
her no more for the day. He had filled his
quota of her.

The next few weeks were going to drive
him mad. He couldn't get the image of her
in that bikini out of his head. She was a
beautiful woman. He had thought that from
the day he had met her, but he never
imagined her to look like that beneath her

clothes. Not model-like beautiful like Jazz. But naturally gorgeous. Unassumingly sexy. The kind that snuck up on you and gut-punched you.

And she had worn white. White against that light brown skin that had grown increasingly sun-kissed as the day went on. And that bikini top that was tied in a bow, right between her breasts, just begging to be untied, begging for a revelation.

He grew hard every time he thought about it. She had shocked him at the beach when she undressed. He felt like a randy teenage boy again, but more than that, he didn't want anyone looking at her. He didn't even want to see her, so he took her deep into the water, thinking that would cool him down, but it was probably a bigger mistake, because he got to feel her breasts pressed against him and her legs wrapped around him. He got to feel her fingers graze down the scars on his back and her lips on his ear. He had been so incredibly erect then. She hadn't known. Her legs were wrapped too high around his waist.

There was no denying his attraction to her or the heavy guilt he felt experiencing it. She was supposed to be his principal and to want to touch her, to peel her clothes off, to run his lips all over her curves and bends, broke every rule.

What made it worse, what made his guilt pound in his chest, was that he had spoken to her father tonight.

"How is she?" he asked.

"She wants to hear from you, sir."

"I can't speak to her."

He wanted to ask why, but it wasn't his place to question his boss. "She is used to working. She doesn't know what to do with herself."

"I know . . . She's like me that way. I worked my ass off until I got to where I needed to be. She doesn't need to work. She needs to play."

"She needs to know the truth, sir. From you."

"Whelan, are you telling me what I should do with my own daughter?" There was an edge in his voice.

"No, sir. Wyn is no biddable girl. She's smart. She'll find out."

"She won't have time to dig if you keep her distracted."

Cullen felt his gut clench. "What do you want me to do?"

"Whatever you have to do, damn it. I wired money into your account. You give her what she needs, even if she doesn't know she needs it."

She needed her own damn father to speak to her. She needed reassurance. But Bates was garbage. "How long do you think it will be, sir? I can't keep her here forever. She'll get restless. You know her."

"Just until I get to the bottom of the leak and sort this thing with her birth mother out."

"She wasn't adopted, was she?"

"She's mine. But I suspected you knew that already. You were former military intelligence."

He shouldn't care. His job was to keep Wynter safe, to keep her occupied. Not to care about the details of her life. He had never cared about the personal lives of anyone he had worked for before. But for some reason he did care about Wyn's and he was more than curious about what the truth was behind the scandal.

He had hung up the phone with his boss hours before, but sleep never came. Just thoughts of Wynter and how he was going to get through the next few weeks.

There was a knock on his door. He hadn't locked it tonight. He hadn't even closed it all the way this time.

He sat up, placing a pillow on his lap to hide his manhood and he opened a book that he kept on his end table before he told her to come in.

He was glad he had the pillow over him because her nightwear almost caused him to groan aloud. It was a simple baby blue nightie, but the material was so thin that he could nearly see through it. He could see the outline of her breasts and that her nipples were hard and standing at attention. His eyes scrambled up to her face when he realized that he was staring at her body just a little too long. "What's the matter, Wyn?"

"I didn't mean to bother you, but I saw that your light was on and I was wondering if you had an extra blanket."

"Are you cold? You can turn down the AC. You have full run of the house."

"I sleep better when the room is cold. I just like to swaddle myself in blankets."

"There's a little closet in my bathroom. You should find a blanket there."

She nodded and he watched her walk away. He would have gotten up and gotten it for her, but if he did she would see how affected he was by her. He'd rather her think he was inconsiderate.

"You've got a huge tub in here," he heard her say.

"I do. I told you, you should have taken this room."

"My room is more than lovely," she said,

reemerging from the bathroom. "I wasn't taking your bed."

"But I feel like shit every time you go into that room and I come into this one."

"Why?"

"Because you deserve better."

She tilted her head and studied him. "Why do you think that? I'm comfortable and I have everything I need. Why do I deserve more than anyone else? Because my father is paying you? The luck of the draw is the only reason I grew up having what I have. I'm no better than you. You've risked your life to protect others. For the last twenty-eight years I have simply existed."

And that right there was why he liked her. She wasn't entitled. She could have been. It seemed almost impossible that she wasn't. He wasn't a fan of her father, but maybe he had raised her right. He had raised her to be kind and generous and sweet. "You've more than existed. Don't sell yourself short."

She gave him a little smile. "I don't want to bother you. I'll get out of your hair now."

"You aren't bothering me. I can't sleep." It sounded, even to his own ears, like an invitation to stay. But he didn't want her to stay. Hell, he didn't want her in the same house as him. She looked too alluring. She smelled too sweet. She made his hands ache with the need to run themselves all over her body.

"Is something on your mind?"

"Yes."

You.

She set the blanket down on the edge of the bed and climbed in next to him. He wished she hadn't done that. His body became even more aware of hers. He wasn't sure what was wrong with him. He had been around her before. He had seen her every single day for the past year, but something had changed. Or maybe nothing changed. Maybe these feelings just intensified. Maybe they had been dormant inside of him. Maybe seeing her at her most vulnerable made him want to protect her even more.

"You want to talk?"

"About why I can't sleep?" he asked, looking at her.

"About anything. I'm surprised you stay awake during my lectures. If you need to get to sleep fast I can tell you the etymology of some words."

"I quite like your lectures. Especially the one about the evolution of words over time. I never went to university. I feel like I'm getting an education."

"You were just a kid when you joined the

military. Were you scared?"

"I was, but anything was better than living with my arsehole father."

"Was it that bad?"

"Yes," he simply said.

"Do you miss Northern Ireland?"

"I grew up in Belfast. There are parts of my country that are so beautiful that you'll want to cry, but I didn't grow up there. It was poverty and violence where I lived. I haven't stepped foot back there since I left."

"There's no family there you want to see?"

"I think about the little ones every now and again." He shook his head. "I guess they aren't so little any more. They're in their twenties now."

"Your siblings?"

"Yes. Maeve and Liam. My aunt took them out of Northern Ireland when my mum died. They lived a very nice life."

"And she didn't take you?"

"No, I was fifteen. I could look after myself. Besides, my pop wouldn't have let me go."

"Why not?"

"He didn't want to be alone."

She made a soft noise and inched closer to him, her shoulder brushing his. "Will you take me to the market tomorrow?"

"I'll take you wherever you want to go.

125

Just say the word. You know that."

"You're saying that as if nothing has changed in the past forty-eight hours."

"What's changed?" he asked, already knowing.

"We're in bed together in the middle of the night and neither one of us is wearing many clothes. You know things changed the moment we arrived on this island."

"I'm trying to pretend they haven't."

"Why?"

"Because it makes things more complicated."

She surprised him by getting on her knees and cupping his face in her gentle hands and pressing her lips to his forehead. They lingered there for a long moment. He shut his eyes briefly. Warm, soft lips on his skin. He had been kissed before, but never like this. At least not since he was a kid. It was odd . . . It was comforting . . . And because it was her, he found it arousing.

"Sometimes things just have to be complicated," she whispered.

She climbed off his bed and left the room with the blanket she had come for, closing the door behind her. He sat there for a moment, his skin still tingling from her lips, his body buzzing from her nearness.

He wanted her. There was no denying

that. But he would have to deny himself the pleasure of her body. She was his to protect. To take care of. She wasn't there to satisfy his needs. He would have to find somebody else for that. But tonight he would have to take care of it himself. He slipped his hand into his underwear and took his erection in his hand. He touched himself, thinking about her, wanting things he knew could never have.

"How long do you think we can keep this from her?"

Wynter sat on the floor in the hallway just outside of her father's study, straining to listen to the discussion on the other side of the door.

Her father had finally come home. This year he would be there for her birthday. He had promised this time. He was to be her birthday present. The only thing she had wanted was one weekend with him and her mother as a family. She had been so excited when she had heard from their housekeeper that he had arrived. She stopped her violin lesson and ran down to his study to meet him, but the door was closed and she heard her mother's muffled voice coming through the wall. Mother never raised her voice. Wynter wasn't even sure she had ever heard her yell, but now she was yelling. The walls were thick in the house,

127

but Wynter could hear her.

"She's going to want to know where she came from."

Wynter couldn't hear her father's reply. He didn't yell back. He wouldn't yell back. But she wished he would. She wanted to know what he was saying.

Were they talking about her? They had to be. Who else? She had been asking her mother if they could go to South Africa this summer. She wanted to see the orphanage where she was rescued from. She wanted to meet the people who had taken care of her. And she hoped . . . even though she had never said a word about it to anyone, that her parents would see another child there, one who was just like her and take them home.

She was born during apartheid. According to what she had been told, she had been born a crime. It had been illegal for black and white people to love each other, illegal for them to create a life, to even live near each other. It sounded so horrible to her. It had sounded like a horrible place, but it was a beautiful one and she wanted to see it. See the nice people there. She wanted a brother or sister. Someone to play with. Someone else to love. She didn't want another horse, or some expensive thing she would never use. She wanted to not feel so lonely. Or so very alone in the world.

But no one would take her to her homeland. No one would even talk to her about it. Wyn kept asking. But maybe she should be asking why they wouldn't take her there instead.

She strained to hear her parents' voices, but her mother had stopped yelling. Heavy footsteps came pounding toward the door. She scrambled to her feet and ran around the corner, her heart pounding. She didn't know why she ran. She should have been braver. She should have walked into that office and demanded to know what they were talking about, what was the truth. But she hid around that corner, too scared to confront them. And she hated herself for it.

Wynter smiled at Jack as he sat at the counter in the kitchen of the community house. Cullen had taken her to a supermarket that morning, where she stocked up on vegetables, spices, and healthier snacks for the community house. They all seemed to eat like teenaged boys there, even Jazz. It made her wonder how Jazz kept her body looking so incredible. It also made her a little bit jealous in more ways than one. No one was ever alone here if they didn't want to be.

She loved the idea of a community

kitchen. Of sharing what they had with each other.

The story of how this place came to be was one she still didn't know, but she would like to. They needed each other, it seemed, and they needed this place because they didn't fit anywhere else in the world.

"You're going to spoil us, Miss Wyn," Jack told her with his gleaming white smile. "King is the only other one who likes to cook here and there's just so much grilled meat a man can take. Plus, no one likes to stare at his ugly ass in the kitchen. You are a much more beautiful sight."

"I'm not ugly," King complained. "I just ain't a pretty boy like you. Throw a wig and a dress on you and half the men in my unit would have tried to date you." King, who was in charge of chopping the veggies for the pasta salad she was making, popped another piece of cucumber in his mouth.

"King," Wyn said, "I don't think you're ugly, but if you keep eating everything you're chopping, there won't be anything left to make the salad with."

"I'm sorry, love," he said bashfully. "I'm just so hungry all the time." He had arms the size of tree trunks and the height of a basketball player, but she thought he was awfully cute in that moment.

"Yes," Darby chimed in, "the man needs to consume a small family's weekly food supply in a day to maintain that kind of bulk. If King gets hungry and there's no food around, we have to lock him in a cage so he doesn't go pillaging in the next village for sustenance."

"Don't be dramatic. I just get a bit grumpy, is all."

"I bought plenty of food. There's cold cuts in the refrigerator. Cullen and I stopped at the little bakery in town and got some really beautiful bread. Make yourselves a sandwich. The pasta salad will be ready soon."

"But I'm not finished chopping," King told her.

"You are relieved of your duty. I will finish."

Wyn took over the rest of the chopping while Darby and King went to the refrigerator. She smiled as she heard the men exclaim over the food she bought. Cullen told her it was too much and that *she* didn't have to buy anything for the community house. But she had ignored him and piled the cart high. This was just a small way of paying his friends back. They had all been so kind to her since she had arrived. She knew it must be strange for them to have an outsider here.

"Tell me about yourself, Wyn," Jack said to her. He really was devastating to look at, especially when he turned that smile on. It was easy to see how women fell for him. He probably didn't need to seduce them at all.

"I'm very boring," she said truthfully. "I teach at a university and do some translating for the local and federal government."

"You've got to be more than just your job. We all are."

"True," she said, but her career had defined her the last six years or so. There was no real life for her outside of it. It was all she had. "I'm pretty sure that I am the dullest person in this community. All of you have lived so much more life than I have."

"What about your family? Are you close?"

She paused before answering him. There was pain there, right under the surface, a short jab in the chest. "No. We aren't very close. I'm an only child. My dad worked a lot. I never saw much of him. My mother is nice, but my father was the center of her universe."

And he had cheated on her, she didn't say. Probably more than once.

It must be such a slap in the face for her mother. But she knew her mother would never leave him, because she had grown up in poverty in the south and Wyn's father gave her everything she could ever want. Her mother had felt rescued and she excused all the inconsiderate things he had done over the years.

"I had one of those fathers too," Jack said.

"What are you two talking about?" Cullen said, walking in.

"I was just trying to get to know Wyn better," Jack said. "Her father is a workaholic. So is mine."

"Yeah." Cullen walked around the counter to where Wyn was and wrapped his arms around her waist and kissed her bare shoulder. It was a pure possession move, a message for Jack. A show for the others, but Wyn still got tingles on her skin. She leaned into Cullen, liking the way his body felt against hers. "I'm guessing when your father is a four-star general there isn't much time for play."

"No, and that's why Pop is still pissed that I left the military before it turned me into a humorless war-obsessed old son of a bitch."

"Dads can really suck sometimes," Wyn said.

"Damn right, girl," Jack said.

"I agree," Cullen murmured.

"I loved my dad," King added, ever positive. "He was a saint. Treated me mum like a queen."

"Oh, shut up about your loving and supportive family, King." Jack grinned at him. "Nobody wants to hear about your happiness when we're bitching."

"I am blessed. Now get off your pretty ass and come get a sandwich before I eat all the bread."

Jack got up and walked toward the other men. "There were four loaves there. There had better be bread left."

"Do you want a sandwich?" Wyn asked Cullen.

"I'll make one in a minute." He was still holding on to her, his chin resting on her shoulder.

"I was offering to make it for you."

"You don't need to do that."

"I want to do it. I see the way you eat. You never take more than you should. You eat just enough to stay alive. You never overindulge." She paused for a long moment and then lowered her voice. "You eat like someone who has been hungry before."

He stiffened slightly. "I have been hungry before," he whispered.

"When you were in the military?"

"Before that. The military gave my life structure. I never went hungry there. I grew up very poor. Things got worse after Mum died."

She could sense a sadness in him last night when they briefly spoke about his family. Separated from his siblings, left with a father he hated. She turned in his arms and looked at him. "Let me make you a sandwich. Please."

"You really want to make me a sandwich, don't you?"

"Yes," she whispered. "You've done so much for me the past year, let me do something for you."

"I did my job. You don't need to thank me for that."

"You had hot tea waiting for me after my lectures. You always seem to know when I'm cold. You stockpiled extra lip balm this winter because you know I always lose mine."

"You figured that out?"

She nodded. "You take care of me."

"I don't do much."

"It means something to me."

He looked at her for a long moment and then closed the distance between their mouths and kissed her gently on the lips. It was the first time their lips had made contact and she felt an intense spark that had traveled through her entire body. It wasn't a deep kiss. It wasn't sexual, but it made her want more of him.

She wasn't sure if it was the sunshine or the tropical setting or the sweet-smelling air, but she was developing this deep need to be closer to him. She had never felt that way about anyone. She knew feeling that way about her bodyguard, about someone who was paid to stay with her, was wrong. They all left in the end. When the paychecks stopped coming, the people she had cared about the most stopped seeing her.

It was foolish to get attached.

"Sweet, lass," he murmured.

She felt like being foolish today. She knew she shouldn't do it, but she had spent her life denying herself. She reached up, looping her arms around his neck and kissed him, deeper this time, her mouth opening beneath his. He kissed her back, his arms tightening around her.

He broke the kiss and looked down at her again, a change in his eyes. Their affection was only supposed to be for show. But that wasn't for show. That was real and she could see the arousal in his eyes.

"No," he said.

"No?"

"You're not allowed to kiss me like that."

"Like what?"

"In a way that's going to get me in trouble."

He pulled away from her and walked outside.

CHAPTER 7

"That sounds like fun," Cullen heard Wyn say a few days after their kiss. "When can we go?"

"Right now," King told her. "I've been wanting some ice cream. There's a shop across the street from the site that puts a whole pint of ice cream on one cone."

"That sounds like a stomachache waiting to happen," Wyn said, her face scrunched.

She was at ease with his friends. He wasn't sure she would be, because looking at her now, anyone would be able to see that she didn't fit in with them. They had all seen action during war. They all had scars and wounds that cut deep. Some of them had done things in the name of their country that would probably make Wyn faint and yet she was there, in her classic but sexy sundress with her good posture and proper speech, hanging out with them and genuinely looking as if she were having a good time.

Could she be pretending? Putting on a good show?

No.

She was too pure for that. Her face betrayed her every emotion. She liked them and he appreciated that.

"His stomach is like a garbage disposal. One day I'm afraid it's going to back up and explode. We're all going to be up to our knees in beef and chips and protein powder," Darby said.

Wyn giggled. Cullen had tried not to stare at her. It was a hard habit to break. His only task this past year was to watch her every move, anticipate her every whim. But he wasn't supposed to do that here. Still, his eyes zeroed in on her. He had never heard her laugh like that. It was sweet.

"Sorry!" She slapped her hands over her mouth. "I just got an image of that in my head."

"Don't be sorry for laughing, sis," King said, squeezing her shoulder with his massive hand. "You don't ever have to be sorry for doing that here. Now, come on. The ice cream shop doesn't stay open all day, so let's go. Darby, you're driving."

"Where are you going?" Jazz walked up to the patio. Cullen hadn't seen very much of her the past couple of days. She got like this sometimes. She needed to be alone, to disappear for a while. They all knew to give her space, to not go off in search of her.

"To see the pirate's castle and get ice cream." The smile had dropped from King's face. There was an intensity in his eyes that reminded Cullen that he was more than the friendly, affable giant that most of them saw him as. He seemed angry.

"Are you going to invite me on this outing?" Jazz asked, her hand on her hip, as if she were challenging King.

"No. You're not invited. Neither is Cullen."

"Excuse me?" Cullen turned to face his friend. "Why not?"

"We like your girlfriend better than you," Darby said.

"It's true," Jack called from the hammock he had been dozing in.

"You coming with us, Jack?"

"I'll meet you at the ice cream shop after you finish with the castle. I've got an errand to run and then I've got to take a couple for a sunset flight around the bay."

"That sounds so romantic," Wyn said.

"It is." Jack hopped out of the hammock and sauntered his way over to the rest of them. "Just say the word and I'll take you up."

"Cullen needs to decide when he would like to go."

"Oh, sweetheart, just like with today's outing, Cullen will not be invited to that one. It will just be me and you and the orange-purple sunset."

Wyn's cheeks grew a little red as she smiled. "Darn. It has always been my dream to be with two men as the sun set."

Cullen's eyes widened at her naughty little joke. She took him off guard again and it wasn't for the first time.

"That was good, Wyn," Jazz said, her gaze still appraising. "I didn't think you had it in you."

"There's a lot you don't know about me, Jazz," she said quietly, before turning to King and Darby. "Gentlemen, there's a pirate castle to see and ice cream to be had."

"Well, then. . . ." Darby offered her his arm. "I think we should go."

A few moments later they were gone. Jack and Jazz were both facing Cullen, neither one of them looking at ease. "What?"

"Marry her," Jack said.

"What?" both he and Jazz said at the same moment.

"You heard me. Marry that girl. If there is any happiness to be found in the world, you'll find it with her."

It was then Cullen was reminded that for all Jack's good looks and charm, he had a darkness in him too. He was a POW. Captured and held for months. Out of everyone in the group, he talked the least about his time away.

He was like Jazz in a way. He used his charm the way Jazz used her fierce attitude and sex appeal. Like a shield. Keeping everyone from getting too close. But unlike Jazz, who sometimes confided in King, Jack spoke to no one.

"I didn't think you believed in marriage, Jack," Cullen said.

Jack shrugged. "Marriage works for some people. Wyn's the type of girl you marry and if you can't see that, you're a complete dumb-ass."

"What about me?" Jazz asked with her hands on her hips. "Am I the kind of girl you marry?"

Jack turned on the devilish grin that made most women melt. He stepped closer to Jazz, grabbed her by the waist and kissed her neck. "Jasmine, my sweet, beautiful princess. I would marry you in a heartbeat. But we can't get married. We're too hot." He kissed the other side of her neck. "We'll go to bed once and end up burning this whole island down."

"We would," Jazz sighed. "It's a shame. We would make the most gorgeous children."

"I'll make you a deal. If you still haven't found your soul mate by forty, I'll make a baby with you."

"Deal." She grinned at him, but it faded away. "You really think Wyn is worth marrying? That's huge. We don't invite outsiders in."

"He brought her here. That says something. The boys love her. I like her."

Jack said he liked her. Not that she was hot or that he wanted to take her to bed. But he liked her. Those words made the hair on the back of Cullen's neck stand up.

Rationally, he knew that Wyn wasn't his, but she felt like his. In another world she might have been his. But in this world he couldn't have her. Not the way his body craved her.

"I'm serious, Jack. Don't try it with her."

"I'm not trying anything with her. She doesn't want me. She wants you. It's all in her eyes. You can tell so much about a woman from her eyes."

She had kissed him. Well . . . he had kissed her first. Just lightly on the lips, because she was sweet and kind and she had wrapped herself around him. He controlled it. He had wanted to cup her face in his hands and kiss the breath out of her. He knew he couldn't do it. That was too much and he had too little control. But then she turned around and kissed him, deeper than he had kissed her, with her mouth open and her tongue sweeping in. He had broken the kiss and looked down at her. Everything was in her eyes. Everything was in her kiss.

There was something there between them, but he didn't want to acknowledge it with her, so he told her *no.* To not kiss him like that. To not make him want her more than he already did.

"She's a good girl, Jack."

"Maybe a little too good for you."

"I agree," Cullen said with a nod.

"I'm going to catch up with them. You two enjoy your day."

He left Jazz and Cullen alone on the patio. "Your *girlfriend* is getting rave reviews from the boys."

He didn't miss the emphasis on the word *girlfriend.* "Why don't you like her? She hasn't done anything to deserve your dislike."

"It's not that I don't like her. I just don't trust her."

"You don't trust anyone. You were a spy. It's in your nature."

"I do trust some people, but not her or this relationship. Are you sure she's not running a scam?"

"What kind of scam would she be running? You think she's a gold digger?"

"I know you have some money socked away, but it's not that she's after."

"Then what?"

"She's a little too perfect. A little too well-bred. Are you sure she's not a spy?"

"What secrets do I have that she would want? I haven't been in intel in over five years. And I didn't even work for the United States."

"I'm sure you have secrets. I don't know what it is about this girl, but there's something not right about you two and I just can't put my finger on it."

"I could say the same thing about you and King. What happened between you two? He's not happy with you."

"Nothing happened," she said a little too quickly. Jazz was good at hiding her emotions, but she couldn't hide hers right now. He saw a flash of pain in her eyes.

"It wasn't nothing. King is mad and I'm damn well sure it was your fault."

Her eyes went wide with outrage. "He's not perfect. How do you know it wasn't his fault?"

"Because I know you and you're harder to get along with than a wet cat. He's the most patient out of all of us and if he can't be bothered with you, then you must've done something to cross him."

"It was a difference of opinion. That's all."

"Apologize to him. He'd kill for you, but more importantly, he'd die for you. Stop being an arse and tell him you're sorry."

"I'll think about it."

"Don't think about it too long. Don't let your pride get in the way of your friendship."

Later that night, Wyn sat on the edge of her bed, looking out the window at the paradise around her. The sky was black, but the moon was bright and huge and, unlike at home in D.C., she could see every star in the sky. She was tempted to go outside and walk around in the balmy darkness, but she knew she couldn't. Cullen would probably hear the door open and spring outside to see what she was up to. She wouldn't disturb him tonight. But the need to go outside was strong and she wondered if she could climb out the window quietly.

The day had been lovely. She had immensely enjoyed her time with Darby and King. The two men made her laugh and King treated her with a warm protectiveness that felt brotherly. He had bought her ice cream and gave her a mini-tour of the island. If this was a normal vacation she would have been very happy, but tonight the tears were rolling down her cheeks and she couldn't stop them.

She had run away from her life. Her career. Her home and routines. But she was in paradise with wonderful people and she should be enjoying herself, but she couldn't fully, because she was thinking about all she had left behind, the scandal that forced her away, and the mystery of her birth.

There was a knock on her door.

"Yes?" She wiped her eyes and sat up straight.

Cullen opened the door slightly and poked his head in. "I just wanted to check on you. I saw that your . . ." He trailed off. "You've been crying."

He pushed the door all the way open and walked in. He was shirtless again, all of his brutal scars on display. He only wore sleep pants; his feet were bare and barely made a sound as he walked across the wood floors.

"I'm fine."

"If you tell me that those were happy tears that made your eyes so red, I'm going to say you're full of shit, lass."

She smiled, knowing that he knew that

she liked when he called her that. "I'm fine. Really. Please, go back to bed. I hope I wasn't making too much noise."

"You weren't. I just wanted to see how you were." He sat down next to her on the side of the bed. "You're not well."

"I think I should go back to D.C. soon. Everything has been so lovely here, but I feel like I'm running away. I just left everything behind."

Cullen shook his head. "It hasn't been a full week. The reporters are still swarming your house, waiting for you to appear. You can't go back. They won't give you any peace."

"But I don't know anything. They can hound me if they want, but they won't learn anything. Pretty soon they'll get tired."

"Maybe, but they'll tear your life apart in the process. You're a person who likes peace. I know that about you."

"What life did I have? I had my work. If I go back home, I could learn the truth. I don't believe the letters were made up. I want to know who my birth mother is."

Cullen's jaw tightened. "You think the media is who you would like to find that out from?"

"I want my father to tell me. But he won't speak to me and that tells me a hell of a lot, more than any reporter could."

"I don't see how going back will make things better. If the news breaks, we can easily access it here."

She shut her eyes and took a deep breath. Her chest started to feel like it was closing, little fingers of panic squeezing around her heart.

The not knowing was the worse. The most painful.

Her father didn't respect her enough to tell her the truth. He still treated her like she was a child, too simple to understand the complexities of an adult relationship. Or maybe he was trying to save her opinion of him. He didn't want her to know he was a cheater. But this was worse. The silence made her think less of him.

She felt Cullen's large, warm hand on her cheek and she opened her eyes to look at him. His face had been so unreadable to her before, but this time he couldn't hide what he was feeling. She could see the concern there.

Things were changing between them. A little more each day. Complicating an already too complicated mess.

"Stay with me," he whispered.

She wasn't sure if he meant here on the island or in that moment. "I'm okay now."

149

"You're not. But you try to put up a good front."

He was so close to her. His hand on her skin. His large body looming over her. She could smell his clean scent. Feel the warmth emanating from his body. It was making her heady. She took a deep breath. "I think I need some air."

He nodded. "Get your shoes and something to cover your shoulders with and meet me at the back of the house."

She walked outside to see that he had changed into shorts and a T-shirt. For a moment she wondered if she should head back inside and change her clothes, but he grabbed her hand and led her out onto one of the trails that snaked off from behind his house. It was gorgeous outside. Just a light breeze blowing through the trees. The extreme heat of the day was gone; the humidity had died down. For a little while she forgot about her problems and just listened to nature around her: the sound of the birds, insects, and the wind blowing through the trees. The stars had been brighter than from the other side of her window and she watched them and the moon as Cullen led her down the trail. She never once looked where she was going or asked him a question. She trusted him. She wasn't sure when it had happened, but she had trusted him for a long time in a way she had never trusted anyone.

He made her feel safe.

She heard running water and she looked up to see a small waterfall coming from a rock formation that fed into a crystal-clear pool. The moon was so bright that it was almost as if there was a spotlight shining down on it.

"I come here when I can't sleep sometimes," Cullen said, his accent almost as soothing as the sound of the water. "There's a lot of shitty things that happen in this world and it makes you wonder how God would let them happen, but then there are little pieces of perfect like this and it reminds you that even though there is bad, there is always good." His hand reached up and stroked her cheek. "Please, don't cry, Wyn."

She hadn't realized that she was, but she was emotional and his words were so beautiful. "I don't know why I'm crying."

"Because you're hurt."

She rolled her eyes. "I hate feeling sorry for myself. There are people who are worse off than I am."

"But you want a mum and a dad who'll love you like you need."

She locked eyes with him. "Who loves *you* like you need?"

"Who says I need love?"

"I do. Everyone does."

He tilted his head. "We weren't talking about me. We were talking about you."

"What if I want to talk about you? I'm supposed to be in love with you. I should know more."

"I'm a dull man." He grabbed her hand again and tugged her slightly closer. "Slip off your shoes. The water is nice. It's feel like a warm bath."

Wynter kicked off her sandals and sat on the edge of the little pool. Cullen was right; the water was bathlike. "How did you find this place?"

"It's on our property. It was one of the things that sold me on the place."

She looked back at him. He was still standing behind her. "Why am I sitting here by myself?"

"You're a bit sassy today," he said as he sat down beside her.

"Am I? Sorry. I don't mean to be rude."

"Don't apologize. I feel like I'm seeing the real you and not the person you present to the world."

"Do you think I'm not genuine?"

"Don't go twisting my words." He looked

at her for a long moment. "You're perfect, Wyn. From the way you lift a fork to the way you walk across a room. Never a misstep. Never a wrong choice. Never a thing you do without grace or class."

Perfect? She almost laughed at the thought. Her entire life she had felt like a fumbling imposter and here was this man, telling her that she was perfect and it was hard for her to believe. "You see me in a way that no one ever has."

"I look at you sometimes and wonder how you could manage to be so perfect all the time. It has to be exhausting."

"I was raised thinking my parents had saved me from an orphanage in South Africa. That I was born as a crime during apartheid and that no one wanted me until my father came along and saved me. My mother used to tell me that I could never make him look bad. That everything I did or said was a reflection of him and my choices in life could affect his dreams. I felt a heavy guilt and this unbelievable pressure to always do the right thing. Not the right thing for me, or because I thought it was right, but the right thing for my parents. Now I don't know what to do or think or how to behave."

"There's no one here to impress. No one

here gives two shits about your father. You don't have to watch what you say or how you act. You're free here. Why be in such a rush to go back to a place where you have to wear a mask? It's hard to take your mind off what you left behind, but enjoy your time here. Enjoy your freedom."

"I'm not sure I know how. My whole life has been so structured. What do you think I should do?"

"I think you should stop asking others what they think you should do. What have you always wanted to do? Steal a car? Jump out of a plane? Take an exotic lover?"

"That last one sounds interesting. I'll have to give it more thought, but there is one thing I've always wanted to do and now seems like the perfect time to do it."

"What is it?"

"Skinny-dip."

She heard him inhale sharply as she stood up, took off her cardigan and pulled her nightgown off over her head. She was nude beneath it and as soon as her skin felt the breeze, tingles broke out along her skin. Her nipples tightened. Cullen was looking at her. No, he was more than looking at her. He was staring with a mix of arousal and shock in his eyes.

She stepped into the water, trying not to

be self-conscious. It had been a long time since she had been naked in front of anyone. It took a lot for her to reveal herself to someone, to be intimate, but with Cullen it was different. He knew her in a way no one did. He saw sides to her that she didn't even see herself. Swimming naked wasn't something she thought she would ever have the chance to do. It seemed too naughty, too decadent for the daughter of a wealthy, powerful man who was raised to be quiet and humble and sheltered. It was something she might not have done last week, but this week things were different. This week she was in paradise with a beautiful man. This week she could pretend she wasn't the Wyn who always played it safe, who always did what she was told.

"This water feels so good," she moaned and she submerged herself fully. "Come join me."

"No."

"No?" She looked up at him. His face had slipped back into his neutral mask. He was her bodyguard again, her highly trained security expert. "Why not?"

"I could lose my job."

"I would rehire you. Besides, who would ever know? It is just you and me and the moonlight."

"No."

"But you want to?" She swam closer to him.

"This is not about what I want. This is about what is right."

"Is it wrong to come swimming with me?"

"It is when you are naked as the day you were born."

"Why? It's just skin. It's just a body. Everyone has one. What's the difference between swimming with me now and swimming with me at the beach the other day?"

"You know damn well what the difference is."

"I don't. You held me close that day. You ran your hands all over my body, my legs were wrapped around your waist, your lips touched my ear as you spoke into it. Our eyes connected. We were close."

"It was hard for me that day," he said, swallowing.

"Because you didn't want to touch me?"

"Because I wanted to touch you too much."

"So touch me."

"I can't, because unlike before, there are no other people around. It's just you and me and the moonlight, like you said. There's no one to stop me. There's no one to keep things from going too far. I'm only a man, you see. I've only got so much self-control. I cannot cross that line with you tonight, because there is no going back. You're hurting right now. You want something to take your mind off your troubles and you can't use me that way, because you'll get back to your life and you might regret this. And I don't want to live as one of your regrets."

She was quiet for a moment, trying to absorb all he had said. She *was* sad. She *did* want to distract herself from her thoughts, but . . . but. . . . She wouldn't regret swimming with a beautiful man in the moonlight. She would never regret the feel of his hard body against hers, or the way his beautiful brogue was like balm to her soul. She didn't want to use him. She wanted to give as much to him as he had given to her.

"How could I regret something that would make me happy?"

He sighed and stood up, stripping off his clothes. Her eyes widened as she got a full view of his erection. She grew aroused every time he got near her, but this time she felt a hard throbbing between her legs.

"I live to make you happy," he said before he backed up, took a running start and cannonballed into the pool. His splash was huge, completely soaking her.

He remerged, his hair slicked down on his

head. He grinned at her and she was stunned for a moment. His smile was so beautiful. She had seen him smile at his friends over the past few days, but this was the first time she was a recipient of his smile. How had she ever thought of him as cold? How could she have not seen the man who was there just beneath the surface?

"I'll race you to the other side of the pool," he said before taking off. She followed him. They didn't touch that night, but she couldn't recall another time she'd had so much fun.

CHAPTER 8

The next morning when Cullen got up, his house was empty. He had suspected that Wyn went to the community house to make breakfast for everyone like she usually did. He was tempted to follow her there, but he stayed behind at his house.

He needed space from her.

They had spent nearly all of last night together, not rolling around in bed as he had sometimes dreamed about, but swimming, playing in that warm pool of water. Neither of them dressed. He had been naked in front of his fair share of women, but this time he felt even more exposed, stripped down.

He enjoyed himself with her. Enjoyed himself in a way he hadn't with any other woman and he hadn't laid a single hand on her.

At first it had been torture, seeing her naked body glide through the water, seeing

159

the way she looked at him, with a kind of innocent expectation. He was never a man who was easily convinced. He could never be manipulated. It was what made him good at his job when he was working for British military intelligence. But he had a difficult time saying *no* to her. He didn't like looking into her eyes and denying her. Last night he had wanted to give in and throw every one of his principles away and just make her feel however she wanted to feel.

But he was still on the job, working for her father. He owed some loyalty to the man, but it was getting harder and harder to stay loyal to someone who was purposely hurting the person they were supposed to love the most.

He pulled out his cell phone and dialed Bates. The man picked up immediately.

"What it is, Whelan?"

"Wynter wants to go back to D.C."

"What? She can't go back there. The media is still swarming. Another letter has been released and I'm nowhere near finding out where the leak is coming from."

"I could track that that information for you, sir. My background is —"

"I'm fully aware of what your background is, but your job is to take care of my daughter."

"She's upset, sir. You can't expect her to sit still and wait until you issue the order that everything is okay."

"Wynter will do as she is told."

"Respectfully, sir, I'm not so sure about that. Your daughter is her own person. She wants to speak to you."

"I have nothing to say to her."

"You owe her a conversation."

"You don't get to tell me what to do. You work for me and that can change in a heartbeat."

"You're going to fire me? For what? Asking you to speak to her? I've been with her for a year. She trusts me and right now she'll listen to me a lot faster than she'll listen to you. I could tell her some things."

"What exactly are you saying?"

"I'll put her on the first plane back to the states," he lied. "I'm sure you can find someone to replace me within a few hours."

"Are you blackmailing me?"

"You damn politicians are so full of secrets, you think everyone is out to get you. I don't want anything from you." He paused, trying to calm himself. "I can't look at her being so upset. It wasn't in my job description."

Bates actually laughed. "You can't handle an emotional woman? I know the feeling.

I'll double your salary. That's more money than anyone like you could ever dream of making."

"It's not about the money. Just talk to her. Reassure her. Hell, lie to her if you have to, but she wants to hear from you."

"I can't," he said quietly. "I could never bear to see her in pain. I can't hear it in her voice. It's the one thing I'm not capable of. You're right. She not a baby anymore. I can't fix this with a pony or an expensive trinket. She won't take a simple explanation from me and I can't lie to her."

"So, you want me to deal with her pain." It wasn't a question. It was what he was telling him to do.

"Yes. You don't love her. It won't hurt you the same way."

Cullen's stomach tightened. Maybe he didn't love Wynter like her father did, but there were feelings there and seeing her in pain bothered him more than he could express.

He ended his call, showered and dressed before heading to the community house. It was a very late start for him. It was nearly noon, but he and Wynter had stayed out nearly all last night and when he got back he slept soundly. The only thing that could have made his rest even better was if he could have shared his bed instead of sleeping alone. When he walked up to the house, he spotted Wynter sitting at the counter with Jack. It wasn't the smiling, flirty conversation he was used to seeing Jack have with a woman, but a serious one. That made him more concerned than if they had been flirting. He had tried to push his jealousy away. It *was* jealousy. He was man enough to admit it.

Jack was probably a better match for Wynter. His father was a four-star general. His mother was the daughter of a former vice president. He was from a better family, highly educated and highly respected. No one would think twice if the two of them turned up as a pair.

Cullen was from pig-shit Irish. Raised by a drunk. A school dropout who only got his education because he was lucky enough to get into the military. He didn't deserve to sit at the same table as Wynter Bates and yet he wanted more than just to sit at the table with her. He wanted more than just to take her to bed. He wanted to drink up every part of her like he was a dehydrated man and she was the only thing to keep him from dying of thirst.

She must have felt his eyes on her, because she looked up at him and smiled. "Hello, sleeping beauty." She got up from the stool and walked over to him, taking his hand and immediately walked around to the side of the house.

"What's the matter?" he asked her.

"Nothing." She cupped his face in her soft hands and pulled his lips toward hers. He couldn't think for a moment. The anticipation of kissing her had wiped his mind clean. There was a deepness to her kiss, a passion that he hadn't expected. It drew him in, made him unable to pull away, unable to do anything except return her kiss. He grew aroused immediately. His hands closed around her waist and suddenly he felt too hot in his clothes. He wanted to strip them off, strip her bare, but he remembered who he was and where he was and where he had come from.

He broke the kiss. Her lips were pink and swollen and she sighed. She was killing him.

"What the hell was that for? You're only supposed to be kissing me in public and you are never supposed to kiss me like that."

"I don't want you thinking that was for show. I want you to know that I'm kissing you because I want to. Because I needed to."

He let out a long breath and pressed his forehead against hers. "Why do you need to kiss me this morning?"

"Were you on the phone with my father this morning?"

He hesitated for a moment before answering. "You overheard?"

"Not everything, but enough." She kissed his chin. "Thank you."

"I didn't do anything."

"You care."

"No one wants to see anyone else hurting."

"That's not true. The world is full of people who don't care about anyone else's pain, much less would do anything to prevent it." She kissed down his neck and he shut his eyes, enjoying the feeling of his lips on her skin.

He had to push her away, but he didn't want to. Not yet. It had been a very long time since anyone had touched him like this. Maybe no one ever had. Maybe he hadn't allowed them to.

"What were you and Jack talking about?"

"His family."

"You were?" Jack wasn't one to reveal much to any of them. But he was sharing with Wynter. He couldn't blame him. It was the way she looked at a person while she was listening. With her head tilted and her eyes focused and full of understanding. She

165

was the type of woman who could make a man spill state secrets. He thought only Jazz had had that power, but Wyn had it in a different way.

"Our parents know each other. I've had dinner at his house in Maryland when I was a kid. Clearly, I didn't bring that little tidbit up."

"I'm glad you didn't."

"Do you think he knows who I am?"

"Not yet. Stop talking to him."

"Stop talking to him? I can't just stop talking to him."

"Of course not. You're too gracious for that. He likes you. All my friends like you."

"Not Jazz."

"She doesn't trust you."

"Is there anything I can do to change that?"

"Besides leave? No."

"You won't let me go."

He shook his head. "I won't let you go." Not yet. He couldn't.

"I'm assuming you didn't get any further with my father. He still won't speak to me?"

"He doesn't want to face you."

The sadness crossed her face and it hit him in the gut. He understood her father, but he still didn't understand how someone could be so without honor. How he could refuse to face her.

"So now what? How long is this supposed to go on?"

"Not forever. I promise. Until then, just try to enjoy yourself."

He told her to try to enjoy herself when she was there. And she *could* enjoy herself. There were parts of her day when she was perfectly happy, when she was with King or Jack or Darby. When she was cooking or swimming or just chatting. She loved the beauty of her surroundings and if it weren't for the uncertainty hanging over her head, this would be the best time of her life.

Cullen had tried to help.

You owe her a conversation.

But her father wouldn't give her that. It was the only thing he had ever denied her, except the truth.

Wynter refused to take his refusal. She refused to wait for him to explain. She snuck away the next morning, making the long walk into town. There was a little coffee shop she had seen when she had gone grocery shopping with Cullen. One that had Wi-Fi. She had taken her iPad with her, the one she brought along with her when she foolishly thought she was going to be able to catch up on reading. But her mind couldn't concentrate on fictional words. She craved fact.

The coffee shop was quiet, sleepy in a way that the one she frequented in D.C. could never be. No one was impatiently waiting for their order. There were no flustered baristas trying to get through a huge line of caffeine-deprived customers. She ordered a large cup of coffee and a guava turnover. She had planned to get right to work, but she didn't turn on her iPad at first. She sat there and sipped her strong, piping-hot coffee as she stared out the window at the ocean in the distance. There was a breeze blowing, causing the palm trees to sway gently. Everything was so calm. So blue and green and vividly gorgeous. Her hometown wasn't like this, but she wondered if there was beauty there that she was missing, which she had taken for granted because her head was so focused on work. There was nothing else to distract her. No family or love or even close friends. Just work.

A sadness swept through her. That wasn't much of a life at all.

When she left here that would need to change. There was fun to be had. Joy to be experienced. How had she forgotten that?

She had only been on the island for six days, but she had already learned that one thing about herself. She was preventing herself from living a fuller life.

She turned on her iPad and connected to the internet. She didn't have to perform a search for her father's name. His picture was splashed on her homepage.

THE MISTRESS AND THE FUTURE MR. PRESIDENT

Wynter's eyes poured over the article. Another letter had been released. There was a photograph of it. Big, loopy feminine writing on folded notebook paper. It wasn't on scented stationery. It wasn't sealed with a kiss. It somehow made it more real for Wynter.

The contents of the letter were below the picture, but Wynter couldn't bring herself to look at it yet. Her eyes kept going back to the picture of her father. Her entire life, she had been told he was an important man. He looked important in his designer suit. He looked powerful.

She had believed in his politics. In taking care of veterans, in fighting corruption, in educating the people on their rights. But what if it all was a sham?

She forced herself to read the letter. It was the second one released, but it was written before the other one, the more explosive one.

W,

I still remember the first time I saw you. You were in your office. Your shirt-sleeves rolled up. Your tie was off. Your shirt was unbuttoned at the collar. I had never seen a man so beautiful. I was supposed to vacuum your floor, but I was terrified to interrupt you. I knew you were working on something that would change the world. And now I'm working on something that will change the world. You helped create her, of course, but I'm growing her and I can tell she's going to be healthy and strong and brilliant just like her father. I'm trying to stay happy, but it's hard for me here. I can only go outside for an hour a day and you know how jumpy I get, how I can't stay still. How I vibrate with energy and some-times just want to run and run until I feel free, but I can't do that here. Every-one keeps telling me that I have to be careful for my baby, so they watch me all the time. I would never hurt her. You know that, don't you? I'm going to try harder this time. And I know it will be okay, because I have you in my corner this time. I don't have to be alone.

I'm sorry for what happened. I know you say you're not upset with me, but sometimes I think you are. Sometimes, I think you won't ever be able to forgive me. You don't look at me the same way. I think out of everything that happened that kills me the most. I love you. I love you more than any man I have ever known and I want to be with you, in whatever way we can. Will you come see me soon? My belly grows every day. I need you to see it. To rub it. To hug me and tell me everything is going to be okay. Promise me you will.

All my love,

G

"Are you okay, ma'am?"

Wynter looked up to see a young woman in an apron beside her. It was then she realized she had tears running down her cheeks. "Yes. Excuse me. I'm fine. I was just reading something incredibly sad."

She had gone back to the compound after that and laid low for the rest of the day. All the other members of the community had been preoccupied with their own things. Jack went to work. Cullen was helping Darby and King fix something that had gone wrong in one of the currently unoccupied cottages.

Jazz was the only one around when she

walked up to the community house later that afternoon. She was rummaging around in the refrigerator, looking for something.

"Damn it," she cursed. "Sometimes I can't stand living with all men."

"Really?" Wynter asked, causing Jazz to stiffen. "I'm starting to think it is better to live with all men than all women."

"Sometimes I think it might be better if I lived completely alone."

"I lived completely alone. You can't blame anyone for eating the last of the ice cream, but there's no one there to fill up the quiet times. No one to have dinner with. No one to talk to or laugh with."

"Aren't you a goddamn ray of sunshine today?"

Wynter shook her head. "Sorry. I just meant that what you have here is nice."

Jazz looked at her suspiciously. "What's your plan? How long are you going to be here?"

"I'm not sure. Maybe another week or so."

"And after that? What is your plan for Cullen?"

Wynter knew that Jazz could sniff out a lie a mile away, so she chose her words very carefully. "I think you should be asking him what his plan is for me."

"You don't know?"

"He's hard to read and he's not one to talk about his feelings. You know that."

Jazz nodded. "None of us are. Except for King." She frowned. "Someone who used to beat the shit out of people for a living shouldn't be so damn sensitive."

"I think he would be a good father. I could just picture him with a houseful of kids. They would never go for one second thinking they were unloved."

"You're romanticizing it. No one is a perfect parent."

"Of course not, but I think King would be a great one."

"What about Cullen? Do you think he would be a good father?"

"Yes," she answered carefully. "I'm not sure he wants children, though."

Jazz raised her perfectly sculpted eyebrow. "You've never had that conversation?"

"No. When Cullen and I met, I don't think he ever intended for us to be a couple, much less a serious couple. There's a lot of conversations we haven't had. There are some we might never have, but I promised myself that I was no longer going to live in the past or the future. I can only live for now."

"You sound like a self-help book."

"Maybe." She smiled at Jazz. "I haven't

lived an eighth of the life you have. I promised myself that I would never be like my father, but I'm more like him than I want to be. All I've done is work. I don't want to look back twenty years from now and see that all I have to show for it is nothing."

"Is that why Cullen brought you here? To give you an experience you've never had?"

"I don't know. I think he probably felt sorry for me. Things have been rough at home."

"What happened?"

"Ah." Wynter shook her head. "I will only tell you about my dark and twisty secrets if you tell me about yours."

Jazz's lips curled into a slight smile and Wynter was struck by how gorgeous she was. Cullen wouldn't be with her because King loved her. She wondered where the pair would be if a nearly twenty-year friendship didn't stand in the way. "Touché. Keep your secrets, girl. Lord knows we've all got them here."

Cullen had barely seen Wyn that day. He had been working on one of the empty houses. A storm had done some damage to the roof during hurricane season and now they were finally getting around to fixing it.

It was one of the cottages they rented out. It was on the far side of their property, with its own entrance from the road. Well away from their crew's homes.

It was how they brought in income during the tourist season. They each had their own jobs. Jack recruited and transported guests. Darby maintained the grounds. King did most of the upkeep on the cottages and Jazz took care of the marketing, website, and books. Cullen just helped out wherever he was needed, whenever he could. He worked most of his time off-island, while the others stayed on nearly the entire year, taking small jobs here and there whenever the offer was juicy enough. His friends were experts in acquiring information. Normally, he would turn to them if he needed help, but this time he couldn't. He would have to let go of his own secrets in order to do that. Protecting Wyn's privacy was his number-one priority.

He needed to find out who her mother was. Bates needed to be the one to tell her and Cullen was still holding out hope he would, but in the meantime, he was gathering all the information he could. It would be his present to Wyn before he left her. He had made up his mind. As soon as he returned to D.C., he was going to resign. The lines were already blurring between them. He was feeling things for her he shouldn't feel. He thought the island and this charade they were playing was to blame, and maybe if they returned to D.C. and back to their normal roles, whatever was between them would fade away. But if he was being honest with himself, he would admit that maybe these feelings weren't new. Maybe he had felt them for her long before he had ever felt her body pressed against his. And that was no good. Even if he still worked for her when they left here, he wouldn't be able to forget how her mouth tasted, or how her hands felt when she brushed them over his scars. He would want more of her. More than he deserved.

Wynter was on the other side of the dinner table from him, sitting in between Darby and Jack. She was listening to Darby tell a story about growing up in the desert in Australia, with a aboriginal mother.

"She's sad today," he heard Jazz say from beside him.

"What?" He turned to her, surprised by her observation.

"Your girlfriend is sad. You should probably find out what's wrong with her."

"I agree with Jazz on this one," King said. "If someone with no feelings can tell, then it's incredibly obvious."

176

"I have feelings," Jazz shot back.

King's expression hardened and he shook his head. "Yes, you feel things. Annoyance, anger, disgust."

"I want you to stop being mad at me," she said seriously. "I don't like it."

"Now we both have things we don't like."

"King . . ." For a moment Cullen saw something that looked very much like vulnerability cross Jazz's face. She kissed King's shoulder. "I hate it."

He shook his head again and turned back to Cullen. "Make sure your woman is happy, okay? I'm going to bed early." He got up from the table and walked away.

Jazz stared after him and it made Cullen wonder what the hell had happened between his friends. He had always known that King had loved Jazz, but the last time he was there he had suspected that something had been going on between them. Now he was certain. But they were adults and their relationship was something they were going to have to figure out.

He had his own issues.

He turned his attention back to Wynter. He knew she had been upset, but he didn't know how to fix it. He had placed a few calls today, but her father had covered his tracks extremely well. There was a reason he wanted to keep Wynter's birth mother a secret and it wasn't just because she was the product of an affair. It had to go much deeper.

In order to pull his attention away from Wynter, Cullen got up from the table and started clearing plates. He cleaned the kitchen. Night had already fallen on the island. They would have to return to their cottage soon. It was the hardest time of the day for him. He lay alone in his room, knowing that she was just a few feet away, in her bed, barely dressed. He couldn't distract himself with other things. He couldn't escape her.

"Let me help you."

She came up beside him, drying the dishes, her arm brushing his as he they worked. They didn't say a word to each other, but his friends were right. He could feel her sadness today. It was heavier than before and as soon as they were done in the kitchen, he took her hand and led her back to their cottage.

"It's our turn to cook tomorrow," she said. "What do you want me to make?"

"Stop thinking about tomorrow and what I want. Just relax."

"Sorry. I can't seem to. You know how much I'm used to working."

"I do. Why don't you go take a bath in my room? Actually, I'm not giving you an option. I'll run it for you." He brought her into his bedroom.

"You don't have to do that. I can run my own bathwater."

"I know, but why should you have to when I'm willing to do it?"

"Don't be so nice to me. I'm not sure I can take it today."

He looked down at her. Her sadness was so deep. It looked as if tears were going to form in her eyes at any second. He pulled her close and wrapped his arms around her. He knew he shouldn't have done it, but he couldn't help it. "What's the matter, pretty lass?"

"Nothing." She rested her face against his chest and wrapped her arms around him. "I'm just tired."

She was lying to him, but he didn't push. He knew what it was like not to want to have someone invade his private thoughts. "Let me run you a bath."

"Mmm," she moaned. "Can we just stay like this a little while longer?"

"Yes." He didn't want to let her go. He knew he should, but he didn't want to. He wasn't just giving her the comfort she needed, he was getting something in return.

He rubbed his hands down her back and shut his eyes. When was the last time he held somebody like this? When was the last time he felt this kind of warmth?

He had fallen in love, or what he thought was love, with a girl right before he went into the military. Her name was Lola, but he was never really sure if that was her actual name or one she had invented to escape the life she was handed. She was a street kid like he had been, born and dragged up in East London. Her family was shit, just like his was, her mother kicking her out every time she had a new boyfriend. She was a thief, mostly stealing food, but she could lift a wallet in less than ten seconds.

She would disappear for days and when she would return, she would be bruised and damaged and he would hold her. Not quite like this, but he would cradle her, comfort her, wanting to save her from all her troubles when he could barely keep himself afloat.

He was feeling that now. The need to save Wyn, but she didn't need saving.

He felt her soft, warm hands slip up the back of his shirt, her fingers tracing his scars. There wasn't another time he could recall allowing this to happen, letting someone touch his scars like this. He used to try to hide them, embarrassed by them, but it had become too much of a chore, yet still he never talked about them. He never allowed a lover to caress him there, but that was because he had never let another woman touch him like this. There had been sex before, but no intimacy. But this was intimate. The fact that her warm lips were pressed against his neck was intimate.

"You're kissing me."

"I am," she said, briefly lifting her lips from his neck.

"You shouldn't be."

"I know." She kissed his chin and up his jawline. These were no longer sweet kisses; they had turned arousing. She was trying to seduce him. He grasped her shoulders and set her away from him. He couldn't think with her body pressed against his.

"What are you trying to do to me?" he asked her seriously. He had never felt this way with anyone else.

"I'm not trying to do anything," she whispered. "Whenever I'm close to you . . ." She trailed off.

"What? Say it."

"I want to touch you. And I want you to touch me."

"Why?" He didn't understand her. Why was this attraction was so strong now?

181

"Because you turn me on in a way that no one has and even hours after I touch you, I still feel you. I still think about you. I will go to bed thinking about you and will run my hands all over my body, wishing they were yours."

He felt a sharp spike of anger — not at her, but at himself, because he was about to do something stupid, something he couldn't take back.

He grabbed her by the waist and pulled her close to him. "No sex." He unzipped her little floral printed dress. Her back was the opposite of his: smooth, not marred by grotesque scars.

"Why can't we have sex?" she asked as he kissed her shoulder.

"You know why." He peeled her dress down, revealing her body to him. She wasn't as outrageously curvy as Jazz, but he found her so incredibly sexy. Even the way she held her head as she looked at him. She held herself with grace all the time.

"I don't."

"I work for you."

"You work for my father."

"Same difference."

"I don't care. You are my equal." She kissed his lips. "I want you."

He groaned. She was going to be his

downfall. "No sex." He unhooked her bra, taking his time to look at her. The last time he had seen her naked, her body was dripping with water as she swam in one of the most beautiful spots on the planet. It had been the most erotic moment of his life. He wanted her then and he wanted her even more now. "You're gorgeous, love."

He ran his fingers across her collarbone and then pressed his lips there. He almost didn't know what to do with her. He felt like a boy again, overwhelmed by the fact that he was actually getting to be with her. His boss's daughter. The woman he was sworn to protect. He wasn't protecting her now. In fact, he felt guilty for what he was about to do.

She reached for the hem of his shirt, pulling it off his body. She kissed his chest. "You're much tanner than you were a week ago. I think island life agrees with you."

Did it agree with him? He had never felt more conflicted in his life, but it did feel different being here. This place was always his escape, but he wasn't sure he could ever return here without thinking about her.

"Kiss me."

He sighed as he obeyed her wishes. He couldn't just give her a simple kiss. He couldn't kiss her without getting swept away. He backed her to the bed, pushing her down on it and pulling off her underwear.

He paused to look down at her. It was a mistake. She wasn't just gorgeous, with her curvy body and her hair spread around her on the bed. It was the way she looked at him. There wasn't just arousal in her eyes, there was something more. Something he couldn't name, but she gave him a shy smile and he felt his heart slam against his rib cage.

She was going to take a piece of him when she left. He crawled onto the bed and covered her body with his. She welcomed him, curling her arms around him, her lips finding his again.

She wrapped her legs around him, rubbing herself against his erection. He was harder than he had ever been. He wouldn't survive like this. He pulled himself off her. She groaned. But he didn't leave her for long. He kissed his way down her body. He had to keep himself controlled. She wasn't like the usual women he slept with. She was more important. More precious.

He flicked his tongue across her nipple. She gasped. He never recalled taking so much time with anyone. But he liked going slow with her. Hearing her moans. Seeing the change in her face when he did some-thing she liked.

"Cullen . . ." She grabbed his hair and gently pulled. "Is this how you get people to tell you all their secrets?"

"What?"

"You're torturing me."

"I'm not torturing you. I'm pleasing my-self."

"Let me please you. Take your pants off."

"No sex." He shifted his body lower, plac-ing his head between her thighs.

"I can't believe you're being so stubborn about this."

"Deal with it." He touched her between her legs, her wetness coating his fingers. She was ready for him and it took all his strength to stay where he was. This night was not about his pleasure, but hers. He opened her lips and licked inside her. She moaned and her entire body tightened. She tasted sweet. She smelled even better. He licked her again, this time placing two fingers inside of her. She cried out his name and a troubling thought filled his mind. He didn't want anyone else to see her like this. He didn't want anyone else to touch her like this. A powerful sense of ownership overcame him. She wasn't his. She could never be his and yet he knew he would kill anyone else who tried to touch her.

He took his time with her, sliding his fingers inside of her, sucking on the most sensitive part of her. It was more for him than for her. He wanted to see what she liked, experiment with caresses and speeds.

He could imagine himself inside her, so tight and wet. Her legs wrapped around him, her lips near his ear, moaning his name, feeling her breath against his skin.

He felt as if he were about to explode. Her fingers curled into his hair and she started to shake as orgasm overwhelmed her. He couldn't miss out on this moment. He got on his knees, unzipped his shorts, fisted himself and pumped to completion, his climax hitting her belly. Shame immediately filled him. He had lost control. But she seemingly could read him. She grabbed his hand and pulled him down next to her. She wrapped her arms around him and kissed the side of his face. "I don't want to leave you right now."

"Stay." He knew he should send her away, but that would seem cruel. Plus, he didn't want her to go. He felt surprisingly raw in that moment.

He placed them beneath the blankets and gathered her close.

"Do you know why I don't want to leave you?"

He looked into her eyes, his heart beating a little faster. "Why?"

"Because I can't. My legs don't work. You turned me to mush."

He grinned at her. "Stop it."

She kissed his shoulder. "I'm not sure I'll ever walk again."

He laughed and pulled her closer. She was trouble. And for the first time in a long time he wanted to be in the kind of trouble he couldn't get out of.

CHAPTER 9

Wynter woke up when the sun streamed through the windows. She slept through the night. That hadn't happened since she had left D.C. almost two weeks ago now. It could have something to do with the warm man who was wrapped around her. She turned in his arms so that she could look at him. His hair had grown out since they had been there, his skin darkened from the sun. He was the most beautiful man. She lifted her hand to touch his slightly bearded cheek. She wasn't sure what the hell she was doing. She was in his bed. She had been more intimate with him than she had been with any man in years.

He was her bodyguard. Rationally, she knew this couldn't go anywhere, but her life had been turned upside down and their relationship had been turned upside down as soon as she stepped foot on this island.

She didn't want to be rational right now.

She just wanted to feel good. She wanted to touch and be touched by a man she was incredibly attracted to. She had promised herself that when she returned to her normal life, things were going to change, that she was going to live her life instead of simply being a witness to it. But why wait until she got back to D.C.? She was going to live right now.

"Good morning, lass," his said in his deep, sleepy voice. His soft accent made her insides turn to liquid.

"Good morning."

He touched her hair, wrapping a curl around his finger. "I like your hair like this."

"Do you? My mother would never let me wear it like this when I was a child. She used to straighten it herself. It was one of the few things she did for me herself."

"She wasn't around much?"

"No, it wasn't that. We had servants to do everything else. My mother grew up the daughter of a maid and a groundskeeper. She hated that her parents had to serve people for their entire lives. People who weren't even kind to them. She swore she would never be like them, and when she met my father he was just a kid starting out in the tech industry, but she saw that he was going to make something of himself and she rode it out. And now she lives the life of a queen. I wonder if she thinks the wealth is a trade-off for my father never being there."

"She loves him. Sometimes people will overlook some things to be with the people they love."

"You sound like you know that from experience."

"My mother stayed with my father when the world thought she should have left him. He could barely support us. Too angry or lazy or drunk to keep a job. My mother had to work two jobs, taking in people's washing and working nights at the local pub. Plus, raising us lot. We would have been better off without that noose of a father around our necks, but she stayed with him. One time, when she cried over not being able to pay the rent, I asked her why she was still with him. All she could say was that she loved him. And I thought love just wasn't enough."

She felt sad for him. Sad for what his childhood must have been like. Sad that there seemed to be no love at all for his father.

"I want to say I wouldn't put up with anyone's shit, but I can't say that for sure, because I've never been in that kind of love before."

"No?" His eyes widened a bit.

"Why do you seem surprised by that? You know what kind of life I live."

"Yes. I see the way men look at you wherever we go." His fingers traced the line of her jaw. "They can't take their eyes off you."

"That's not true." She often felt invisible. Or maybe she tried to be invisible for all these years. Her father always sought the light. She shied away from it whenever possible.

"It is."

"Then why haven't I been asked on a date in a year?"

"Maybe because I won't let a man anywhere near you."

She was surprised by his admission, but she didn't want to read into it. "You're the reason for my lack of orgasms."

"You could always give them to yourself." He grinned at her. "In fact, I'm hoping you do."

"What other choice did I have? Should I have called you?"

"You barely called me for anything." He pressed his lips against her bare shoulder. "You wouldn't let me drive you to work. You wouldn't even let me pick up your damn takeout."

"I felt bad."

"Why? I'm supposed to work for you around the clock. I didn't feel like I was earning my pay."

"I bet you feel like you're earning it now."

"No," he said and she could see the guilt in his eyes. "I feel like I should turn in my resignation. Being naked in bed with your principal isn't a part of the job description."

"Who says you can't have fun at work?"

"We can't do this anymore," he said as he pressed his lips to hers. "When we get out of this bed we go back to the rules we had before. You can only touch me in front of my friends. When we're alone we keep our hands to ourselves."

"How can I agree to that when you are running your hands all over me?"

"I can't seem to stop, Wyn. And that's the problem." His hand slid down her back, cupping her behind.

"Why is it a problem when it's what I want?"

"I have my integrity. How am I supposed to maintain objectivity? How am I supposed to speak to your father if I'm carrying on with you behind his back?"

"I don't give a damn about my father."

"I've always done what's right. I've always been professional. I can't slip anymore."

"After today, right?" She pushed herself closer to him, feeling his erection against her thigh.

"After we get out of this bed," he said, right before he gave her the hottest kiss of her life. Her entire body caught on fire in that moment and she knew that no matter what he said, that this wouldn't be the last time they would be here. It wasn't just one-sided. He wanted her. And the longer they were together, the harder it was for them to stay apart.

He slipped his hand between her legs, groaning when he found her slick with desire again. This morning she wasn't content to lay back and be touched. She wanted to touch him too. She reached out and wrapped her fingers around his thick manhood. She couldn't get the image of him from last night out of her head. The way he looked at her as he knelt over her, his hand pumping furiously. He wasn't pleasuring himself, he was relieving the intense pressure that built up inside him. She didn't want that to happen today. She wanted to share in this moment together.

His eyes focused on hers and a question appeared in them.

"You need to let me touch you," she told him.

Why should he give to her and not receive any love in return? She slid her hand down his shaft and he seemed to relent, his entire body relaxing. He closed the gap between their lips and kissed her as he began to stroke her in slow circles. There was no frenzied rush. He had told her as soon as they left this bed they would be going back to normal. It was what Cullen told himself he wanted, and Wynter would respect that, but right now she was in no rush to get out of bed and it seemed that he wasn't either.

They kissed and touched each other's bodies, but as much as she wanted to make this feeling last forever, his fingers were too efficient and she found herself shuddering with climax. He followed soon after her and for a few long minutes they just lay wrapped up in each other, neither one of them wanting to move.

"I know you said that we would go back to normal as soon as we left this bed, but how about we go back to normal as soon as we leave this room? You promised me a bath last night and that tub is big enough for two."

He thought about it for a moment, but then kissed the side of her face. "A promise is a promise."

Cullen wasn't sure what to make of the scene before him. Jazz and Wynter were sitting together at the patio table with bottles of nail polish before them. They were laughing. Together.

"This looks like a five-year-old has done this," Wynter said, looking at her hand.

Jazz glanced down at her own fingers. "I can't do my right hand either."

"Yours looks way better than mine."

"I don't think yours looks so bad. The nail polish is old. I haven't bought any in forever."

Wynter reached for the nail polish remover. "You want to get a manicure and pedicure with me?"

Jazz looked absolutely stunned by the invitation. "Really?"

"Yeah." Wynter's eyes lit up. "And maybe a massage? Is there a spa around here?"

"I'm sure there is. I've never been to one before."

"No? I was pretty sure you're the kind of woman a man likes to pamper."

"She is," Cullen said. "But Jazz doesn't allow anyone to take care of her."

"I take care of myself."

195

"Taking care of yourself requires more than money. You have to do some self-care as well," Wynter said to her.

"You're one to talk. When's the last time you've done something for yourself?" Cullen asked Wynter. He had been with her nearly every day for the past year and he had never seen her indulge at all.

Wynter looked up at him, her head tilted slightly to the side, a smile in her eyes. A little mischievous smile played around her lips. "You're the thing I do just for myself."

He couldn't help but to grin back at her. Her sexiness shot straight through him and the urge to close the distance between them and kiss her nearly overwhelmed him. He remembered this morning in vivid detail, her naked body pressed against his in the bathtub. They had just touched each other, but there had been laughter and long kisses. He couldn't recall another time he had enjoyed himself like that with a woman without sex. "You're a cheeky lass."

He knew that they shouldn't have done any of the things they did last night and this morning, but he couldn't regret any of it. It had to stop before he got in any deeper. It would be hard enough to forget her as it is.

"Do you two need to be alone?" he heard Jazz ask.

"No." He shook his head and pulled his eyes away from Wynter's. "You two should go enjoy yourselves. There's a hotel in town that just opened. I'm pretty sure they've got a little spa. You could probably get an appointment if you call right now."

"Are you talking about the Blue Cove Inn?" Jazz asked.

"I think so. Enjoy yourselves." He was glad that Wynter had suggested they go out together. Cullen had been a little worried about Jazz the last few days. She seemed slightly lost without King, even though he hadn't gone anywhere. Something had clearly happened between the two and Cullen had hoped that it would sort itself out. Things would never be the same if there was a rift in the group. Jazz and King both needed this place. They all did, but the two of them had come here to heal. This couldn't be the scene of their heartbreak.

It was hard when your best friends were in love with each other and too damn stubborn to do something about it.

"Let me go back to our cottage and get my bag. I'll meet you at the Jeep in ten minutes."

"Okay," Jazz agreed. She looked unsure for a moment, her nature naturally distrusting, but she looked vulnerable too, which was a very new, very surprising side to her.

She stood up and when Wynter was out of earshot, she walked over to him. "I don't hate your girlfriend," she said.

"High praise indeed." He nodded.

"I mean it. She's . . . sweet. She's not trying to get anything. There's no scam there. She's just a nice person."

"You say that with some disgust."

"I was trying to find something wrong with her. I was actively looking for something to be wrong with her." She shook her head. "What the hell is the matter with me?"

"You were in too long. You were trained to question. Not to trust. That life is over now, Jazz. You can take people at face value now."

She let out a long sigh. "Maybe one day I'll be able to do that." She gave his shoulder a slight squeeze and walked away.

Cullen felt a little guilt as Jazz got further away from him. Wynter was a nice person, but they were lying, presenting themselves as a couple when he knew they weren't. It didn't matter how attracted he was to her, or how he felt whenever he was near her. It was a lie. One that he could never reveal to them, even after Wyn returned home.

It was important to protect Wyn's identity and his friends' comfort and seclusion. He knew they wouldn't be able to be themselves around her if they really knew who she was. But still, even with the best reasons, he felt a little pit of uneasiness in his belly. He hated lying.

He heard the phone ring from inside of the community house. It was rare that anyone called that line. He heard Darby answer the phone and he was about to walk away when he heard Darby call his name.

He looked back at the patio and looked back to see Darby standing there with the cordless phone in his hand and a concerned look on his face.

"It's your sister."

"My sister?" He hadn't seen her since she was a girl. He had lost track of his siblings, not because he couldn't find them if he wanted, but because they had led such a different life from his. They had escaped the worst of their father and Cullen didn't want to be reminded that they got the chance he never did.

"Yes. She says her name is Maeve and that your Aunt Sheila gave her this contact information."

He nodded. He had given his aunt the number when the uncle who took him in in London had died. He told her to only contact him in an emergency, but he had never thought she would use it. He didn't have a family anymore. Whatever it was could be taken care of without him. "What does she want?"

"I think you should hear it from her."

"What does she want, Darby?" he asked forcefully.

"It's your father . . . He's had a stroke."

"So? The NHS will take care of him. Tell her to call me back when he dies. I'll chip in for the funeral."

CHAPTER 10

Cullen winced as he peeled his shirt from his back.

It was sticking to him, to his open skin.

He was surprised that he could still feel pain. He had so many scars on his back that he didn't think he was able to feel anymore. He was numb. He had been numb as his father slashed his back the first few times with his old belt. But then that feeling had bubbled up inside of him. The one he had been feeling more and more as he lived in this dark little house.

He didn't remember what happened exactly. It was all a blur to him. But now his fist throbbed. His knuckles were raw and bloody.

His father's face flashed before his eyes, the blood spurting from his mouth, the look of shock in his eyes, and then the recognition, the bit of soberness that came before the second blow.

He couldn't do it anymore. He couldn't allow

himself to be hit. He couldn't stay here with his father, because he was going to turn into him.

He realized it was starting to happen yesterday. He had found one of the bottles of whiskey his father had hidden around the house. He picked it up and looked at it for a long time before he took the top off and took a long swig.

He wasn't sure why he did it.

He felt the burn for minutes after he had swallowed his first drop and part of him wanted to do it again, to drink more, to feel whatever it was his father felt that made him so tied to this brown liquid.

But then he heard his father stumble through the door and he looked up to see a dirty, stinking shell of a man. Cullen had always thought he was good for nothing, but he was far worse without his mother.

He never realized that she was the glue holding that broken thing together.

Cullen didn't want to be him. He couldn't allow himself to turn into him, living on benefits in a council paid for by the government.

Today when he hit his father, he wanted to do it over and over again until the feeling stopped bubbling inside of him or his father stopped moving. He didn't remember which one of those things happened. He was turning into the man he hated: a violent son of a bitch who couldn't control himself.

He couldn't allow that to happen.

He grabbed his schoolbag out of his closet and started shoving the few things he had into it, along with the money he had scrimped and saved from doing odd jobs around town. It was enough to get him a train ticket to London and a few meals. It was enough to get him away from this bloody, miserable life.

He walked out of his room to see his father on the floor, leaning against the wall where Cullen had shoved him. He could smell the booze emanating from his skin from across the room, but that's not what shook him, or the fact that his father's face was bleeding. He was crying. Sobbing. A blubbering, drunk fool.

Cullen shook his head and headed for the door.

"Where are you going?"

"Fuck you."

"You can't leave here!" There was panic in his eyes.

"You'll not hit me again."

"No, I won't."

"What?" He wasn't sure he heard him correctly.

"I won't hit you again, boy."

"You won't get the chance, because I'm

leaving. You won't have me to push around anymore."

He scrambled to his feet, but he was too drunk to stand up straight. He wobbled as he walked toward him. "I don't want you to leave me." He grabbed Cullen by his shoulders. "Please. Stay here."

He had hated his father for so long, but as he looked into his bloodshot eyes, he thought of him as pathetic, more than anything. "I'll not be a part of your hell, old man."

He pushed him away and walked out the door. He heard his father wail, but he didn't look back. There was no point.

Cullen woke up when he heard his cell phone ringing from his nightstand. He sat up, rubbing his hands over his face, trying to shake off his dream.

"That was me calling you," he heard Wynter say. She was standing in the doorway of his bedroom, cell phone in hand, concerned look on her face. "Can I come in?"

He felt like hell. She had been scared to come into the room, because the last time he had dreamed like this he had grabbed her, hurt her, thinking she was somebody there to hurt him.

"Are you sure you want to?"

"What a stupid question to ask."

She walked in the room, climbed into his bed, and snuggled beneath the covers like she belonged there. He hated to admit that when he went to bed tonight he had felt like something was missing.

It was her.

"I'm sorry I woke you."

"It's okay." She rested her head on his chest. "I ended up where I wanted to be in the first place."

He had that troubled feeling sneak up inside of him again. He knew he shouldn't allow this to continue, but he wasn't sending her away tonight. "How was your day with Jazz?"

"I like her. I think she's sweet."

"No one has ever described Jazz that way."

"They don't know her."

"You've known her for two weeks. I've known her for years. How could you make that assessment?"

"You know I study how languages evolve over time, right? People are the same way. They evolve. I'm sure she's not the same person she was when you all met. I'm sure that none of you are the same people you were when you met."

"I don't think I've changed very much."

She made a soft noise. "What happened today after we left?"

"The boys and I did some more work on the damaged cottage. We missed you at lunch. Especially King. He wants more of that chicken salad."

"I'll make more in the morning. But you know what I meant. What happened with you after I left?"

"Why do you think something happened to me?"

"Because you were quiet tonight."

He grinned at her. "And how is that different from any other night?"

"I don't know how you do it. You answer every question correctly. You kept track of everything going on and everything said, but you weren't with us tonight."

He set his hand on her cheek. He couldn't lie to her. He couldn't say everything was fine when it wasn't. "You know me better than I would like."

"What's wrong?"

"My sister called."

"Your sister? I thought you hadn't seen her since she was a child."

"I haven't."

"What did she say?"

"I don't know for sure. I didn't speak to her. Darby did. She was calling to tell me that my father had a stroke."

She looked up at him. "I don't know what

question to ask first."

"He should be dead already," he admitted. "He was a miserable drunk. He was alone. He should have been dead."

"It sounds like you want him to be dead."

"I thought I didn't care if he lived or died, but I'm thinking I do want him to be dead. Every time I look in the mirror and see the scars on my back I want him to be dead and more than that, I want to be the one who killed him."

She inhaled sharply. "Your father did that to you?"

He nodded, realizing that he had never told anybody this before. King knew, but he guessed and they had never spoken about it. This was the first time Cullen was sharing this part of himself. "You thought it was some old war wounds. They are, but the war took place in my own damn house."

"How could he beat you like that?"

"It was every damn day. I couldn't breathe the wrong way without feeling his fists. He hit me until I could hit back, until he knew I was stronger than he was, until he knew I wouldn't take it anymore. The day I left, I had beat him bloody and he begged me to stay. With tears in his eyes, he begged me to stay."

"What did you say to him?"

"Nothing. I was disgusted. It was all I could do not to spit on him."

"You hate him."

"I don't want to give him that much space in my head. In some ways he did me a favor. I would have never joined the military if it weren't for him. Being in a combat zone was easier for me than living with my father. Special Forces training was easier than being in bloody Northern Ireland with the man who was supposed to love me."

"If you could survive him, you could survive anything," she said, more to herself than to him. "You're not going to see him."

"Why should I? Why should he see how I turned out? He wanted to break me, like he broke himself."

"What about your sister? Why didn't you talk to her?"

"I don't know. It was too much to take in at the moment. It's been years since I had seen or heard from them. And when I do hear from her, it's to tell me our father has had a stroke. What the hell does she want me to do about it? The bastard never did anything for us."

"She doesn't know how bad it was for you, does she?"

"No. She doesn't need to know. They got

out. They shouldn't give another thought to me."

"How could they not think about you? You are their brother. There must be some love there, even if you haven't seen each other in fifteen years."

"How could there be love there? They don't even know me."

"But you knew them. You didn't love them when they were little? You didn't miss them when they were gone?"

"I did miss them."

It was a double blow. First his mother died and then the little ones were taken away. It was for the best, but it still felt like they were ripped from him. And with them went the only remaining bit of life that remained in the house.

"Call your sister. Even if you don't want to see your father, call your sister. You should know her and your brother. I'm sure they want to know what kind of man you turned out to be."

"They're going to want to know why I hate him so much. Do I have the right to tell them? Do I have the right to kill the good memories of the man they loved?"

"The fact that you care about affecting their feelings for him makes you incredible. They have to realize that there was a reason your aunt took them away. They have to have some memory of how he was before they left."

"They were so young. Mum shielded them from the worst of it."

She had made excuses for him.

Da is sick, she would say when his head was in the toilet after a night of drink. *Da is working,* she would tell them when he wouldn't come home some nights.

"Maybe they think your father is a saint and maybe you don't want to tell them the truth, but at least you should speak to them, just to see how they turned out. Aren't you curious? Don't you still want the best for them?"

"Shut up, lass," he said softly as he kissed her forehead.

"I wish I had a brother and sister. Someone to share a history with."

"Enough already, Wyn. I'll call Maeve tomorrow. You've convinced me."

"Good." She yawned. "Can I sleep in here tonight?"

It made sense to tell her no. He shouldn't get used to her being in his bed. One night without her and he missed her. Two nights with her and he would start to crave her. But it seemed cruel to send her away. There was also the small fact that he didn't want to. "I'm not kicking you out, love."

"Thank you."

"You're not afraid to sleep in the same bed with me?" he asked seriously. She was smart not to touch him when he was in the middle of his dream. They both wouldn't forget what happened the last time she did.

She frowned at him. "Why would I be?"

"I have those dreams sometimes. The last time I hurt you."

"That was my fault. I snuck up on you. You know I'm here with you. You'll feel me all night. You'll go to sleep knowing that I'm beside you and I'm going to sleep knowing that you would never do anything to hurt me."

He felt like he had been kicked in the gut. He had never felt like this before and a selfish part of him wanted this forever. Someone who he was comfortable with. He could never relax. His career, his life, had never allowed it, but here he was with her now, not wanting to move. Enjoying this feeling more than he should. He could try to keep her on this island, in this safe, warm bubble forever, but he knew eventually she would have to go back to her life and he would have to leave her there.

He could only have her here like this for a little while. He should enjoy it. He should forget about his duty and his loyalty to her father, but he worked for the man, took his money to finance his retirement. "Good night, sweet girl." He kissed her forehead. He wanted to kiss her lips, but he knew he wouldn't be able to stop. He wanted to make love to her. He wasn't sure how much longer he could hold out. She would welcome him if he tried, but tonight wasn't the right night. He still felt raw about the news of his father. Making love to her would be like balm to his wounds, but he didn't want to use pleasure as an excuse to forget.

When he made love to her, he wanted them both to be in the right mind-set, not trying to forget, not trying to soothe. There could be no regrets afterward, no misplaced thoughts during.

"Good night, Cullen."

The next morning Wyn had left Cullen sleeping in his bed. His bad dreams haunted her. She knew she wasn't supposed to wake him, but the sounds he was making last night . . . It was anguish. It was the only word she could use to describe it. She couldn't take the sound and stayed in her room as long as she could before she went to him. She didn't know if she could comfort him, but she had to make his nightmare stop. She thought he was going to tell her he had been a prisoner of war, tortured by some foreign entity. But his own flesh and blood had done that to him. It made the scars on his back even more horrific. To beat him so ruthlessly and repeatedly for years was unthinkable. He was a child. He had been powerless.

And now the man had had a stroke and Cullen seemed torn about how to feel about it.

She couldn't blame him.

Her relationship with her father was complicated, but it was nothing compared to how Cullen felt about his father.

She walked to the community house to find Jazz sitting on the edge of the pool. Her feet dangling in the water. "Good morning."

"Good morning. I already made coffee. You don't have to do it this morning."

"You're up early today."

"I'm always up early. I just don't come up here. I used to take walks with King in the morning, but . . ." she trailed off.

There was a sadness in Jazz that had lingered this past week. Jazz, who was so strong, so confident, seemed like a fraction of her old self. Wyn had only known her for a short while, but she knew that something had happened to her. Something with King. She used to wish that someday some man would look at her the way King looked at Jazz.

"Why don't you walk anymore?" She sat beside Jazz, slipping her shoes off so she could put her feet in the warm water.

She looked down at her hands. They had spent the entire day together yesterday, getting manicures and massages. It was a good day for Wyn. The best she'd had in a long time. She didn't have female friends. There were no girls in school she had been close to. She was too much of an outsider, even though she had grown up in privilege just like them. Her adult life had revolved around work. No time for friends. No time for herself. It was nice to be out with another woman. To chat about silly things. About men. About hair. She had always considered herself a serious person, but sometimes it was fun not to be serious. She wondered if that was a part of having a friend. Having the fun times like yesterday and then the times like today, where sometimes just listening was needed. "He's been busy in the mornings."

"We've all noticed that something isn't right between you two. Do you want to tell me what's going on?"

She looked at Wyn, her guard going up momentarily, but then coming down just as quickly. This was as new for Jazz as it was for Wyn. This type of friendship. "He wants more than I can give him."

"What does he want?"

"Everything," she whispered.

"You love him," Wyn told her.

"I don't believe in love."

"I don't believe you. You wouldn't be this upset if you didn't love him."

"He needs a nice girl like you. One who likes to cook and hold hands and raise children."

"I would like to think of myself as more than a girl who just likes to cook and hold hands. I'm a woman with a doctorate. And if you think that's all King wants, you're a fool."

"I have killed people for calling me nicer names than that."

"I'm not scared of you." She shrugged. "We're friends now. You won't kill me. I'm pretty sure King doesn't want a nice, quiet woman who just likes to bake. He wants a former secret operative, or spy or CIA agent, or whatever insane job you had before you came here."

"I started off as a Marine. Most of my family told me not to join up. They wanted me to go to beauty school. They wanted me to do something girls did. But my grandfather was so damn proud of me. He told me to get the hell out of the Bronx and I did. I was a damn good Marine and then I got recruited into the special service and it was almost six years before I stepped foot back on American soil. A lot happened to me in those six years. In that time, I came to the realization that I could never be somebody's wife. I could never be somebody's mother. I'm too fucked up."

"You can have anything you want, Jazz. You are a lot of things, but you are not broken."

"Says the woman who probably grew up with the perfect childhood. Oh, I forgot. You have daddy issues. What happened? He didn't hug you enough? You turned out okay. You're a damn PhD."

"Don't do that. Don't get nasty so you'll push me away. I'm the product of an affair. I've only seen my birth mother once, when she tried to kidnap me. My only memory of her is sobbing as three men pinned her to the ground and then carried her away. I may not have been a spy, but I've got my shit. We've all got our shit."

Jazz surprised her by resting her head on her shoulder. "I've been kidnapped too. For three weeks."

"Don't try to one-up me! We're talking about you and King."

"There's nothing to talk about. I think I might have to leave this place by summer. I'm going to ask Jack to buy out my share."

"Don't do that. Don't run away."

"I'm not. I've just gotten good at knowing when to move on."

"Good morning, ladies." Wyn heard Cullen's voice from behind them. She turned to see him, looking at them with a curious expression on his face.

"Hey, Cullen." Jazz got to her feet. "Your girlfriend is one of those touchy-feely types. I thought we banned them from here."

"I must have missed the meeting where we came up with that rule."

Jazz walked into the house and poured herself some coffee.

"It's hard living with a group of spies," Wyn said, getting up and walking to Cullen. "You all have so many secrets."

"We're not spies. At least, not all of us." He grabbed her by her waist and pulled her close to him. "How did you sleep last night?"

"Fine."

He searched her face. "I didn't wake you again?"

"No."

"Then why does it look like you didn't get much sleep?"

"Do I look bad?"

"No, you look beautiful. I can see it in your eyes. You're tired."

"I was thinking about you," she whispered.

"You two are gross," Jazz commented.

"Gross?" Cullen raised a brow at her. "Like I haven't had to sit through years of you and King giving each other hot looks across the table. You think none of us could tell? We were just polite enough not to mention it."

"Shut up, Cullen."

He shook his head and returned his attention back to Wyn. "I'm sorry." He lowered his voice to a whisper. "I never meant for my burdens to be yours."

"They are not burdens to me. You should be happy. That's all I want."

"I'm going to call Maeve now. Then I want to do something for you. Where can I take you today?"

"To lunch. I want to take Jazz with us."

He nodded. "Of course." He kissed the side of her face and let her go, walking away to make his phone call in private.

"Do you guys usually celebrate Cullen's birthday?" she asked Jazz.

"No. He's never been here on his birth-day."

"I would like to throw him a party with balloons and party hats and a big cake."

Jazz frowned at her. "I don't think Cullen is a party hat kind of guy."

"I know. That's why I want to have a party for him and I want you to help me plan it."

"Is it going to be a surprise party?"

"I'm not sure. Do you think we can keep a secret from a former intelligence officer?"

"We can try."

Darby had saved Maeve's information for Cullen, the older man knowing him better than perhaps he would like. "I knew you would come looking for this," he said as Cullen walked into his cottage.

"Wyn made me feel guilty."

"No." He motioned to the armchair in his living room. "You already felt guilty, but Wyn made you come to terms with it."

"I didn't tell her about my father, but she knew something was up. She can read me."

"That's what happens when you find someone to love you."

"To love me?" He shook his head, knocked off-balance by the statement. They were just pretending. Though sometimes being with her felt like the most real thing he had ever experienced. But still, it wasn't real. He had just spent nearly every day for almost a year with her. She trusted him. He protected her. It wasn't a typical relationship.

"Yes. Love you. You act like that is a foreign concept."

"I don't know. She's lovely like that with everyone. You should see her with Jazz."

"But I'm not talking how she is with everyone else. I'm talking about how she is with you. About how well she knows you and how you allowed her to know you. You can't say that anyone else does. Not even us."

He nodded. He knew he had feelings for her, that he'd had them for a while now, but he knew nothing could come of them. They would be going their separate ways and all he would have of her were his memories. Of the way she felt curled into him. Of the way she smiled at him. Of her lips pressed softly against his. It would have to be enough. He turned his mind away from her and the thoughts of being without her.

"Thank you for taking her number. It saves me the trouble of tracking her down."

"The fact you would have to track her down tells me a lot. You don't know where she is, because you purposely don't want to know where she is."

"What makes you say that?"

"Where's your father?"

"In a Belfast care home. He's been there since he shattered his legs in a car accident."

"And how do you know that? How do you know about the accident? You haven't talked to him since you left home."

"That's not true. I spoke to him when I finished basic training."

"Almost twenty years ago?" He raised a brow. "How do you know where he is?"

"I looked this morning. He hasn't moved. He hasn't changed. I knew I could always find him if I wanted to, but I didn't want to because I have nothing to say to the bugger."

"How long did it take you to find him?"

"Minutes."

"Why don't you know where your siblings are?"

"Wyn asked me the same thing. I'm still thinking about that."

"Don't think about it anymore. Call." Darby left his chair. "Stay here to do it. I'm heading to the house for coffee."

"Thank you, Darby."

"No need to thank me. I didn't do anything."

He walked out, leaving Cullen sitting there

with his sister's number clutched in his hand. He was nervous. He realized that's what he was feeling. He had been numb for so long, but in the past few weeks he was feeling things more than he had since his mum had died. It was troubling.

He remembered the day his aunt had come to take his brother and sister away. His father had locked himself in the bedroom, saying he didn't want to see the "bloody cow" who had come to take his kids.

At first Cullen thought his father didn't care, but he must've. He had to. It was a loss. Plain and simple. It was almost as bad as losing Mum.

His brother was trying not to cry as he carried his little bag on his back, but Cullen could see he was torn up. He couldn't look at the boy. It was too damn difficult, but Maeve . . . She had been even worse. She was too young to understand the finality of it. For days after the tragedy, she kept asking when Mum was coming back, and when their aunt had come to take them, she reached for Cullen, confusion in her eyes and asked why he wasn't coming with them.

Someone has to take care of Da, he told her. But he had wished in that moment that the man had been dead. That someone had killed him instead of Mum. He wished he could have gone away too. Leave their shitty house. Leave their poverty behind. But he knew that that life wasn't meant for him. That someone had to stay behind.

He forced himself to look down at the number that was now crumpled in his hand. It wasn't a foreign number, but one from the States. Miami. He knew it well, because before he came to work for Wyn, he had lived there, protecting his arms-dealer boss.

He dialed his cell phone quickly, his fingers moving faster than normal. It took three rings before she picked up.

"Hello? Cullen, is that you?"

Her voice was soft, lightly accented, sweet. It suddenly made him miss his homeland. He had never been back. He had never wanted to go back, but sometimes he missed people who sounded like him, who knew what it was like to have grown up there. "Yes, Maeve. How are you?"

"Why didn't you want to talk to me yesterday, you arse?"

He grinned, remembering that sweet little Maeve had spirit. "I don't know. I haven't seen you since you were a baby. I was thrown off."

"I'm well grown now. I'm going to be twenty-five soon."

"In May. I haven't forgotten. Mum said you were her spring gift."

"You haven't forgotten, have you? How have you've been, Cullen? That question seems very inadequate for speaking to your long-lost big brother. But still, I'm wondering how you've been."

"I'm fine. I'm good, actually."

"You joined the military. We heard you went straight to the top."

"I've done all right for myself. How are you, little one? What are you doing with yourself?"

"I'm in school, studying to be a therapist."

"A therapist? That's the most un-Irish thing I've ever heard. We don't go on about our problems."

"I know that, brother. Which is why I came to the States. Americans love to talk about their problems. They go on and on. I love it. It makes me feel better about my life."

He smiled again. Twenty years had passed, but it was as if it hadn't. She used to ramble on as a little girl and he always listened, finding her too cute not to. "How was your life after you left? Were you treated well?"

"Auntie was good to us. She wasn't lovely like Mum, but we had it all right. I know you didn't," she said softly.

"No."

She paused for a moment. "He told me he beat you."

"He told you that?"

"Cleansing his soul after the accident, I guess. You know about the accident, don't you?"

"Aye. He was drunk. Smashed into a wall. He should have died."

"Yeah, but he didn't. I feel like he is one of those people who just hangs on so he can be miserable. I used to wonder why he never wrote or called. Why he never visited us once. We were his children. I thought he loved us. And then I thought it might have been too painful for him because of Mum, but then I went to see him and I talked to him for a little while and I realized that he's a selfish bugger. It's not just addiction. He's clean now, but he is the most thoughtless person."

"You were better off not knowing him," Cullen said. "He wouldn't have added anything to your life."

"He wanted to see you. He talked about you. He's hurt that you left him."

"I don't know what to say to that," Cullen said, thinking about the day he walked out. "I don't want to see him."

"I'm not suggesting you do. I'm just telling you what he said in case you ever wanted to know if he still thinks about you."

"I'm sure he does. Blaming me for everything that went wrong in his life after I left." He shook his head. "How bad was the stroke?"

"Bad. His body isn't strong enough to recover. Too many years of booze. Too much damage."

"I figured as much. Are you going back to see him?"

"Would you think less of me if I didn't?"

"Would you think less of me if *I* didn't?" he countered.

"He told me what he did to you. He tortured you. That's what it was, Cull. It was torture and then he blamed you for leaving him. I wouldn't blame you if you spit on his grave."

"I know that, but why do I feel so damn guilty for not wanting to see him?" He wanted to take his mind off the old man, even though he knew that he was the reason for his sister's call. "How is Liam? What does he think about it?" he asked, speaking of their brother.

"Liam's all right. He lives in London with his girlfriend. Works in an office. He has a nice little life."

"Did he go with you to see him that time?"

"He did. He tried to maintain a relationship with him, but Liam learned too late that even though he's in a care home and has been clean for years, the addiction is still there. Liam took him out to lunch for his birthday and he got stinking pissed. And the next day he called him, demanding for Liam to bring him booze. It broke his heart. Liam didn't want to see how broken he was."

"Is he going to see him?"

"I don't know. He's the closest. I'm not sure if I can get away long enough to go to Northern Ireland or even if I could afford to go. He doesn't feel like a father to me. I've seen the man once in twenty years. Am I supposed to feel love?"

"You haven't seen me in twenty years. Do I feel like a brother to you?" he asked, finding himself afraid of her answer.

"I don't remember ever loving him, but I do remember loving you, Cull. You let us sleep in your bed for two days after Mum died. You used to carry me on your shoulders around the garden. So, I guess I'm saying if you had a stroke, I would come see you."

He laughed. "I've missed you, Maeve."

"Why didn't you keep in touch?"

"I don't know. At first it hurt too much. I

figured you were happy where you were and if you talked to me, you'd know I was miserable with him. I didn't want you to know that. And then later on, I worked some very dangerous missions. I wasn't allowed to say where I was and frankly, half the time I went into them expecting to die. I couldn't have done my job to the best of my ability if I was worried about who would miss me if I died. It was better that I was alone."

"And now, Cull?"

"I'm not alone now." Immediately he thought of Wynter. Not of his friends who he built a community here with, but the woman who was surely only temporary in his life.

"You can have us, you know. I don't want to be a stranger to you anymore."

"Then you won't be."

He spoke to her for a little while longer, and when he hung up, there was a lightness in his chest and it felt a little bit like hopefulness. He had never felt that way before.

CHAPTER 11

Wynter lingered in the living room that night, not wanting to go to bed yet, even though she was tired. It had been a long day, full of her trying to keep her mind off the mystery of her birth. She and Cullen had taken Jazz to lunch. They had gone window-shopping in town and they popped into a little convenience store to get some cold drinks before continuing their walk through town, when Wynter saw a newspaper with her father's face splashed on the cover.

PRESIDENTIAL HOPEFUL DENIES KIDNAPPING CLAIMS

She had to stop herself from snatching the paper off the rack. Jazz was there. Nothing much got past her, even though she was preoccupied with her own issues. She would know something was up. Wyn had to make herself walk in the other direction. She had to pretend she was studying the arrangement of crunchy snacks that she didn't give a damn about, all so she could calm herself.

But Cullen was too observant. It was like he could feel the shift in her mood. He had come over to her, a paper neatly tucked beneath his arm.

"Find anything you want?" He placed his hand on her back. She couldn't recall how many times she had felt his touch there. Before, it was purely professional. Walking her through a crowd, or placing it there when he leaned in to speak into her ear. Sometimes his touch was the only touch she had during those days. She had never realized how comforting it was.

"I think you know what I want."

"I'm not sure you're going to find what you're looking for here."

"We can go to the bigger market if you want," Jazz said, coming up behind them.

"No, it's fine." She turned to face her. "I'm not sure I'm even going to find it on this island. I think I'll only find what I want at home."

"You're not at home. The best thing about being here is the opportunity to experience something new," Jazz said.

She had looked over to Jazz and nodded in agreement, but still there was a sinking feeling in her stomach, a huge sense of

230

embarrassment that her father had gotten involved in such a huge scandal.

Still, she tried to take her mind off of it for the rest of the day. She genuinely tried to enjoy herself. Cullen made sure that he kept them busy and it was nice. Not having one, but two people there to take her mind off things. They all did that for each other. Took their minds off of things that were haunting them.

But now it was night and all she had facing her was her bed and a sleepless night. The newspaper sat on the kitchen table. Untouched. She wanted to look at it, but she was afraid to see what was inside of it. More truths about her father that she didn't want to know, didn't want to believe.

"What are you doing out here?" Cullen asked her as he walked out of his bedroom. He was shirtless and beautiful. His normally pale skin even darker after spending the entire day in the sun.

"I'm avoiding going to bed."

"Why?" He frowned at her. "You're tired. I know you didn't get much sleep last night."

"My mind spins."

"Did you read the article?"

"No. I almost don't want to look."

"There's no mention of you in it, if you're

curious." He sat down on the couch beside her. "No pictures. I think we're safe from anyone discovering who you are."

"That's not what I'm worried about. I'm more worried about what my father did to that woman. I thought I knew him, but now I'm not sure what he's capable of."

"I wish I knew what to say to you. You know his character better than I do."

"There's nothing you can say to me. But I would like to know how the conversation with your sister went."

He smiled and it was the most beautiful thing she had seen all day. "She's an adult, but she still sounds the same. Still full of sass. Still sweet. I knew I had missed her, but I never realized how much until I got the chance to speak to her again."

"Are you going to see her?"

"Eventually." He nodded. "I want this mess with your father to be over with before I go see her in Miami."

"She's in Miami?"

"Yes. She's going to school there," he said with some pride. "She loves being in the States. She loves the heat of Miami and the people and the cultures. You should have heard her go on about the food she's eaten since she's been there. I've been gone so long that I forget what it's like to be in

Ireland, but it's a world of difference. Life seemed so much less colorful there."

"You have no urge to go back to Ireland?"

"No. I never thought I'd want to live in America, but I can't see myself living any place else. Except for here. I could spend the rest of my life here with no regrets."

"Where else do you love to go in the States?" He had been with her for nearly a year and yet she felt like she was just getting to know him. Like she was getting to know him in a way that few did and his words almost felt like a gift to her.

"New York. I lived there for a year when I first started doing private security. Everything you need is in a ten-block radius. You can see people in a dozen different colors and hear a dozen different languages in a day."

"You can get lost there," she said softly.

"Yes, if you want to get lost. But you can also find yourself there. I can imagine one can create a community wherever they go."

"And you chose to make yours here."

"Yes. These people were my family when I thought I had none."

A touch of sadness swept through Wyn at his words. She had parents. She had family on paper, but she didn't feel like she had a community. There was no sense of home.

No soft place she could land if she fell. But she could create one. She could be like Cullen and that gave her hope.

"Do you ever want a bigger family?" she asked him. "Children of your own?"

He was silent for a moment. "I haven't thought about it. My lifestyle never seemed to be able to fit a family of my own before. I would have to give up my work to have that. I couldn't raise children and do what I do. I could never be like my father. I cannot be absent. I'd rather be childless than be a shitty father."

"You would be a good father," she told him.

"Why do you think that?"

"You take care of people. You take care of me in a way no one else ever has. You could just be doing this for the paycheck and you probably are, but I don't feel that way. I feel like you care."

"I take pride in my job, and would go above and beyond for anyone under my protection, but you are different. I'm not just protecting you. You know that, don't you?"

"I feel like I'm a giant pain in your ass," she said with a watery laugh. "You brought me here. To your home. To the people who mean the most to you."

"How is that a burden on me? I believe if there was a choice between keeping me or you, I would lose the competition. I think your cooking has won the hearts of my friends."

"They are very nice people."

"I'm out of the godforsaken cold weather and I don't have to worry about any hardened criminals coming after you like I did when you were translating for the jails. Bringing you here has made my life easier."

"I'm preventing you from seeing your sister." That weighed on her a bit. He wanted to wait until this scandal blew over, but how long would that take? How many more things would creep up before it ended? Would there ever be an end?

"You're not stopping me from seeing my sister. I haven't seen her since she was a girl. A little while longer won't make much of a difference. I don't think I would have called her if you hadn't pushed me to." He grabbed her hand. "Don't be such a cry-baby," he said with a soft smile. "You're looking for reasons to be anxious."

She nodded, feeling comfort in the weight of his hand in hers. "What are you going to do about your father?"

"I still don't know. He smashed his car into a wall years ago and has been in a care home ever since. He blames me for leaving him. I'm not sure why he wanted me to stay behind when he hated me so much."

"Do you really think he hated you?"

"He beat the shit out of me daily for years. I don't know much about loving a child, but I don't think that's how you go about it."

"If he hates you and you hate him, then why are you still so unsure about what to do about him?"

"What do you Americans call it? Closure? There's a rawness inside of me when I think of him. It never goes away. It's just beneath my surface. I want it to go away. I'm not sure that's possible. He hasn't changed. Maeve told me he's the same selfish bastard he always was. So what's the point of seeing him if he's only going to make my rawness worse?"

"Or it could get better?"

"Or it could get better," he agreed.

"I would go with you," she told him and when his gaze sharpened on her, she wondered if she had said the wrong thing. "If you wanted."

He touched her cheek and then pressed his lips to hers. It was a gentle kiss, but it took her breath away. "It *was* a mistake bringing you here. I can't think clearly when

I'm with you."

"Maybe it's a good to be a little muggy-headed sometimes."

He kissed her again. His eyes closed this time. "I need you to go into your room and lock the door."

"Why?" She rested her head against his. "I want you."

"Please, Wynter. I don't ask you for much, but I'm asking you for this."

He was right. He had never asked her to do anything for him, so she would do what he had asked. She would lock herself away from him, falling asleep thinking about how much she wanted to be in his arms.

When Cullen woke up the next morning, he found the newspaper that he had bought yesterday was missing from the kitchen table. The headline was accusing Wynter's father of kidnapping. They teased another letter from his lover that would prove that he had. It was all speculation from everyone stateside. There were letters only signed with a G, by some mystery woman who never was produced. There were no facts. No hard evidence.

It could all be fake, some news stations claimed. A huge ruse designed by someone who wanted to bring down Bates and his future presidential campaign. But Cullen knew that the woman existed or had existed once. Bates admitted that much to him, and that there was someone who was leaking the letters. Perhaps a former staffer, someone close enough to be able to access his personal belongings.

But whoever the leaker was hadn't been determined. He knew Bates was working to find out who had put such a huge wrench in his life. Cullen was interested too, and he wondered if the leaker understood that what he or she did didn't just affect Bates, but his family. Specifically, his only child, who most of the speculation surrounded.

He remembered Wyn's tortured expression yesterday and wished there was something he could say to her to reassure her. But there was nothing he could say. Her father might have kidnapped that woman, forced her away until her baby was born and ripped the infant from her arms.

Might was the wrong word. Did. Bates did do that. It wasn't a possibility. It was true. Cullen reread the letters that had been released to the media. Bates had kept that woman hidden somewhere that she couldn't escape. But why?

It seemed needlessly cruel. His wife had to know about the affair when Bates brought home a baby. It didn't seem to be a reason to imprison someone.

But more importantly: What happened to the woman later? Could Bates have had her killed? He knew those thoughts were going through Wynter's mind. They could be true. She wanted to know the truth, but maybe this truth would hurt too much.

Cullen found himself going back to Darby's house. His friend had been one of the best operatives in the business. His entire life centered around gathering information. Cullen had met him over ten years ago at a lavish party, when he was very new to military intelligence and counterterrorism. Darby seemed like a real-life James Bond to him. Charming, debonair, classically handsome — all the things that Cullen was not.

He could convince a mute man to sing. He could learn any information in a matter of moments. He was better than Cullen in every way at his job, and even though he had retired from that game, Cullen still knew he was who to go to for help.

"A visit? Two mornings in a row?" he asked in his Australian-accented voice. "I don't think any of your other long-lost siblings called."

"No. I came to walk with you this morning. Do you mind?"

"Of course not. I was heading to my favorite trail."

They headed out on the path behind Darby's house. He'd picked this plot of land that backed up to the nature preserve. It was some of the most beautiful landscape in the world, but it wasn't an easy hike. But for someone like Darby, who had grown up in rougher terrain in the outback, this was paradise.

"It's humid as hell out here," Cullen said to him. "I don't know how you do this every day."

"I spent nearly ten years in Eastern Europe. It was so cold there I thought my fingers were going to break off and fly away in the wind. This is beautiful weather. I'll never leave here. Never."

"Once you're here, it's hard to want to go back to another life." He wasn't looking forward to the day when he would have to send Wyn away, even though having her so close to him was complicating his life in a way that he had never imagined. But the thought of not being here with her weighed heavy on him. In the end, he had signed on to do what was best for Wyn. Not for himself.

"Why did you come to me, son? I know

you weren't aching to come walking with me when you have that beautiful girl waiting for you in your cottage."

"I'm here about her."

"Oh?" Darby raised a brow.

"I know I don't have to ask for your discretion here. But I need you to do something for me and not tell anyone about it."

"Of course."

"It's about Wynter's father."

"Warren Bates."

Cullen stopped in his tracks. "You know?"

"I know you're in serious trouble. You broke a cardinal rule. You're never supposed to fall for your principal. You lose objectivity. You make mistakes. You do stupid things, like bring her to a place filled with former spies."

"I know." He wiped his hand over his now-damp face. "I've been with her for a year. No vacation days. No weekends. I told myself it was because her father was paying me loads of money, that she was easy to look after, but then I found myself finding excuses to see her when I knew she didn't need me. I was fetching her damn tea in the mornings. I was Special Forces, for fuck's sake. That is not what I do. But she makes me want to do things I have never wanted to do."

"Clearly. I'm the last one who'll pass judgment on you, son. But why did you bring her here? You could have gone anywhere."

"To keep her safe. I knew she would be the safest with you lot. I also wanted you all to meet her. If you hated her, then I would know I was cracked."

"You're not cracked," Darby said gently.

"I didn't think I was."

"What do you want to know about her father? He's a billionaire and a politician. A man like that has many secrets."

"Do the others know who Wyn is?"

"I don't think so. They took her at face value. They trust you. Plus, they see how you look at her. What is there to question?"

He felt guilty, because even though Darby knew much more than anyone else, he still didn't know everything. He didn't know that they were pretending or supposed to be pretending. That they weren't really a couple. He didn't know that Cullen had never made love to her. He didn't know he was still trying to not cross that final line and that when they left, she would go back to her life and he would try to forge a new one alone.

"How do you know about her?"

"Because unlike everyone else, I keep track of what's going on everywhere. They are trying to hide from the world. I want to know everything about everyone in it. I saw her in the papers. There's a good shot of you ushering her through a park."

"Her father is a sneaky bastard. She's his biological child. There was no adoption. No orphanage. He admitted that much to me, but he refuses to tell her. I know her birth mother worked for him, but I can't find any records of his employees the year before Wynter was born. He had those files scrubbed. I have found records for every other year. His finances are clean. He doesn't seem to be involved in any other illegal activities, but I can't find any record of this woman."

"Do you think she's dead?"

"I don't know. So far the only letters that have been released are from right around the time Wynter was born. She could be dead. He definitely kept her locked up. This was before he was trying to run for office. I keep asking myself why. There wouldn't have been such a scandal. Mistresses have had babies before."

"But he kept Wynter." Darby's expression turned thoughtful. "Have you ever considered that maybe he and his wife planned this? That they couldn't make a baby to-gether, so they got a child another way?"

"But they could have used a surrogate. IVF. They have money and with money comes choices. Kidnapping is too much. The author of those letters was clearly in love with Bates."

"Maybe she was *too* in love. Maybe she was obsessed with him. Bates could have gotten rid of her to protect his family."

Cullen nodded. "You could be right. I wish I could get Mrs. Bates in the room. I have a feeling she knows everything."

"You think he's told her everything?"

"Yes. He may have cheated on her, but I've seen them together. They are a united front. He wouldn't be where he was without her."

Darby made a soft noise. "This is a hell of a mystery."

"Aye."

"I'll see what I can do. Give me a week. Maybe two."

"Two weeks? You sure, old man?"

He nodded. "Gives me something to do."

"You know if you ever need anything from me, Darby . . ."

"I know, son. But you gave me a lot when you invited me to come live here. No repay-ment needed." Darby stopped to take a drink of water from his canteen. "I hope you don't think you're getting out of the rest of this hike with me. We're just getting started."

Wynter was usually up and out of the house before Cullen left his room. But that morning had been different. The house was empty when she arose. Cullen was nowhere to be found, so Wynter continued on with her morning as she normally did. Going up to the community house, making coffee and starting breakfast for whoever was around.

Cullen didn't have to check in with her. He didn't have to tell her where he was going. But it still didn't stop her from wondering. For the past year, she had started her mornings with him every day. Back in Washington, he would be at her house by seven, dressed in all black, looking every inch of the bodyguard he was.

He would ask her what her plans were for the day and if there was anything she would like him to do for her. Then he would wait for her while she would finish getting ready, walk her to her car, his hand always gently resting on her back. He was her silent strength, her comfort. And now that she was here on this island, she could admit to herself that she used to miss his presence on the weekends when he wasn't with her the entire day. She could admit now that she never let him drive her, like she did with her other bodyguards, because she had been attracted to him all along and her body couldn't handle his closeness.

He was a very large part of her life. They couldn't go back to the way it was when this was over. They knew each other too well. He knew her shockingly well and now she knew him. She could read his moods, feel his hurt.

He thought they had gotten too close, but she still wanted to get closer. On the surface, she understood his hesitation. He took pride in his job. He followed the rules, but they couldn't ever go back.

They couldn't pretend that anything they did was professional anymore. Because it wasn't. It was personal.

Maybe she could let it go if she knew he didn't want her. But he did want her. She felt it in his kiss, the way he looked at her and the way he cared.

They were here in paradise. He could let go with no repercussions. No one would know what went on between them except them.

She had followed the rules her entire life. She had always been good. She had tried to be the perfect daughter, but that ended up getting her nowhere. This time she wanted to do something for herself. This time she wanted to feel good.

Cullen emerged around lunchtime, shirtless and sweaty. She was so busy looking at him that at first she hadn't noticed that he was with Darby.

She had been with Jazz that morning, planning the little party they were going to have for his birthday. It was nice to see this side of Jazz. She was incredibly organized, but she was creative too. An artist. She had sketched out the patio and all the decorations. She had even colored it in, making the vision come to life.

She blushed when Wynter praised her work, embarrassed by the compliments. It made Wynter wonder if anyone had ever done that before. Jazz seemed to ooze confidence. She was highly trained, specially chosen to serve her country in a deeper way than most. How did she not know how special she was? Something had happened to her along the way. Something that had stripped all her confidence.

"Is that where you were?" Wynter stood up and walked over to Darby and Cullen as Jazz put the party plans away.

"He tried to kill me," Cullen panted. "He

took me on a trail with fallen trees, enormous bugs, and the steepest damn incline on the planet. It was terrible."

"You were a bloody combat veteran. This hike did you in?"

"Yes. I haven't seen combat in twelve years. My current principal doesn't require much of me. I haven't had to dodge a bullet in over a year."

"You're growing soft." Darby shook his head.

"You're a machine," Cullen shot back. "I feel like you're training for the apocalypse."

"One can never be too prepared."

"You're red." Wyn frowned at him. "Did you wear sunscreen?"

"If I tell you yes, will that prevent us from having this conversation?"

"There's no conversation needed. I just want you to know that if you got some highly preventable disease and died just because you didn't wear sunscreen, I would be heartbroken and devastated."

"Heartbroken and devastated?" He looked at her for a long moment and frowned. "Those are strong words."

"Yes. That's why I said them. It's hard to imagine my life without you in it," she said truthfully.

It struck her in that moment that she

might be falling in love with him. Or maybe she had been falling in love with him for a year now, she just hadn't realized it.

"You're making me feel bad," he said softly.

"Good." She kissed his cheek, feeling off-kilter. "Wear some damn sunscreen."

"Yes, ma'am."

"You'd be a good interrogator, girl," Darby said with a little smile on his face. "You sure as hell cracked him quickly."

"She's spent a lot time in interrogation rooms," Cullen told them. "Maybe she picked up some techniques."

"Why were you in interrogation rooms?" Darby asked her, seeming surprised.

"When I'm not teaching, I spend many of my days translating for the local and federal court system in D.C. I've work with the FBI a few times as well."

"You've translated some sensitive things, have you?"

"Yes." She nodded, not sure why Darby's eyes had sharpened on her in such a way that made her wonder what he was trying to figure out.

"Have you ever translated something you think someone might want to get back at your for?"

"Yes." She nodded. "I've been threatened before."

"What?" All the softness drained from Cullen's face.

"It was before I knew you. I translated some letters from a gang member, confessing to the murders she committed. She told me she was going to slice my throat after I testified in court. But it was her fault. Anything that you send from the prison system is subjected to be intercepted and read."

"You were just doing your job," Jazz said.

"I was."

"I don't like it when she translates in police stations," Cullen admitted. "I wish she would work in an elementary school."

"I'm just saying what they are saying. Most people are very happy to see me, because I am giving them a voice."

"I understand that, but I don't have to like it."

"You don't."

"You work too much," Cullen told her. "What's it going to take for you to take some time for yourself?"

"That's easy," she said. "I need something else to fill my days and give my life some meaning."

"What would that be?" His eyes were

locked with hers and for a moment it was so intense that she needed to look away.

"More people to love." She turned away then and went back to working on her plans with Jazz. She had revealed too much. But she didn't regret it. She had promised herself that she was done with that emotion.

CHAPTER 12

Dinner that night had been a little more special than usual. It was Jack's turn to cook. He was never one to do anything typical and tonight was a perfect example of that. He was one of those people who made friends with everyone. All he had to do was flash that grin of his and he could usually get whatever he wanted from someone. He would have made a good intelligence officer. He could tailor his personality to make whoever he was trying to get something from feel at ease. It was a gift. But he wasn't in intelligence like the rest of them had been, which made him almost an outsider in their little group.

They never excluded him, but he kept himself a little away from them, using his charm as a shield. It made Cullen wonder what his real personality was and if anyone ever got to see it.

"So they just gave you those lobsters?"

Jazz asked as she sat at the little bar on the patio.

"Yes. And the steaks and the shrimp. And could you hurry up with those drinks, Jazz? My glass is starting to feel lonely."

Jazz had made pitchers of rum punch that were delightfully sweet, but dangerously strong. None of them were big drinkers. Maybe a glass of wine or a couple of beers at dinner, but tonight four pitchers of the fruity concoction had been consumed. Everyone was a little more mellow. They lingered a little longer after dinner.

"It's coming," Jazz told him. "I don't understand why people just give you stuff."

"It's because they like me. Can't be that hard to understand."

"It's because you flirted like hell with the restaurant owner's wife. You made her feel so good that she acted like giving you hundreds of dollars' worth of seafood was doing her a huge favor," Kingsley said from his spot by the pool.

"I *was* doing her a favor. It would have spoiled."

Jazz smiled as she walked over to him to refill his cup. "You're so full of shit. I'm surprised you haven't drowned in it."

"I'm not good at many things, but keeping my head up is one of them." He grinned back at her.

"I think that's something that you all excel at," Wynter said.

Cullen glanced at her. She was maybe four or five feet away from him. Laying on a chaise lounge, the moonlight washing over her. She had her eyes closed and a little smile on her face. He had to stop himself from going over there, sweeping her off her feet and taking her back to their cottage.

He was breaking down. Every interaction he had with her made him want her more. But he needed to keep his wits about him, because he wasn't sure he was going to be able to walk away from her if he didn't.

"Do you want another drink, Wynter?" Jazz asked as she walked over.

"Yes, please." She held out her glass. "This stuff is delightful. What's in it?"

"Very strong rum and magic."

She giggled as she took a sip. "I love magic."

"How many of those have you had?" Cullen asked her.

"Two? Three? I don't remember." She sat up. "Should we dance? I feel like we need to celebrate tonight."

"What are we celebrating, Wyn?" he asked her, knowing the drinks had gone to her head.

"This night." She sprang out of her seat and ran into the house. A few moments later he heard disco music pouring through the Bluetooth speakers. Wynter reemerged with a huge smile on her face. "Who is going to dance with me?"

"Spies don't dance," King said. "Especially to disco music."

"Why not?" She walked over to Jazz, grabbed her hands and started dancing. He never thought Jazz would comply, but he saw her guard drop again and she danced with Wyn.

Wyn spun Jazz around, which was a feat, because Jazz was about five inches taller than Wyn, but it caused both women to laugh. It caused all of them to laugh. Cullen looked over at King. He had been purposely ignoring Jazz for days now, but tonight his eyes were glued to her. There was such intensity there. Such aching need. Cullen looked away, feeling like he was intruding on a private moment.

He looked back over to Wyn, who was giggling now. There was sweet girlishness to her still. He never thought he would find that appealing. He liked harder women. A year ago he would have said Jazz was much more for him than Wyn.

And maybe if King didn't look at her with

such pure, naked desire, things might have been different. But there he was, staring at Wyn as she danced in the moonlight and he just hoped he didn't look at Wyn with the painfully obvious need that King showed while looking at Jazz.

"Hey, ladies." Jack got up from his seat and danced over to them. "You got to let me in on this action. I'm standing here watching one of my fantasies come true."

"I'm fairly sure you've danced with more than one woman on multiple occasions," Jazz said dryly.

"But I have never danced with two women as stunning as you."

"You're so full of it."

"We should go skinny-dipping," Wyn announced.

"Little Miss Prim and Proper wants to go skinny-dipping?" Jazz raised a curious brow. "Have you ever done it before?"

"Of course," she said proudly. "With Cullen. He has the most beautiful body. You should see it."

"Okay." Cullen sprang from his place and grabbed Wyn's hand. "I think it's time we called it a night."

"Why?" She wrapped her arms around him and shut her eyes. "You are very beautiful." Her breath smelled like fruity punch and just a hint of rum. It wasn't unpleasant; neither was the way she felt like warm liquid in his arms.

"Thank you, lass. It's getting late. We should go home."

"But the dancing isn't over."

"For us it is. Good night, everyone."

"Good night, Captain Killjoy," Jack said. "I might as well go out. You all have become so damn boring in your old age."

"I'm not boring!" Jazz frowned, offended by the remark.

"You want to go out with me, then?"

"After ten? No way. I gave up those late nights when I stopped seducing powerful men for their secrets."

"See? You're boring."

"You think because you fly planes and drink shots that you're some kind of bad boy? I've danced with sheiks and eaten off of solid gold plates in private jets while state secrets were being discussed. Just thinking about those days still makes my heart race. You drinking shots and sloppily making out with drunk women doesn't make you exciting. It makes you a basic flyboy with nothing better to do on a weeknight."

"Ouch," Jack said.

"Damn," King added. "You just verbally castrated the man."

"My balls are still intact." Jack grinned. "That's why I love you, Jazz. Your words hurt so good." He kissed her cheek. "I'm about to go do what a flyboy with nothing better to do does on a weeknight." He winked at them and disappeared behind the house.

"Was I too harsh?" she asked King.

"Your tongue is like a knife sometimes."

"It makes me unlikable," she said.

He shook his head. "Only to those who don't know you."

She walked over to him and curled herself into his lap. He stiffened at first, but then he relaxed, wrapping his arms around her. Jazz kissed him and Cullen knew that it was only a matter of time now. She was never openly affectionate.

"Let's go, Wyn," he whispered to her.

She sighed, but agreed, and he led her back to their little cottage. He was hoping she would go to bed, but she didn't. He didn't go either. He knew if he did, he would just lie there awake for hours. So he sat with her on the couch and allowed it when she wrapped herself around him and placed her lips on his throat. They felt good there. Her kisses were starting to feel familiar. They were soothing. He had never experienced that before.

"What do you think is going on with Jazz and King?" she asked him.

"I'm not sure. I suspect they have been sleeping together for some time now, but it may have been something casual that had turned into something much more."

"Or they told themselves it was casual when it always was much more."

"Yes. You're probably right."

"I know a secret about Jazz."

"You do?"

"She likes babies."

"No she doesn't."

"She does. That day we went to the spa, there was a young mother who was struggling with her two kids. She was about to break down and cry when Jazz went over to help. She helped wrangle the two-year-old and then she picked up the screaming baby and like magic, she quieted it. The kid just stared up at her, mesmerized, as she said little silly things to him."

"It was a boy? That explains it. Most men find her irresistible. It doesn't matter the age."

"You're missing the point. She liked the babies and she told me if I told anyone she would dislocate my arm."

"But you're telling me?"

"Well . . . yes. But you can keep a secret.

She thinks we're a serious couple, so of course I would tell you. Couples tell each other everything."

But they weren't a serious couple and yet she knew more about him than anyone. "Have you told me all your secrets?"

"What secrets do I have that you don't know about?" She kissed his throat again.

"Have you ever been in love before?"

"I thought I was in love when I was a teenager, but looking back on it now, I wasn't. He was just the first boy who made me feel special. What about you?"

"I was a teenager. She was a girl I thought I could save, but she was much more broken than I could handle."

"Is Jazz broken?" she asked, taking him by surprise. "She thinks she is."

"I can't answer that. She's sacrificed a lot for her country. Some might even say her soul."

"What happened to her?"

"I don't know the whole story. I just know that she was used as bait. Her job was to seduce powerful and dangerous men. She's one of the most beautiful women in the world and her government used that face to protect their citizens. I know Jazz had to do some things that disgusted her and I don't think she's come to terms with it."

"Don't you all go through that?"

"No. I never had to use my body to get something."

"That makes me sad. She wouldn't like it if she thought I was sitting here feeling sorry for her."

"No." He rubbed his hand over her bare shoulder. "Let's talk about something else."

"Will you kiss me?"

"Yes, but only a little bit." He slid his hand across her cheek, pulling her face upward until her lips touched his.

She moaned and he knew they had to stop. She was too arousing. "I think we should have gone skinny-dipping tonight."

"You're drunk."

"A little," she giggled. "But I don't know what that has to do with anything."

"I don't want anyone else to see you naked. I shouldn't have seen you naked, but I have and I'm a selfish bastard who wants to keep that image all to myself."

"It's just skin," she whispered. She stood up, swaying slightly on her feet as she hiked up her dress and removed her underwear.

He was frozen, mesmerized by what she was doing. She straddled him. He could feel the heat radiating from between her legs through his shorts. "What are you doing?"

"Getting closer to you."

"No."

"*No* to getting close?"

"You know what I'm saying *no* to."

She tilted her head and looked at him. Even her look was arousing. "You don't want to have sex with me?"

"I'm not going to have sex with you tonight." He wouldn't lie to her. Want had nothing to do with it. He was so hard he couldn't think straight.

"Please," she whispered. "I want you so much."

He wrapped his hands around her hips. "You're killing me."

"It won't take long. You don't have to move. Just sit back and let me do all the work. Let me make you feel good." She kissed him then and he was powerless to stop her. Her lips tasted sweet; her body felt so damn good pressed against him.

He was being tested. He had been captured behind enemy lines before. He had been questioned, punished, abused, and he never broke, but now he was breaking. She was more powerful than anyone else on the planet. She was causing him to break.

"Stop it," he said to her, but even he didn't believe his refusal.

"Look at me." He opened his eyes, obeying her. She was so damn sexy. Her lips were swollen from their kisses. Her hair was curly and wild. Her eyes were filled with lust. "Say yes."

"I can't."

"Say yes? Or be with me?"

"I can't," he repeated, because he wasn't sure he could manage other words.

"You want to."

"That is not the question. You know I want you."

"You don't have to be worried about your job. If you don't make love to me, I'm going to have you fired." She giggled and he remembered that she had had too much to drink, that she wasn't clearheaded.

He couldn't have sex with his principal, his employer's daughter, especially now when she was drunk. That knowledge gave him just the strength he needed to act.

"Damn it, Wyn." He lifted her off him. "No."

He walked away from her and left the house, not looking back to see the hurt on her face, not looking back because he knew he wouldn't be strong enough to say *no* a second time.

Wyn had left the house early the next morning and went to the little coffee shop in town so she could search the internet without anyone in the compound seeing what she was doing. She also escaped the house because she didn't want to face Cullen. She had been so horribly embarrassed about what transpired between them last night.

One moment, he was staring at her with sleepy, arousal-filled eyes; the next moment he looked so angry with her. She had thrown herself at him and she was ashamed. She had misread things. He didn't want her like she wanted him.

He had rejected her too many times. She wasn't sure she could face him again. She had tried to search for flights home, but she was sidetracked by the details of her father's affair making headlines once again.

Another letter had been released. No date. Not signed with a name again.

How could you do this to me? I was fine. I was better than before. I should have never told you what happened to her sister. I did what I did to save her. I'm trying. I'm listening. I obey all your stupid orders. There are people here watching me all the time. Every step I take, I have someone behind me, telling me where to go and what to do. You did this to me! You are keeping me here and you can't even face me to tell me why you are doing this to me. I won't take it. It's cruel. It's hurts. You stole from me. You stole my second chance and I'll never forgive you for it.

Wyn had sat back for a long time and just stared at her screen. The letter produced more questions than it had answered. The media had seemed to go crazy with the news. There was a sister? Another child.

Wyn had a sister? It was hard to wrap her head around. She didn't even know for sure that she was the missing child her father's mistress said was stolen from her. There were no facts to back it up. But there was her gut. And she felt it deep in her gut that she was the child that woman had been talking about and she wasn't the only one she had given birth to.

Where was she? Was she still alive? And if not, what the hell had happened to her? Wynter wanted to know, but part of her was scared to find out. What if she found out that both her parents did terrible things? How could she come to terms with it?

She had nearly spent all day out of the house, returning to the compound around four.

"Where the hell have you been?" Cullen leaped from the couch as soon as she walked in the door. "I've been sitting here all damn day thinking the worst."

His accent was so much thicker when his emotions ran strong.

"I went into town."

"Without telling me? Without telling anyone? What the hell is your problem?"

"I'm fine. I was at a coffee shop."

"All day? You were there all day? Almost eight hours?"

"I went for a walk on the beach. I stopped for ice cream. You don't have to worry. I was never in jeopardy. Your job isn't in danger."

"This isn't about my fucking job, Wyn. It's about you disappearing for hours and no one knowing where you were. I was nearly out of my mind."

"I thought you needed some space today."

"From you?" He frowned.

"Of course, from me." Her eyes stung with tears and she turned away. "I'm sorry about last night. I'm embarrassed and ashamed of my behavior. I didn't mean to upset you with my joke. You know I would never do anything to risk your job."

"For fuck's sake, Wyn. You sure as hell don't know how to read a situation." He grabbed her shoulders and spun her around.

"What?"

"I want you. We've established that. It's gotten to the point where I can't control myself, but last night you weren't sober. You were giggly and silly and so damn sweet."

She shook her head. "I'm confused."

"I've been with you for a long time now. I know you. I know you wouldn't have said or done most of those things if it weren't for the alcohol."

"Maybe I wouldn't if I were in Washington, but back then I thought I knew who I was and where I came from, but everything has changed and the rules I've played by no longer exist. Why should I censor myself? Why should I play the good girl and tiptoe around what I want? I can't do it anymore, because doing so was slowly killing me. If you don't want to be with me, I can accept it, but being around you like this, pretending for the sake of your friends, isn't working for me. It's made things so much more complicated."

"I know." He shook his head and turned away from her. "I crossed lines that I thought I would have never crossed. I asked you to do this and never thought about how it would affect us. Or maybe I did. Maybe I knew I could never have any part of you if things stayed as they were, but with this, I could have some of you and still tell myself

I was doing my job."

"But why do you have to hold back? I've wanted to be with you for a year."

"For a year?" He seemed surprised by her statement, but it was true. She had just been denying it to herself. "I have never made love to a woman who wasn't sober. There can be no doubt in my mind that being with me is what she wants. I don't ever want you to wake up the next morning and regret what we have done."

"I would never regret it."

He took a step toward her and placed his hand on her cheek. He leaned in for a moment, and she thought he was going to kiss her. "When I make love to you I want you to be clearheaded. I don't want alcohol to dull any of it. I want you to remember every moment of it. Every touch. Every kiss. Every sensation. I don't want you to come to me for comfort or distraction. And I don't want to come to you simply because I've lost control. If we do this, I have to know for sure that it is something neither one of us will ever want to take back."

His words made her insides turn to liquid. No one else ever had the power to make her melt with words alone. "I'm very sober now. I promise you I won't forget a thing."

He laughed. "I'm still mad at you for

disappearing on me like that." His eyes searched her face. "I was worried."

"That someone kidnapped me? That's only happened once and I'm fairly sure the woman who tried to take me was my mother."

"What?" He shook his head. "There was an attempt made before?"

"Yes, when I was a child. You knew that. That's why I have always had private security since."

"I didn't know that." His eyes narrowed. "You think the person who tried to kidnap you was your birth mother?"

"Yes."

"Why?"

"It was the things she said. I didn't make the connection until recently. She called me her baby. She said that they kept me from her. I thought she was just some crazy person, but now it all makes sense."

"Why didn't you tell me this sooner?"

"I don't know. I assumed you knew my story."

"I knew you were a billionaire's daughter. I knew he wanted you protected. Beyond that, I knew nothing else."

"Does it matter?"

"Yes, it matters. How old were you when she tried?"

"Ten or eleven."

"What did she look like?"

"Blond. Blue eyes. Beautiful." Wyn shut her eyes as that day came flashing back to her. "I remember the way she cried when they pinned her to the ground. It was more than a sob. She was wailing and I felt bad for her."

"She was in pain, Wyn. She must have loved you."

"Yes, but why the hell did my father take me away from her? He could have left me with her. Paid her off. I could have grown up on the other side of the country."

"It's a good question. Mrs. Bates loved you, right? She never made you feel like you were less than her own child?"

"No. I felt very loved by her. She used to tell me she thanked God daily that my father brought me to her."

"Do you think he did it for her? Stole you so she could have you?"

She shook her head, not sure she was comfortable with that notion. "I — I don't know what to think anymore."

Cullen watched as Wyn rubbed her temples. His mind was racing a mile a minute. He could only imagine how she was feeling. "Sit down." He took her hand and guided her to the couch, but he was too antsy to sit beside her.

She had just revealed a very important piece of information to him. One that lead them to the woman who had given birth to Wyn. One that made him believe that she could still be alive.

He knew that she hadn't died in childbirth, nor had Bates had her killed shortly after.

But she had been stashed somewhere. Purposely kept away from her child.

There was no doubt in his mind that Wyn's would-be kidnapper was her birth mother. He didn't know many women who would just allow their child to be taken from them.

"Do you know what happened to her after they stopped her?"

"No. I was whisked away."

"Did anyone say anything to you after? Did they try to explain?"

"No. The next day I had armed security with me and that was that."

"Damn it, I wish I had more to go on."

"I need to know what happened to her. Another letter was released today. It was short. There was another child. A girl. She wrote that she should have never told him what happened to her."

That was big news, but it didn't clear anything up. Only added more questions.

"She's dead?"

"I don't know. The letter didn't say, but it sounds like something happened to her."

It was a troubling thought. But it made more sense than him stealing Wyn just so his wife could have a child. But then again, it could still be plausible. Bates could have planned this. Seduced a vulnerable woman so he could take her child. It all seemed too sinister.

This whole damn thing was a mess. But without this mess he wouldn't have ever gotten this close to Wynter. It was selfish of him to be glad for it. He got to kiss her lips. To hold her hand. To smell her skin. To feel her close to him as she slept.

Today, when he didn't know where she was, he nearly went out of his mind. He wasn't afraid for her safety. He was afraid that she had left him and the thought of it made him feel sick in his gut.

The thought of not seeing her daily, not seeing her in her most natural state, gave him a feeling that he could only describe as panic. He didn't panic. He didn't do sadness, but he thought about not being with her and there was misery there. Like something deep and profound would be missing if she was gone.

He didn't like feeling that way. He didn't want to examine what it meant, because he already knew. He was in love with her.

He had been denying it for so long now, but that's what it was. He was in love. In real love for the first time in his life and he knew that it couldn't go on forever. He wanted her. He wanted every inch of her, but he knew it couldn't last. He wasn't right for her.

There was too much shit in his past. Too much damage. And she had so much going on herself. She had been lied to her entire life, enormous secrets had been kept from her, her identity a mystery. His entire career had been about keeping secrets — even now, he knew more about her past than she did. She needed a nice man with no PTSD, no scars, no trauma. One who could give her a big family with a bunch of kids. A worldly guy who could keep up with her brains. She needed someone who could match her passion. She had so much of it. She deserved that. He needed to find out who her mother was so this could all end. He could go back to his life. Find peace.

He sank on his knees before her and buried his head in her lap. Her hands immediately came up and she buried her fingers in his hair. "You seem tortured by this," she said to him.

"Yes."

"Why? I don't expect you to find my birth mother. You were only supposed to keep me away from the media."

"I want happiness for you, Wyn." He looked up at her.

"Even with all this going on, I'm happier here than anywhere else I've ever been."

"Lush scenery and warm ocean air will do that to anyone."

"You think?"

"Why do you think I'm going to retire here?"

"It's more than that and we both know it."

"You have to go back to your life one day. You have to decide what it is going to be after all this is over."

He stood up, not able to take her touch anymore. He wanted more and more of her and he was afraid he wasn't going to be able to escape this without everlasting damage.

"I have been thinking about that," she told him. "There's so much I want."

"You have to find a way to have it all."

"Is it possible for anyone to have it all?"

"Maybe not everyone, but you can."

"What if what I want involves you?" She

whispered the question, her heart in her eyes.

"Don't ask me that. Not now."

He couldn't take it. Darby said that she was in love with him, but he couldn't believe it. He couldn't be sure until after this was all over and everything was calm and she didn't need to lean on him so much.

It could all be a phase for her. Something she got caught up in while being in one of the most beautiful places on earth.

And that's why he needed to keep himself grounded. He couldn't allow himself to be swept away.

"I need to go see Darby. Will you stay here?"

She nodded. "I'm not going anywhere."

Chapter 13

When Cullen arrived at Darby's cottage, he was surprised to see that Kingsley and Jack were there with him. They stood when he walked in.

"Did I interrupt something, lads?"

"No," Jack said. "Did you find her?"

"Wyn?" He nodded. "She came back about an hour ago."

"We were going to go out and look for her," King said. "You're usually so damn calm, but I knew it was serious. I could tell there was something up."

"You could tell?"

"We all could tell, son."

"I'm losing it, Darby. I can't go back into the field in this state."

"You're retired," King reminded him. "There's no objectivity you have to keep. It's okay to be worried about your girl."

"I think you should tell them," Darby said. "About Wyn. You can trust them like you trust me."

"You're holding something back from me?" King asked him. "I've known you longer than anyone here."

"I know, but this isn't just about me. It's about Wyn."

"What about Wyn?" Jack asked. There was an edge to his voice.

"She's my principal. I work for her father."

"So basically you're telling us you brought your work home with you." Jack grinned. "You broke a rule. A big, fat rule. I love it."

"Damn," King said, shaking his head. "You're still on his payroll?"

"Yes. But not for long." He paused for a moment. "There's more, but I don't want Jazz to know. She won't forgive me." All the men nodded, knowing their friend well. "She's Warren Bates's daughter."

"Who?" King asked.

"Don't you ever read a bloody newspaper?" Darby asked.

"You know I don't. The entire point of moving here was to be as disconnected from everything as possible. Plus, I'm from London. I don't keep up with Americans."

"He's a tech billionaire from D.C.," Jack answered. "He ran for Senate in Virginia a few years ago. He's trying to launch a presidential campaign. My family knows him." He shook his head. "Are you telling me that Wyn is his daughter?"

"Wynter Bates. The story they put out was that she had been adopted from an orphanage in South Africa. But letters were leaked to the media that put everything into question."

"Letters from who?" King asked.

"Bates's mistress. She gave birth to his child. A girl. The girl was then taken away and the mistress was kept locked up somewhere."

"And you're sure this child is Wyn?"

"The letters don't prove it," Cullen responded. "There's no dates or even a name signed to them, but Bates admitted to me as much. He wouldn't admit it to his own daughter, though. He's refused to speak to her since the news broke."

"He would have to explain himself." Jack sat back down. "I can't believe that Wyn is his daughter. I've seen her before. I was a teenager. She accompanied her parents to a dinner party at my house. She was one of those timid types. Couldn't make eye contact. Too shy to say more than a few words. I can't reconcile that the woman who suggested we go skinny-dipping is the same person who was too nervous to hold a conversation with my older brother."

"This process has changed her," Cullen admitted to them. "She's tired of following rules and being the perfect daughter."

"Which is why she is sleeping with her bodyguard," Jack said.

"Don't be an asshole, Jack," King said. "It's more than that."

"Sometimes I'm afraid it isn't," Cullen told them.

King shook his head. "No. Don't listen to Jack. Wyn's not like that. She can't hide her feelings. Everything she feels shows on her face."

"I still can't believe she's Bates's daughter," Jack said. "She's the type of woman my parents would love for me to marry."

"Even with the scandal?" Cullen asked him.

"Yes. You don't know how the rich and powerful work. If Wynter's father becomes president, he can do all sorts of things that would benefit my father and his career. He would love to have a daughter-in-law who could help him curry favor."

"But knowing you, you wouldn't marry anyone just to make your father happy."

"Hell no. But I like Wyn. Almost enough to not give a shit who her father is."

"Why are you telling us this now, Cull?" King interrupted them with his question.

"Because I need your help, lads. Wyn just told me that she thinks her birth mother tried to kidnap her when she was around ten. That tells me that the mother was alive at least until then. I need to know if there was any record of that. Were the police called? What happened afterward?"

"There was also another letter released today," Darby added. "There was another child. The letter alluded that something happened to that child. I think it's very important to find out what happened to that child."

"It could give us insight into why Bates did what he did," King said.

"I agree." Cullen nodded as he surveyed his friends. "I need you to help me find out anything you can. I've tapped out all my sources. Darby, did you find anything?"

He nodded. "I think so. You were right. He scrubbed his employee files pretty good, but I think I found a first name: Grace. I have my people looking deeper, but most of my contacts are foreign. They don't deal much with American intel."

"Ah." Jack grinned. "I think I can be of service here. There's nothing more fun for rich people than gossiping. Someone will know more."

"That would really help me, Jack. Thank you."

"Of course." He gave a little salute. "Never send a bunch of foreigners to do an American's job."

"Hopefully, I won't need this kind of favor again. Thank you for your help. Please don't tell Wyn. I want to gather all the facts before I share this with her."

"Of course," King said with a nod. "You know you can trust us."

Another week had passed. A week since that bombshell letter had been released. Wyn had tried to take her mind off things and she was doing pretty well. She kept herself busy during the days and there were large spans of time when she didn't think about the scandal or the sister she would probably never know. The nights were hard. They always were.

She hadn't been in Cullen's bed once. She hadn't kissed him when no one was around. She went back to the original rules he had set. She was pretending they were a couple. Pretending to be in love with him in front of his friends.

Only she wasn't really pretending. The love was there just beneath the surface at all times, aching to get out. She would keep it to herself. She wouldn't bother him with it. She wasn't sure he could handle knowing. It might cause him to push her away. She wouldn't allow herself to be pushed away. She had too much pride for that.

She would love him quietly.

"Do you think he has any idea?" Jazz asked as she hung lanterns around the pool.

"I don't know. He's not letting on if he does." Wyn was standing at the bar, chopping fruit for the sangria that she was making.

"What does he think we've been up to for the past couple of weeks?"

"I don't know. I think he's just grateful that I'm not bothering him," she said with a smile.

"You think he's getting sick of you?"

"He would never admit it if he was. He's too polite for that."

"He's not." Jazz grinned. "Cullen doesn't do attachment. He once dropped a girl for calling him at home."

"I don't believe that."

"He doesn't like people getting close. He sure as hell didn't want any woman attached to him. I think that's what I liked about him. He was unattainable."

Wyn stopped cutting and looked up at Jazz. "That was very revealing. You had a thing for Cullen."

"Yes. He's hot and brooding and has that accent. But I knew it could never work. I'm happy he's with you."

"I'm surprised you are admitting this to me."

"You're my friend, Wynter. I have these guys, but it's been a very long time since I've had a female friend. Not since I went into the Marines. I'm happy that he brought you here."

Wynter's eyes started to mist and she left her spot at the bar and went over to Jazz, pulling her into a hug. "I don't have any friends either. It's nice to find another misfit."

"Get off me," Jazz complained. "You're going to make me cry and then I'll have to kill you."

"I'm going to let you go, not because you threatened me, but because we have so much stuff to do."

"There's not that much. I know you were hell-bent on making a cake, but it was easier to order one. It was delivered an hour ago."

"I want to be annoyed with you for doing that, but there was no way I was going to have time to frost and decorate that cake."

"I know. You have to learn to delegate more."

"My mother used to throw massive dinner parties. I was never sure how she got things done, but then I remembered we had servants. She just oversaw everything and took credit for it."

"You don't have servants at home?" Jazz asked.

"No. Why would I need servants? I live alone."

"Would you have them after you have kids?"

"No." She shook her, head thinking about it for a moment. "There's no shame in having others help you. I don't know how I would be able to work and take care of my family without help. But I would like to think that I could do it all if I want."

"Cullen wants you to cut down on working."

"I know, but is that fair of him to ask that of me, when his entire life revolved around work?"

"No. It's a goddamn double standard. No one asks men to cut down on their work so they can raise a family. They get patted on the back just for being around. But Cullen isn't all about work anymore. He's here with you. His life now revolves around you."

But she was his work. Jazz didn't know that and the closer that they got, the guiltier she felt about it. How could she tell her who she really was without Jazz hating her? She was going to have to leave one day. What would happen to their friendship? It saddened her to think that she would never see her again, never know how her life turned out.

Cullen could keep her updated, but she wasn't so sure he would be around when this was all over. They couldn't go back to the way things were and they couldn't continue on as they were. She was a planner. She had always looked ahead. But the only thing she could do now was to take things day by day.

Sometimes it was exciting, but sometimes she hated it. She hated not knowing.

"You went quiet on me," Jazz said.

"I was just thinking."

"Cullen would never want servants. I couldn't see him allowing anyone else to do things for him. Maybe you'll be modern and he'll be the stay-at-home dad and you can continue on in your career. I know he wants out of the private-security game. He told us that his current principal was going to be his last. He wanted to retire here and expand our little rental business."

"Did he give a timeline for this?" she asked Jazz.

"No, but I feel like that's a conversation that he should have with you."

"He's not ready for that."

"How do you know?"

"Because I've tried to have it before."

"And he didn't want to talk about it? I'm confused." She shook her head. "You guys are clearly in love. What the hell is his problem?"

She loved him, but they weren't in love. They were a lie. That was the problem. It was starting to hurt to lie.

"I could say the same thing about you and King. You're in love and everyone knows it."

"We weren't talking about me."

"But now we are."

"Nope." She turned away from her. "I'm going to check on Cullen's surprise."

Jazz's departure was exactly what she needed in that moment. She didn't think she could hold up to her questioning much longer.

CHAPTER 14

Cullen watched as Wynter placed a flower in her hair. It was up tonight. Her curls piled on top of her head, a few of them cascading down like a waterfall. He couldn't take his eyes off her as she got ready. He wasn't trying to pretend like he wasn't watching her. She was so beautiful tonight. She wore a long, bright pink halter dress with large white flowers emblazoned on it. She was a goddess come to life.

"Is what I'm wearing okay?" he asked her.

She glanced at him in the mirror. "Why are you asking me? You can wear whatever you want to dinner."

"You sure?"

"Yes." She grinned at him.

He missed kissing her. She hadn't tried to kiss him since that night, when he turned her away. He was regretting it. She had held a little of herself back from him. He missed her and she was in the same house with him.

They held hands in front of his friends. She was lovely and cheerful in front of them. It was what he had originally asked of her. She was giving him what he wanted — only he didn't want it anymore.

"You look so beautiful, Wyn." He came up behind her and kissed her shoulder.

"Thank you."

"I bought you a present today when I was in town."

She couldn't hide her confusion. "Why?"

"You're not supposed to ask somebody why they do something for you. They do it because they want to." He took the little box out of his pocket. In it were flower-shaped earrings with her birthstone in the center. "I think they'll go with what you are wearing tonight."

"That was sweet." Her eyes flashed with tears as he placed them in her ears. "Thank you."

"Don't cry. They weren't much. I just saw them and thought of you."

She turned around and hugged him. He pulled her in tighter. He had missed her hugs as well. Her closeness. Her easy affection. "You are making this harder. I was doing so well."

He didn't respond. He knew what she meant. He knew he was going back on what he had asked of her. It wasn't fair at all.

"Let's go to the house for dinner."

He took her hand and they walked to the community house without saying a word. He could see the big, colorful lanterns around the pool a hundred feet from the house. And as he got closer, he could see the entire patio had been decorated with flowers. It was beautiful. All of his friends were there, dressed in their island best.

They had been in on it. His little surprise. He smiled at them, feeling happiness tug at his heart. In this past few weeks he had felt happiness and torture right beneath his surface at all times, each one fighting each other intensely.

"Surprise," they said in unison.

"He's not surprised," Wyn said. "He was just kind enough not to ruin it for us."

"I was surprised. I didn't figure it out until today when I went in the kitchen and saw the cake."

He had known she and Jazz were up to something, but whenever he saw them, they were huddled over Jazz's sketchbook. He had just assumed they were making plans to decorate the four unoccupied cottages on the other side of the compound. He was genuinely surprised that they had done this. No one had ever thrown him a party before.

No one had cared enough.

His mum probably did, but there was never enough money. Just a little cake and maybe a small gift if she managed to scrape together enough money.

"Have a seat, birthday boy." Wyn lead him to the head of the table and placed a paper crown on his head. "Today you are the king. Let me get you a drink."

He grabbed her hand as she turned to leave him. "You don't have to do that."

"Stop being annoying and let me do this."

He still didn't let her go. He tugged her closer and kissed her. He really kissed her, taking her face in his hands and not letting her go until she went slack. "Thank you for this, Wyn."

"Happy to do it," she whispered.

He let her go, watching her walk away.

"What a lovely girlfriend you have, Cull," he heard an Irish-accented voice say. "She throws a good party."

He frowned for a moment and shook his head, because he thought he saw his mother walk out of the kitchen of the community house. He just sat there, staring at her. Same long, dark brown hair. Same round cheeks. Same sparkling blue eyes. But he knew it couldn't be his mother, because this face was too innocent. Too happy. Too alive.

"Maeve? Is that you, love?"

"You're looking well, big brother." He knocked over his chair as he got up and grabbed her, picking her up and spinning her around like he used to when she was a little girl.

"You're so beautiful," he said when he put her down. "You look just like her." Seeing Maeve was another paradox: Two contrasting feelings fighting for dominance inside him. He was overjoyed to see her, but acute grief struck him as well. He still mourned his mother. Sometimes, it felt like yesterday she was taken from him. "How are you here?"

"Your girlfriend sent for me. First-class and everything. I nearly fell out and died when I saw how posh everything was. They gave me the best meal. Three courses and a wee bottle of hot sauce. It was so darling I snuck it into my bag. I don't even like hot sauce."

He grinned at her, flashing back to when she was a tiny thing and would talk his ear off for hours. "I'll make sure I'll send you home with some real souvenirs."

"Are you crying, Jazz?" he heard King ask.

"Shut up and mind your damn business."

"Jazz helped me do all of this," Wyn told him. "None of it would have happened without her."

"It gave me something to do," she said bashfully. "Now the rest of you — let's get the grill started and this food out. It will give Cullen and his sister a chance to catch up."

The others left and Cullen just stared at his sister for a moment. He had wondered about his siblings over the years, how they had grown, what they looked like. It was surreal to see her here.

"Gosh, Cull. You're a proper grown-up now, aren't you?"

"I am. But so are you."

"I guess. But sometimes I still feel like a kid. You ever feel that way?"

"I think I feel the other way. Like I'm a hundred."

"You've lived a life, have you? An intelligence officer. Your girlfriend told me that I was coming to an island full of them and I best not be too nosy."

"She said it like that?"

"Of course not." She grinned at him. "She's much too posh for that. How did a dirty bugger like you end up with her?"

"I don't deserve her."

"She doesn't seem to think that. Look at what's she done for you. She was asking me if I remembered anything you liked from when we were kids. Like if there was a toy you always wanted or a food you always liked. I couldn't remember anything. Made me feel right guilty, I'll tell you that."

"You were a wee one when you left home. How could you remember anything?"

"I wanted to remember for you. I wanted your girlfriend to give you something from home that would have made you happy."

"She did. You're here. How long can I keep you?"

Maeve smiled at him. "A few days. Wyn made it possible. She got me excused from my classes. Apparently, she is friends with the chair of my department. She said they worked together once. What does she do, Cullen? Flying me out was no cheap thing."

"You don't recognize her?" Her picture had been splashed all over the media. Maeve now lived in the States. She must have seen it.

"Is she an actress? I don't keep up."

"No. She's a professor," he said, feeling relieved. "She teaches at Georgetown. She's got a doctorate."

"Oh. Extra-posh," she said cheerfully. "Does she have a rich, handsome brother out there for me?"

"I'm afraid not."

"Damn. That's okay. I'm just happy you

found someone who loves you so much."

Love. People kept saying that Wyn loved him. He was having a hard time wrapping his head around that. He didn't want to dwell on it, to even think about it, because it didn't matter. It didn't change how he felt about her, his duty to her. "Are you seeing anybody special?"

"Not anyone I would want to tell you about. I'm focusing on school right now. Love will come when it comes. No rush."

"Good girl." He nodded in approval. "Is there anything that you need, Maeve? Anything I can do for you?"

"No, brother. I needed to see you, that was all."

He squeezed her hand. "I'm glad you're here."

Wyn didn't return to the cottage until nearly three in the morning. She was exhausted, but the tiredness was well worth it. It had been a beautiful night. Everything from the decorations, to the food, to the mood had been beautiful.

She would never forget the smile that spread across Cullen's face when he saw his little sister. He had been happy. His life had been a hard one and she knew she was witnessing one of those rare moments when his happiness was pure. She was glad to be there to see it, to have a role in giving him that. She watched him all night as she interacted with his sister. He kept looking at her in disbelief. Almost as if she was an apparition that was going to fade away.

But Maeve didn't. She was a lovely girl, full of laughter and sweetness. It was hard to believe the two of them had come from the same mother and father. Cullen's life had been so different from his siblings. He had been through war well before he had become an adult. He had been homeless. He had served his country. He had learned secrets and witnessed death and had escaped it. He had done nearly all of it alone.

He didn't have to be alone anymore. He had a family. The one he created and the one that was given to him. She was happy for him.

She had tried to be quiet when she walked through the door. Cullen had walked his sister to her cottage and Wyn assumed he had gone to bed while she and King and Jazz put away the food. But her attempt at silence had been for nothing, because she should have known that he wouldn't have been asleep.

He would have made sure she was safe inside before he even tried.

"You're up," she said to him.

He rose from his chair, not saying a word. He walked toward her, a look in his eye she couldn't read. She swallowed hard, feeling anxious. There was no lightness in his eyes. No humor.

"Are you mad that I brought your sister here? I asked the others first if it was okay. They thought it would be."

He grabbed her shoulders and pushed her against the wall. "For someone so smart, you ask the dumbest questions sometimes. That was the kindest, most thoughtful thing that anyone has ever done for me."

"Then why do you look so angry?"

"Because I don't deserve it and no matter how hard I try, I can't pay you back for what you have done."

"I don't want you to pay me back. Seeing you happy makes me happy."

He took her face in his hands and looked at her for a long moment and then he kissed her. She could tell that this time it was different. There was no control this time. There was a kind of wild rawness there that both scared and excited her.

He briefly lifted his lips from hers. "I'm sorry," he said.

Before she could ask why, his hands tore at the back of her dress, pulling it down till it pooled at her feet. He kissed her neck as he unhooked her bra. His hands were so efficient, turning her on as he stripped her naked, making her skin burn as his rough hands passed over them.

She was trembling by the time he removed her underwear. No coherent thought could form in her head. She was just a mass of feelings. Arousal, fear, love, desperation, heat.

"I'm sorry," he apologized again.

He didn't remove his clothes, he just undid his shorts, wrapped her leg around his waist and pushed deep inside of her.

The shock of feeling him there made her cry out. It was intense. She was so wet. His body was so hard, so hot. His mouth was dangerous, kissing her and kissing her, until she couldn't make sense of anything.

His rhythm was fast and rough and furious, but it was what she needed. She clung to him, digging her nails into his back. She had never been with a man like this before and now that she had, she didn't think it would be possible to go back to regular life, to not feel this kind of passion again, to want any other man as much as she wanted him.

Her orgasm was one that overtook her entire body, coming only seconds before his.

He kissed her through it, her naked body loving the feeling of his clothes against her skin.

He was finally still, no longer kissing her, but his lips pressed against hers, his body still inside her.

She spoke first. "If you let go of me, I'm going to fall. I'm jelly."

A small smile spread across his lips and he scooped her into his arms, carrying her to his bedroom. He placed her beneath the covers and then stepped back to strip away the rest of his clothes. She wanted him to look happy, but instead the expression of guilt on his face was undeniable.

"Why do you look so miserable?" she asked as he climbed into bed.

"That was not how I planned it," he said, reaching for her. "I wanted to go slow. I wanted it to last all night. I wanted you to be comfortable. But I lost control. I was too rough with you."

"I didn't want it slow and all night. I wanted it fast and up against that wall. I wanted it with you. Stop treating me like I'm fragile."

"You're not fragile. I've just thought about making love to you for a year."

"Have you?"

"Yes. I used to wonder how you would

respond if I leaned in to kiss your neck when I was helping you put on your coat."

"I would have died of shock."

"Would you?"

"I had no idea. None. You were nothing but professional."

"My thoughts weren't. I knew you were alone across the street at night. I used to think about coming over in the middle of the night and climbing into your bed. I thought about how I would seduce you. What it would take for you to be with me."

"A kiss," she said, giving him one. "Or you could have just asked me."

"I could not be with you with then."

"But now?"

"But now I can't be without you."

Wyn's heart flipped over. She thought she was in love with him before, but she had just fallen deeper in love. She touched his cheek, his skin no longer pale, his hair no longer efficiently short. and just looked at him. She wanted to cement this moment in her mind. She didn't want to forget it. "I don't want to leave here," she whispered. No place, no other moment could compare to here.

"Maeve said this place was perfect. That she'd never seen anything like it."

"Is she like you remembered?"

"Yes and no. I remember a tiny girl. She's a woman now. She looks just like my mum. Same hair, same eyes, same smile. It's hard for me to look away from her. I had to keep reminding myself that Mum had passed."

"It's bittersweet," Wyn said with a nod.

"Yes. It makes me realize how much I miss my mother. But Maeve still has the same personality. The same brightness. I'm glad my aunt took them away. It would have been impossible for them to keep that if they had stayed."

"I'm sorry I couldn't get your brother. He was too far away and there wasn't enough time."

"You've done enough for me." His hand cupped her breast, his thumb absently stroking her nipple. She was relieved that their celibacy was over. They wouldn't have to stop tonight. He wouldn't have to hold back. He was relaxed. She felt the difference in him and she knew that this was special. That few people got to see him this way. "Have I said *thank you*?"

"You've showed me."

"I didn't hurt you?" He touched between her legs. There was a concerned expression on his face.

"No. Stop worrying."

"There's been no one since I've met you,"

he said, stroking her. "I couldn't control myself."

"I . . ." Her words drifted off because his fingers felt too good. "I can't think when you're doing that."

"Who wants you to think?" He pushed her flat on her back and rose above her. "You must be exhausted. You put in a lot of work today. Let me put the work in tonight."

He kissed the base of her throat. "You must be tired too." She reached up and ran her fingers through his dark hair.

"I'm not too tired for this." His lips moved to her shoulder. "I want to go slow this time, but you turn me on so much. You can't see how you look to me."

"I probably look a mess."

"No. You're gorgeous." He dropped more kisses on her body. "Your skin is dewy. Your lips are swollen from my kisses." He picked up her wrist and kissed the inside of it, which was more arousing than she could ever imagine. "Your curls are wild and you have a little, sweet smile on your face that would make a man want to sell his soul just to see. You drive me crazy. In every way. I feel blessed to be here with you."

"Now," she moaned.

"What, love?"

"I want you right now."

"But I'm not done. There are so many places my lips haven't touched."

"Later." She wrapped her legs around him. "Cullen, don't make me wait."

"Yes, ma'am." He slid inside her. "I live to serve you."

CHAPTER 15

Nearly everyone got a late start to the day. Cullen wasn't one to lay around all day, but he had slept like the dead. It was a deep, dreamless sleep that his body needed. The emotion of the night before had left him spent. The sex had too. Great sex tended to have that effect on a person.

He couldn't stop himself from touching her last night. That's why he was afraid to start this with her. He knew his need for her would only grow. He would never be satisfied. He would only want her more. When he woke up, he reached for her again, only to find the bed empty.

It was almost noon, he realized, and they had company. He should have known Wyn wouldn't have stayed in bed when there was a guest to be entertained. He found her at the community house, making another pot of coffee. Everyone was there. Jazz was sitting in the shallow end of the pool, a pair of shades covering her eyes. Jack was dozing in the hammock on the side of the patio. His sister was sitting at the island, with King and Darby surrounding her.

It all seemed right to him as he walked up. Having all these important people in a place he loved.

He greeted everyone and then walked up behind Wyn, wrapping his arms around her waist and kissing her shoulder. "Good morning, lass."

"Good morning." She leaned into him. "Did you sleep well?"

"I did. Why didn't you wake me up when you got out of bed?"

"I thought you might like to sleep in."

"I'd rather wake up with you." He buried his nose in the crook between her neck and shoulder. He loved her smell. The soap. The product she used in her hair.

She turned in his arms, went up on her tiptoes and spoke directly into his ear. "I think we both would know what would have happened if I woke you up this morning. Neither of us would be standing here right now." It was true. Feeling her pressed against him now was doing things to his body. She turned back around and scooped some fruit salad into a bowl for him. "Do you want coffee this morning, Cullen? I can make you some tea as well."

"I'll get it myself, Wyn. You've done enough."

"Pouring you a cup won't push me over the edge. I can handle a little domestic work." She looked at Maeve. "Your brother is incredibly stubborn about letting people do things for him. Please, tell me that you do not share his annoying habit."

"We're Irish, love. It's against our nature to let people do things for us we can bloody well do ourselves, but you won't find me complaining if a beautiful man wanted to be at my beck and call all day."

"Trust me, I'm not at his beck and call. He's done so much for me. Getting him coffee seems like such a small thing."

"She's thrown me my first-ever birthday party and brought my long-lost sister to me. I don't think I'm ever going to be able to match that." He kissed the side of Wyn's face and poured his own coffee.

"Are you two getting married?" Maeve asked. Cullen paused at the question, not sure how to respond.

"We told him he should," Darby said. "I've never seen him like this before."

"Like what?" Cullen asked.

"Happy. You're happy now, aren't you, son?"

"Aye."

"If we're going to get married, you'll be the first to know," Wyn said. "Now, what are you two going to do today?" she asked, changing the subject.

He was glad she changed the subject, but at the same time he wasn't. What were they? How would she classify what was going on between them? He couldn't say that they were just sleeping together. They weren't. It was deeper than that. On this island they could be boyfriend and girlfriend. Here they were equals. Stateside, they wouldn't be. She would go back to being the daughter of a billionaire. He would go back to . . . To what? She was his last principal. He wouldn't work for anyone else again. This little compound was his home. The rental business would turn into his full-time job.

He couldn't ask her to make her life here, to give up working, to just be his wife. Her life was too big for that. But he had no place in her world. The heaviness in his chest spread through him. He didn't want to think about the future, because he didn't want to think about the end of them. Especially since they had just begun.

"You want to explore the island, love? There's a nice place I can take you for lunch on the water. Or we can go to the beach?"

"Exploring the island sounds like fun. Let me go back to the cottage and get ready. I'll meet you back here."

Darby and King excused themselves so they could work on one of the cottages, leaving Cullen semi-alone with Wyn. "Are you coming with us?"

"You should enjoy the day with your sister. You don't need me tagging along."

"What if I want you tagging along?" He took her hand.

"You should create memories just with your sister. Twenty years from now, I want you to be able to look back and think about this day. Take the opportunity now. Who knows what the future can bring?"

"I still want you with me."

She hugged him close. "I'm staying here." She kissed his chin. "I'm going to take a long nap. You didn't let me sleep last night."

"You can lock me out of the room tonight." He rubbed his hands down her back. "You're going to have to lock me out, because I don't think I can stay away from you."

"The door will not be locked. I don't want you away from me."

"We can't ever go back now," he said seriously. "You know that, right?"

She nodded. "If my life didn't take this

turn, do you think we would have ended up here?"

"I don't know," he answered honestly. "One too-long touch might have led to a kiss, which would have caused me to resign."

"I'm glad it happened this way, then."

He was still going to have to resign. He didn't want to tell her that just yet. He wasn't ready to think ahead. He wanted to live in right now forever. "Rest well today, love." He gently kissed her lips. "I'll see you tonight."

Wyn did take the day to rest. She lounged by the pool with Jazz and when the sun finally sapped the rest of her remaining energy, she returned to the cottage she shared with Cullen and slept. But not as long as she wanted to. She had watched Cullen go off with his sister today. He had been happy, his life made a little fuller by Maeve's presence. She was happy for him. Happier than she could ever be for anyone else, but she kept thinking about her own incomplete family. Her lack of answers.

Her gut told her that the letters were real, the sordid details from the scandal were true, but a tiny part of her still wanted to hear from her father that it wasn't. That everything she had heard about him was a lie.

She had had a sister once. More than anything else, that was nagging at her. She tried to push the thoughts away, but it gnawed at her. What happened to her? What did she look like? Would they have been friends? She would never know the answer to these questions, because her sister was gone. Some mysterious circumstance took her away, just like they did her birth mother.

This missing sister was almost a worse pain than an unknown birth mother. The child had been innocent. And Wyn had been loved by the woman who raised her. There was guilt there sometimes when she thought about wanting to know who her father's mistress was.

She was sure she had met her, but if she had the chance to meet her again, would she want to know her? Could they have built a relationship?

All of these ever-flooding thoughts were making it clear to her that she needed to build her own family. To have her own babies. To be with a man who she loved with no secrets between them.

She wanted that life with Cullen, but she had no idea what he wanted and the thought of asking him scared her. It was too soon, even though she had probably fallen in love with him long ago, even though his friends and family were asking them questions about it. She knew she couldn't think in terms of forever with him. Not yet.

There was a knock on her bedroom door a little after four that afternoon. Cullen peeked in.

"Hi," she said, feeling shy all of a sudden.

"Hello, love," he said as he walked into the room. "I thought you'd be sleeping."

"I can't seem to shut my mind off," she admitted.

He climbed in bed beside her. "I understand." He stroked her cheek with his thumb. "I wish things were different. Easier."

She nodded, hating that all she could do was focus on herself here. It was why she threw herself into work. She could think about others. She could give to others. "How was your day with your sister?"

"We had a nice time. I thought it would be different being out with her. Like when she was four and I would take her with me to do the shopping. She always treated everything as if it were an adventure. I thought she would lose some of that as an adult, but she hasn't. You should have seen the smile she gave me when I bought her ice cream."

"You're a good big brother."

"You helped me with that." He looked down at her, his eyes searching her face. "I want you to move into my room with me. I don't want to feel like we're pretending anymore."

"Okay."

"Why do you seem so sad today, love?" He looked worried. "You're not regretting this?"

"No." She shook her head. "I'm not sad. I just keep thinking the real world is waiting for me. My old life is paused in place, ready for me to push *play.*"

"You miss how things were."

"Some things." She lightly kissed his lips. "There are things that I've encountered here I never want to lose."

"I knew how you feel." He pulled her closer, settling deeper into the mattress. She felt comfortable with him. Safe. This was the feeling she was searching for her entire life. She wanted to hold onto it, to believe she could always have it, but she wasn't sure if that was possible. She was worried about how it would be when she didn't have Cullen anymore. "Sleep with me. I've been to bed with other women, but you're the only person I want to go to sleep with."

Being in love was physical. She felt it through her entire body. He said things to her, things that made her feel like he more than just cared. Sometimes she felt like he loved her too. Was it a foolish thought? Maybe, but right now it felt too good to stop thinking it. "I'll go to sleep with you if you promise me one thing?"

"What's that?"

"Make love to me when we wake up."

"That's one promise I'm eager to keep."

It was good not having to pretend anymore, Cullen thought the next day, as he walked up to the community house with Wyn. There was a freedom in being able to express how he felt, in not holding back. His entire life he had to hold back, but now he no longer had to.

The guilt never left him, though. The doubts didn't either. He tried not to think about how things would be if he had never brought her here. If he never created this situation in the first place. It would do him no good.

"I'm making breakfast this morning," he announced when they arrived at the house. His sister was already there, wearing a pretty floral dress. He had never thought that two kids from Northern Ireland would be here together in a tropical paradise, but here they were and where they had been born seemed such a faraway memory that it could have been from another life.

"You cook, brother?"

"I can make a few things. Eggs being one of them. Wyn made way too much food for the party, so we've got a lot of leftovers I can put in them."

"I think some of that ham might be good in there," Maeve agreed, with a nod. "I'll help you."

"Thanks. Wyn, you are to sit down and not lift a finger today."

"I like to do those things. I don't get to do them at home. I want to enjoy the opportunity while I can."

She wanted to go home. He could tell. She was a woman used to working. Used to helping people. She was growing bored on this island, not using her ability and intelligence. He wished he could find a way to keep her happy here. He knew he alone wasn't enough. He would never be enough to satisfy her mind. It bothered him a small bit. In theory it sounded nice to be someone's everything. But he knew himself. He knew he would find a woman like that annoying, suffocating. He wanted her to have everything she needed out of life.

"You're like our mum," Maeve said. "I used to watch her work all day. Washing clothes, cooking and cleaning, helping out the neighbors. It looked exhausting to me, but she never seemed to mind and even as a wee girl, I knew that I could never be like her. She said she needed to feel useful. I sometimes wonder if she had stayed alive would she have burned herself out with all that giving."

"I'm sure your mother worked much harder than I ever have. I have had people taking care of me my entire life. Before it was housekeepers and tutors. Now your brother takes care of me. At first, I bristled at the idea of having him so involved in my life, but now . . . He's gotten to me. I think I need him to take care of me as much as I want to take care of him."

"I would gag at the sweetness of that statement if you didn't make my brother so damn happy." Maeve grinned at him. Her cell phone beeped. Her screen lit up with a text message. "It's Liam." She picked up her phone. "Wants to know where the hell I am. I don't get good reception in my little cottage. It's better here."

"Yes. We made sure the main house had the best reception," Cullen said. "Isn't it one AM there? You should see what he wants. He's probably worried."

She nodded and dialed their brother. "Liam. I told you where I was going. I'm here with Cullen and his girlfriend. Did you think I went falling off the face of the earth?"

"It's Dad." Cullen could hear the graveness in his voice through the muffled phone. Maeve put the phone on speaker. "He's taken a turn. The care home thinks he has another week or so in him."

"Oh." She looked up at Cullen. "Are you with him?"

"No. Not yet. I think we should be there. I'm catching the train in the morning." Liam paused. "I know I shouldn't ask you to come, but I want you to come see him. I don't want to go alone."

"I'm here with Cullen. It's his birthday. You should see all the trouble his girlfriend went through to bring me here."

"I know. And I know what our father did to him, but he's our father and I think if we don't see him before he dies, we'll not forgive ourselves."

Wyn's hand slipped into his. At first, he was too shell-shocked to feel it. It wasn't the fact that his father was dying. That wasn't a surprise. Cullen thought the man would have died long ago. It was Liam's voice. He sounded just like the old man. At least, the version of him that Cullen remembered when he was a boy. He hadn't seen a picture of Liam. He didn't know how he looked, but there must be some of their father in him.

Just hearing his voice took him back to their small home in Belfast. That feeling returned. That tight ball in his stomach that made him want to black out and forget the world.

"I don't know what to do." Maeve sounded helpless.

"Don't let my relationship with him play any role in your decision. I will support you in whatever you want to do. If you want to go, I'll pay for your flight."

"You really don't want to see him, Cull? Not even to tell him to rot in hell?"

"I've said everything I had to say to the man the day I left him drunk and blubbering on the floor."

"I would like to see you, Cullen," Liam said. "I can't get stateside, but I would give just about anything to see you."

Cullen looked down at Wyn. "Will you be all right here for a few days if I go back to Ireland to see my brother?"

He didn't say to see his father. It wasn't why he was going. He was going so Maeve

316

wouldn't have any regrets. He was going so he could see his brother.

"I'm going with you."

"What? I don't know if you should be traveling."

"I'm going, Cullen. There's nothing you can do that will make me stay behind."

He couldn't tell her that he was worried about her safety. Or that reporters might catch on if they made too many moves. He wanted her with him. It was as simple as that. He wanted her with him when he returned home. It would be too hard to step back in time without a lifeline to his present with her to keep him grounded.

It felt odd leaving the island, Wyn thought as she boarded the private flight that Jack had arranged for them. The scenery had soon changed. The lushness of the island had disappeared and all she was left to look at was clouds. There were times when she had wanted to return to some kind of normalcy, but leaving now didn't feel good. They were going to see a dying man and the warmth she had felt on the island had vanished. Maeve was full of nervous energy. She talked a lot on the flight. About everything. About nothing. Wyn knew it was to take her mind off the reason behind this trip.

Cullen, on the other hand, was silent. He had morphed back into the man she had known before they had come to St. Thomas. The one who showed no emotion. The one in all black. The one who only spoke when absolutely necessary. She hated that.

She hated that he could only be comfortable, reveal himself, in one place. The rest of the world would never see him how she knew him. Maybe she didn't want the rest of the world to have that part of him, but she hated knowing that he must be feeling so much and wouldn't give away anything about it.

She got up from her seat and sat in his lap. He looked at her, slightly surprised, like he had forgotten everything that had transpired over the past month and he was just her bodyguard again. But he wasn't. He was the man she loved.

She took his face in his hands and kissed him. It took him a moment to respond, but he did. He buried his fingers in her hair and prolonged their kiss. "I'm here with you," she told him when he let up. "Don't forget that."

"No, love. I won't."

It was raining and cold when they got off

318

the plane a few hours later. She didn't know much about Belfast. She had only been to London when she was in the UK, but she found the part of the city they were in to be surprisingly beautiful.

"It's changed," Cullen said as they drove to their hotel. "I nearly don't recognize it."

"Yeah," Maeve said. "Belfast has changed a lot since you left. It's got a big cultural scene. Fancy restaurants, museums, cafés."

"You might be too little to remember, but they used vans as bombs. Two explosions in less than twenty-four hours. I was walking somewhere with my mates when one went off. We were too far away to get very hurt, but I remember the heat of it. So intense. Hotter than any fire you could imagine. And the glass . . . Little shards of it flying through the air. A piece of it struck my cheek, slicing it open. Mum was out of her mind when I got home that night. She told me to stay out of that area. She didn't know that two weeks later she would be the one to succumb to the violence."

Wyn's throat burned with unshed tears. Cullen's pain was so acute. His face remained that same cool neutral that she had known, but she could hear it in his voice, feel it radiating off of him. She had grown up so sheltered. Alone in many ways, but he had grown up in a war zone. And then he spent his adult life in them.

She grabbed his hand and lifted his fingers to her lips. What else could she do, but let him know that she loved him? Let him know that his pain was no longer his own.

"You're not allowed to cry," he told her.

"You can't tell me what to do," she retorted.

He leaned over and kissed her forehead. Wyn wished she could get a glimpse inside of his mind, but it might be too scary in there. She might not be able to handle what he was thinking.

"I'm sorry, Cull," Maeve told him. "I didn't realize how this would be for you."

"I'm fine," he said. "It's just odd seeing this place so different. It's like leaving your house for a day and coming back to all new furniture. It's still home, but none of it is what you're used to."

They all went silent for a moment as they pulled up to their hotel. Wyn had booked the rooms. She knew how hard this trip would be for him when he allowed her to do so.

"Ah, Wyn. This is swanky." Maeve's eyes went big. "I didn't think college professors made so much money."

"They don't. I translate documents for

the federal government as well. Plus, Belfast is surprisingly affordable. If this was New York or D.C. this would have cost five times as much."

"Still the nicest place I've ever stayed," she said. "Liam texted me and said he was here already. He's waiting in the lobby."

Cullen nodded and stepped out of the car first. He looked back and reached for Wyn's hand. She took his hand and walked into the hotel with him. She was anxious for him, but in a way she felt blessed to be with him, to experience this important event with him.

CHAPTER 16

Cullen spotted Liam immediately as he walked into the lobby. He was sitting in the plush seating area in the lobby. He could tell his brother was nervous. Liam hadn't spotted them yet, but he was sitting in his chair, his leg bouncing up and down. Cullen was afraid he would look just like their father as he remembered him, but Liam didn't. There was no doubt that Liam was his son — their features were nearly the same — but looking at Liam, Cullen could see no sickness in his soul. No bloating in his face. No drunkenness in his eyes. Liam was healthy and alert. There was nothing trashy about it. He looked like a nice young man who didn't live through violent conflict, a man who wasn't plagued with demons every waking hour of the day. Liam wasn't his father and Cullen felt relieved.

He walked up to him and Liam jumped out of his seat. "You look all right," were

Liam's first words to him. "I was afraid I wouldn't be the better-looking brother. Glad to see that I am."

Cullen blinked at him for a moment and then smiled. That cheeky grin had spread across Liam's face and he remembered that his brother was the funny one in the family. A joker. A kind lad. That was the thing that had struck him the most when they had gone. How quiet the house was. How void of laughter and lightness it was.

He grabbed his brother and gave him a tight hug.

"I'm taller. Women like that," Cullen retorted.

"That's what you think." He pulled away from Cullen and the soberness returned to his face. "I'm happy to see you, Cull. I'm glad you are well."

"I am." He nodded. He glanced back at Wyn, who was standing quietly at his side. She had semi-returned to her old clothes since it was so damn cold in Ireland. She wore her cream-colored wool coat and a pair of sensible slacks. Her hair was still in the wild curls he loved and she was wearing the earrings he bought for her on a whim. They were cheap and she deserved something more precious touching her ears, but she put them on every day since he had given them to her.

He wanted to do something special for her, but he didn't know what could be big enough to thank her. She had been there for him in a way no one else had been, in a way he never allowed anyone else to be. He trusted her. He could lean on her. It was a wholly new feeling for him.

"This is Wyn." He grabbed her hand and presented her to Liam. "She's special to me," he said, not knowing how else to describe her. She was no longer just his principal. She wasn't his friend.

Girlfriend wasn't the right word. It wasn't strong enough. Wyn was the kind of woman a man made his wife.

He wanted to be that man, but he knew he wasn't enough for her.

"It's nice to meet you." Liam shook her hand. "One of the things I remember about my brother is that he always fell for the most beautiful girl in the neighborhood. I see he hasn't changed. You might be the most beautiful woman this town has ever seen."

"What an outrageous lie," she said, laughing softly, "but thank you. You are very charming."

He nodded his head and then turned to Maeve and greeted her with a big hug. "I know you all must be tired from your flight.

Go rest up for a while. We can meet down here in a couple of hours for a meal. We need to talk about our father."

"I'll be with you during the conversation, but the decision is up to you. I want no part of it."

"You're the most important to him," Liam said. "You're the only one he really cares about."

Cullen shook his head. "He only cares about himself. We're going to check in. Let's meet back here later."

They checked in and went to the room that Wyn booked for them. It was the nicest hotel room he had ever stayed in. He hadn't been paying attention when she booked this trip, but he knew it must be costing her a small fortune. She had refused to take his credit card, but he would find another way to pay her back.

"You booked a suite?" He looked out their window, high above the city. They had a view of the river before them. It was all lovely, but surreal. He couldn't get over how odd it was to be back here when he swore he would never return.

"I did. I booked ones for your brother and sister as well."

"That was too much, Wyn. You're going to allow me to write you a check for this."

"You know I won't take it. Besides, I used my father's money. Do you think this hotel has any five-thousand-dollar bottles of champagne?"

He sat on the edge of the bed. "Do you think your father would notice or care if you are using the money out of your trust fund? You don't go on vacation. You don't shop. You're driving a ten-year-old car. I think he would want you to use it. He's also a billionaire, love. He has dinners that cost more than this."

"Don't ruin my rebellion for me."

"You call being overly generous to my family a rebellion?"

"I do. I also want them to like me."

"Why do you care if they like you?" He grabbed her by the waist and rested his forehead on her stomach.

"Because you are the most important person in my life and I want the people who are important to you to like me."

How could she be so sweet? He should have refused this job the moment he met her. It was like he had willingly walked into this trap and he never wanted to break free from it. "They like you. They'd like you if you didn't do anything at all. They'd like you for the same reasons that I like you."

"Why do you like me?"

He looked up at her, choosing his words carefully. "Because you are you and being with you makes me feel good."

"How are you feeling?" She ran her fingers through his hair. "Being back here can't be easy."

"I'd rather be back in Afghanistan." It wasn't an overexaggeration. His purpose there was clear. He was there for his queen and country. Here he felt useless, unable to take any action.

"Isn't that where you got shot?"

"Yes." He had been more than shot. He nearly died.

Wyn made a soft noise. "Is there anything I can do for you?"

It felt selfish to ask more of her, but he couldn't stop himself. "Take a nap with me. The only time I sleep well is with you beside me."

"Is that true?"

He pulled her down on the bed so that they were face-to-face. "I wouldn't lie to you." He had demons that threatened to strangle him every time he closed his eyes. But not with her. He knew where he was with her, even as he slept. It was hard for those dark thoughts to interfere when he had lightness beside him.

He wasn't sure he could go back to sleeping alone. But that wasn't a thought he wanted in his head at the moment, so he closed his eyes and drifted to sleep, trying not to think about anything except how good it felt to be with her.

The next morning Cullen met his siblings in the lobby. They were to have a simple breakfast before they set out to see their father one last time. Cullen knew this was the last time. The man was dying and even if he weren't, Cullen wouldn't see him again.

The mood was understandably tense as they sat at the table. Wyn had tried to inject some lightness into their conversation that morning. It helped with Maeve, who was visibly nervous. He could tell she was torn between being a good daughter and a loyal sister. Cullen appreciated it, but he didn't need her to be loyal to him. He didn't want his father's treatment of him, or Cullen's feelings for the man, to color her memories of him. He had stayed quiet last night, like he promised he would, as Maeve and Liam discussed their father's future. There would be no church service. No big funeral. No long line of mourners. He would be cremated. His ashes spread in the countryside, where he had met their mother. Liam had tried to contact their father's family, but he had alienated most of them. It was just the three of them there — really, only two — to care about the fate of Seamus Whalen.

They had gathered into a taxi and ridden in complete silence to the care home. Cullen had turned his thoughts off as the numbness spread through him. He felt like a boy again, in those days after Liam and Maeve had gone and his father was at his drunken worst. It was easier to go numb than to feel pain. He wasn't sure he would have survived the pain. It would have eaten at him, swallowed him whole. He didn't know where he would have been now if it had. Probably dead or in prison. There had been no future for him here. He was afraid that if he came back, he would feel some sort of longing, some deep pang of regret for leaving his home, but he didn't.

He did not regret leaving. He just wished he would have left sooner.

The taxi pulled to a stop. They all piled out in front of the modest facility. Wyn took his hand, her fingers locking with his as they walked in. She was quietly reminding him that he wasn't facing his father alone. He wouldn't have been able to make it through this trip without her. He considered himself a strong man, but he had needed her. He had needed her to sleep, to soothe him, to keep him calm when the raging beast that he used to be threatened to come out.

Everything had gone out of his head as he walked through the care home to the unit where their father was kept. Cullen couldn't make sense of anything he saw or heard. It was all just white noise and bright, unforgiving lights. He did take note of the smell: Antiseptic. Sickness. Death.

"Hiya, Pop," he heard Maeve say.

It was then his eyes focused on his father. He was in a hospital bed, a sheet covering up his useless body. He looked much older than he was. He wasn't even sixty yet, but he looked like a man who had lived a very long, hard life. His hair was shockingly white, not the oil-slick black it used to be. He wasn't big anymore. His presence didn't take up space. He was frail, his skin so translucent that you could nearly see all the veins beneath it.

Cullen felt no fear or anxiety from his presence. It was the first time he had been in a room with his father and was sure that the man wouldn't lift a fist to him. He was still numb, but maybe there was some sadness there. Sadness over a life wasted. He didn't expect to feel that.

His father's eyes focused. They settled on

Maeve, then went to Liam. It was a moment before they went to him. Seamus's eyes settled on him for a long while. They were staring at each other in a silent deadlock in which Cullen refused to look away. Recognition sparked in his eyes and he immediately began to struggle to sit up, but his body wasn't strong enough to accomplish the task.

"Pop, don't," Liam said. "Just rest."

"Is . . . that . . . my . . . son?" Every word was a struggle to get out. Cullen couldn't make himself move or respond. He stood where he was, staring at the man he didn't recognize anymore.

"That's Cullen. He's come to see you," Liam said softly.

"Come here, son."

He wasn't acknowledging his other children. It bothered Cullen. They had come from far away to be with their father as well. Liam had been more loyal to him than anyone and yet they were ignored, not even greeted. All of the attention was on Cullen. It was a feeling he was used to. It was a feeling he hated.

"Say hello to your children."

His father frowned in confusion, as if he didn't have other children.

"Your other children. The little ones." He

gently pushed both Liam and Maeve forward. "They're the reason I'm here. You acknowledge them right now, you old bastard."

"Hello, Liam. Hello, Maeve. Thank you."

They both nodded. It was clear they were both emotional. Maeve was on the verge of tears. Liam didn't look far behind. "How are you feeling, Pop?" Maeve asked.

"My son is here," he answered, looking at Cullen as if Liam wasn't his. "Let me see you, Cullen."

He gave his father what he wanted and walked closer. He was a man now. A decorated veteran. A retired intelligence officer. A man who worked hard and earned what he had. No handouts. No leg ups. He did it alone. He wanted him to see who he was in spite of him.

"You did well for yourself."

Cullen nodded.

"You live in America now?"

He nodded again, not giving him more information than that.

"Is that your girl?" He looked beyond Cullen to Wyn, taking her in for a moment. It was rare that somebody who looked like Wyn was in Northern Ireland. He tensed, waiting for his father to say something about the color of her skin.

"Yes, she's mine," he said through clenched teeth.

"American?"

"Yes."

"She's posh. Good work."

The compliment knocked him off-center. It was so surreal having this conversation with him. His father acted as if nothing happened, like there weren't multiple daily beatings. Like he never had gotten so drunk in a pub that Cullen had to literally drag his passed-out body home. He acted like his alcoholism and his destruction never existed.

And maybe it didn't in his mind. Maybe the alcohol had done in his brain.

"You've seen me now. I'm going to step out and let Maeve and Liam visit with you." He turned to go.

"You're going to leave me again?" The question was clear. His voice had been getting stronger as their conversation continued, but this time his voice was crystal clear, no slurring, no struggle.

"I never wanted to see you in the first place."

"Why? I loved you. I never wanted you to go."

Cullen's anger sparked and rose wildly. His balled his hands into fists and forced himself to stay on the spot. "I had to go. I would have been nothing there with you."

"You could've come back for me. Taken me with you. Set me up in a nice place. I was lonely without you."

"What?" He couldn't process what his father was saying. "You expected me to come back?"

"If you had, I wouldn't be in this bloody place now."

Cullen couldn't say that Maeve hadn't warned him. She told him that his father blamed him, but actually hearing it sent him over the edge. He took off his coat, pulled his shirt over his head, and bared his back to his father. "You did this to me."

He heard his siblings cry out in distress.

"No," his father denied it.

"You beat me bloody every damn day for years. You took your anger and your grief out on me. I didn't deserve it. You were my father. You were supposed to protect me. You nearly destroyed me. I don't owe you a fucking thing." He put his shirt back on. "Good-bye, Pop. I hope you find more peace in the next world than you did in this one."

He walked out. There was nothing more he wanted to hear from him. There was nothing more for Cullen to say.

His lungs expanded as soon as he left the care facility. They hurt, feeling as if a bomb had gone off inside him. He needed to clear his head, to be anywhere but here. A hand reached out to grab him and he swung around, seeing that Wyn was there, heavy concern etched into her face.

"Let's take a walk," she said. He nodded and took her hand. Walking away was what he needed to do, but part of him felt miserable about it.

CHAPTER 17

They had walked for hours that day. Wyn had made sure she held onto his hand tightly as they made their way to the city. It was important for her to make sure Cullen didn't feel alone. But she was glad he confronted his father. Glad he showed him the scars that hadn't healed in twenty years. She didn't know if it had any impact on the man, but he had needed to see them. Maeve and Liam had needed to see them. They had known that Seamus had beat his son, but she was sure that they didn't know how bad it had been until that moment. She could read the shocked disgust on their faces.

But she also knew they were torn. Their father was dying. It was clear as soon as they walked into the room. Wyn had watched them all. Cullen's face had gone to stone. His entire body had as soon as his father had set eyes upon him. It was hard for Wyn to fathom that shell of a man, who couldn't even sit up on his own, was the man who had beat his son like that.

It would have been the same for the other Whelan children as they grew. They hadn't really known their father in his prime, taken away when they were little more than babies. They didn't remember him the way Cullen did. To them, he was just absent. But even when they were in the same room, he was still absent to them. He had only focused on his eldest son. His eyes coming alive. There was happiness there and maybe a little bit of hatred. His father seemed obsessed with him. He blamed him for his weaknesses. He blamed him for not coming back.

Wyn wanted to talk to Cullen about it. But she remained silent for the day. He would have to let her know when he was ready. If he was ready. She decided that her role was just to be there for him.

They walked around the city. Through the parks. He showed her places he had been as a boy. He explained how different they were. How different they felt now that the city was no longer in danger of exploding into violence at any moment.

They were now back at the hotel. The sun was starting to set. Wyn had ordered room service for them. The food had been there for about ten minutes, but Cullen made no move to eat.

"Cullen, you need to eat. You've barely eaten anything in the past two days."

He looked up at her from his spot in the chair by the window. "I'm not hungry."

"I didn't ask you if you were hungry. I told you that you needed to eat. It's not healthy."

He got up and walked over to her. "Would you like to go France with me? Not to Paris, but to this little town on the sea that I went to when I was still in the army. We can have good wine and lay in bed all morning and in the afternoons we can explore the town."

"I would go anywhere with you."

He came over to her, cupped her face in his hands, and looked into her eyes. "You mean that?"

"Yes. Anywhere. I love you, Cullen."

The words slipped out, but she didn't want to take them back. It was something she had been feeling for a long time. He looked at her and then something she never expected to happen, happened. His eyes filled with tears. "Not today, Wyn. Don't tell me that today."

"Why not? I should have told you that yesterday and the day before that and the day before that. I love you. I've loved you for a long time."

Tears streamed down his face. She knew she was seeing something no one else had seen. She felt as if she knew all of him now. There were no secrets. Nothing held back. He pulled her close and kissed her. She could feel his rawness in the kiss. She wanted to soothe him. She wanted to make every ounce of hurt inside him disappear, but she didn't have that power. So she decided just to love him in that moment. She began undressing him, pulling off his shirt, her lips leaving his for only moments. She ran her hands up his back, feeling his scars. She hated that they were there, but she didn't wish them away, because they were a part of him, a part of who he was as a man.

"I don't deserve you, Wyn."

"Don't say that."

"Why not, love?" He picked her up and brought her to the bed, laying her down gently. "It's true. I never dreamed I could be with someone like you. It doesn't feel real to me."

"How can I make it feel real?"

He unbuttoned her pants and slid them down her body. He stared at her for a moment, his eyes taking her in. She felt so beautiful when he looked at her.

"I never want to live someplace so cold again," he told her. "It takes far too long to undress you when you're wearing so much."

"Okay. So we won't."

He finished undressing her and himself and laid beside her in bed, their naked skin pressed against each other. "You'd give up D.C.?"

"Yes," she said, kissing him.

"I would never ask you to do that. You love your job. You're a good professor."

"I can teach anywhere. It's just a job. I want to share my life."

He looked so tortured for a moment, but he closed the distance between their mouths as he placed his heavy body on top of hers. She loved his weight on her. She loved his smell. The way he felt as he entered her body. She had waited her entire life to feel like this. She wished she could have had this sooner. It took going through great pain for her to experience this kind of love. But she wouldn't take any of it back. It was all worth it.

Cullen woke up the next morning with Wyn at his side. Her face was relaxed in sleep, her body curled into his. He never thought he would enjoy having someone so close to him. He thought he would feel trapped, clung onto. But none of those thoughts came into his mind when she was with him. She loved him. She told him she did. She told him more than once. Part of him didn't believe it. Part of him wished she hadn't said it, because he wasn't sure, despite what she said, that he was enough to keep her happy.

It troubled him because he wasn't sure he would ever be able to give her up. He would be stuck on her. Forever. But he didn't want to think about that. No thoughts of the future, or the past, or why they were here. He didn't want to think. He just wanted to be. He kissed the side of her face, not wanting to wake her up, but wanting to feel her skin beneath his lips.

She opened her eyes and smiled at him.

"Good morning, love."

"I love you," she said in return. "Stop looking surprised when I say it."

"I'm not used to hearing that. You should have never told me."

"Why not?" She seemed hurt.

"Because I won't ever be able to get over you."

"Good." She smiled again, and he thought how perfect it was waking up to a smiling woman. "How are you feeling today?"

"Like I don't want to think about anything."

"Is that possible?"

"I don't think so." He sat up. "We didn't eat last night. Let me take you out for a big breakfast. We could drive a little bit out of the city to the countryside. I could show you where my mum grew up. She used to take us there when I was a boy."

"So you don't have all bad memories of this place?"

"No. Not all bad. I have some very good ones. I want to share them with you."

"I would like that."

"I wish it were summer," he said. "It's the most beautiful in the summer."

"We can always come back."

"I don't need to come back. This is it for me. This is my last time. This is my goodbye."

His cell phone rang just then. He reached for it, seeing it was his sister. "Hello, Maeve."

"Cull . . . Pop passed away last night."

It wasn't a surprise. He had known it was coming. He could see death in the man's eyes when he first looked at him yesterday. But still he didn't know what to say. He had wished him dead a thousand times, but now that it happened he had no words. "I'm

342

sorry, love."

"For heaven's sake, Cull! Why are you apologizing to me?"

"I don't know what to say. He was your father."

"He was *our* father . . . I didn't know how bad it was. I didn't know he did that to you." He heard the emotion choke her.

Wyn came up behind him, wrapping her arms around his middle and resting her lips against his scars. "I'm fine now," he said, not just to comfort her, but because it was true. He was fine. There were moments of happiness. Big moments. He wasn't alone. He had a family that seemed to be growing as the years went on.

"He said to tell you he was sorry," she said and then was silent for a long time. "They were his last words. He was sorry, Cullen. I don't know if you want to forgive him, or even if you can, but he said what he said."

He didn't know how he felt about that. He never expected an apology from him. He didn't want one and now he was finding that he didn't need one. It didn't make a difference. He wasn't angry anymore. The rage had faded away; the repressive numbness was gone too and he was left feeling sore. But it was a soreness that would go away in time.

"Thank you for telling me."

"Liam already made the arrangements. No service. Pop didn't want one, anyway. Liam will have the ashes sent to him."

"Okay. Let me know when you are ready to go home and we'll send you. We won't be going back right away. I'm going to take Wyn on a little trip."

He disconnected from his sister, sitting on the bed for a long time, not moving. Wyn said nothing. Her arm was still wrapped around him, her lips still on his skin, reminding him that he wasn't alone.

"How are you, Cull? I wish I knew the right thing to say to you."

He turned around and pushed her body down on the bed, his body covering hers. "I'm glad you are here," he said. He could see the concern in her eyes. She loved him. He was trying to doubt it, but he couldn't because her looks couldn't lie. "I think I feel free."

"He has no hold over you anymore."

"I think I started to feel free yesterday when I showed him my scars. I hid them for years. I didn't like for anyone to touch them."

"They're a part of who you are as a man."

He nodded and kissed the side of her

neck. "Let's get dressed. Our time here is over."

They had been gone from St. Thomas for almost two weeks. Cullen had taken her to the countryside to show her where his grandparents had lived and then they went to France, to that little seaside village that he had spoken about. It had been beautiful, but Cullen hadn't been content to stay there. He said he wanted to show her more. Show her places that he had been while he served his country, places that he had good memories of. He took her to France's wine country and they spent their days making love in a little villa that overlooked the vineyard. Wyn had been happy to be there, to experience it all with the man she loved.

They were happy and went back to St. Thomas. She wished she could have said she could have stayed there forever, but the selfish part of her crept up.

She had a life she left behind. A career. A home. The rest of her life couldn't be spent on vacation. The scandal was dying down. She quietly checked the American headlines every day they were gone. She couldn't continue hiding. But she knew she couldn't go back to the way it was, because she had changed along the way. Her relationship with Cullen had changed. He was still on her father's payroll. He was still supposed to be protecting her. They needed to have a conversation, but she didn't feel right bringing it up now. Not so soon after his father's death.

He seemed fine. He told her he had felt free. But she wasn't sure how true that was.

How soon could a person snap back from that?

He was sitting outside in the back of their little cottage. His eyes were closed. His face turned up toward the sun. She walked outside and sat beside him, slipping her fingers into his. She could remember the first time she had done that, and how he had flinched. He didn't flinch now. He lifted her hand to his lips and kissed the back of it.

"What do you want to do today, love? We could go to the other side of the island. You haven't been there yet."

"That would be nice."

"You don't sound too thrilled about it. We don't have to go. Just tell me what you want me to do and I'll make it happen."

She took a breath, unsure if she should bring up what was on her mind. "I want to talk to you."

"You can talk to me anytime, Wyn." Concern crept into his eyes.

"Cullen!" They heard Jack's voice from the front of the house. Jack never came to visit them here.

"We're back here."

Jack appeared, followed by King and Darby. All three men looked proud of themselves. "We did it."

"Did what?" Wyn asked.

"We found your sister. She's alive. She's been looking for you too."

"What?" Wyn sat there stunned. Her head was swirling with thoughts. She had a sister.

Who was alive. Someone else she shared her genes with.

"She lives in South Carolina with her husband and children. She's about to have another baby."

"My sister?" She shook her head, trying to process this information.

"Her name is Sunny," Darby informed her. "You two look alike." He bent down in front of her and took her hand. "You're right: Grace was the one who tried to kidnap you when you were a girl."

"Grace?" She frowned, not sure she was understanding him.

"That's your birth mother's name. I thought Cullen told you."

"I didn't know." She didn't know he knew

her name.

"Oh . . ." Darby paused for a moment. "Your father came and took her away before the police could come. There has been no trace of her ever since, but we believe she is alive."

"How . . ." She blinked at them, still not sure she was hearing them correctly. "You know who I am?"

Jack nodded. "You look much different than you did when you were a kid. You're gorgeous. I would have never recognized you."

She turned to Cullen. "You told them everything?"

"I had to," he said softly. "I needed help."

"*You* needed help?" She couldn't describe how she was feeling in that moment. There were too many feelings battling inside her, but she felt blindsided.

"Could you excuse us, lads?" Cullen stood up and shook each one of their hands. "Thank you for everything. I truly appreciate it."

The men took that as their cue to leave, each one of them giving Cullen an uneasy look as they went. Wyn sat where she was. She was shaking. She balled her hands into tight fists and buried them in her lap, but it didn't stop her from vibrating. She felt so many things in that moment, but the thing that was rising in her throat, burning in her chest, was anger. She was tremendously angry.

"Wyn . . ."

"You made me lie to them for months. I had to hide who I was. Watch what I said and you told them?"

"I had to. I wanted to find your mother. I didn't want this to be a mystery for your entire life."

"But why didn't you tell me? Why couldn't we have discussed it? You kept it from me! Instead of allowing me to be a part of the process, you let your friends work in secret. Darby has seen a picture of my sister before I have. King knew I had nieces and nephews before I did. Jack knew my mother's name. I knew nothing! How could you?"

"I did it for you."

"You did what for me? Made me a liar? Did you tell them we were a sham too? That you told me I couldn't tell them the truth because you told me they wouldn't handle it well? That my presence in their world would be an invasion of their life? You made me feel like I would be a burden and then you go and tell them like it was nothing."

"We aren't a sham," he said fiercely.

"What we are is based on a lie."

"What we are will always be rooted in a lie. If they knew about your mother or not it wouldn't have changed anything. The way I feel about you has never been a lie."

"But how do we know if it is real? What's to say that if I had come here as your principal, instead of your pretend girlfriend, if things would have gone down the same way?"

"There's always been that connection there. You know there has."

"Why couldn't you just have told me? I don't understand. What reason did you have to keep this from me?"

"I wanted to respect your privacy. I didn't think they would burst in here to tell you. I wanted to be the one to tell you."

"That's not a good answer." She shook her head. "If they didn't tell me, I'm not sure you would have."

"You think I would keep that from you?"

"I don't know! I don't know why you kept this from me."

"I have never lied to you."

"An omission is still a lie. You made me lie. You made me leave my home. You didn't trust me with my own information about myself. You've treated me like I am a help-less idiot that needed to be rescued."

His face went to stone. "I don't know

what to say. There was no malice in what I did."

"I want to go home. I'm tired of being here. I'm tired of not living my life and doing everything that you say."

"I was only trying to keep you safe. It was my job, Wyn."

"It *is* your job. You work for my father. I keep forgetting that. He pays you. He probably told you to keep the information from me. He sure as hell didn't want me digging. You conned me. You probably seduced me to distract me."

"Stop!" he yelled at her. He never raised his voice, but he yelled at her and it made her pause. "Don't say something you can't take back. Do not question my character."

"I want to see my sister." Her eyes filled with tears. "I want to go home now."

He nodded. "You'll be stateside before dark."

CHAPTER 18

The flight back to the States was one of the longest Cullen had ever experienced. Not because the length of the time in the air, but because of the deafening, overwhelming silence from Wynter. He had been trying to protect her, but he had miscalculated. He didn't know why he didn't tell her that he was letting his friends search for information about her. He didn't know why he didn't have a conversation with her about it first. She would have agreed. Finding out who she had come from was that important to her. But he didn't include her in her own life and now she wasn't speaking to him. She could barely look at him.

It was painful. It made him wonder if he had kept things from her on purpose, sheltered her for his selfish reasons instead of for her interest. The headlines in the papers stopped weeks ago. No new letters had emerged. All was quiet. She could have gone back to her life sooner, but she was with him. Consoling him after the death of his father. He allowed her to do so even though he wasn't sad, even though he had felt free after finally saying what he needed to say to him. But he loved her attention, the fact that she loved him and wasn't afraid to tell him. Tell him every day. As many times as he needed to hear it. He had been happy in those two weeks, the happiest he had been since he was a small boy.

He had taken her back to D.C. To her home that had set empty for months. The weather had begun to change. It wasn't so icy cold. Spring was in the air and D.C. had a quiet beauty about it that he had forgotten about in their time away. There was no swarm of reporters waiting outside her door to question her. It was as if life had returned to how it was the day before the news broke.

"Wynter?" Her back was to him as she went through the mail that had accumulated in the time she was gone. She was staring at one letter for a long time. "What's wrong?"

"Nothing," she said without looking up at him. "A job offer. I get them sometimes."

"Do you want to tell me about it?"

"No."

"When are you going to speak to me?" He was tired of her silent treatment. He hadn't meant to hurt her. She should know him well enough to know that.

"How long have they been searching?"

He hesitated before he answered. "I asked Darby to help first. The boys didn't join in until later. I needed Jack, since he had more connections to your world than anyone else does."

"How long?"

"About a month. Maybe a little more."

The hurt flashed in her eyes. "Before you made love to me for the first time?"

"Yes. But what does it matter?"

"You kept pushing me away. All those weeks. And then one night you give in. What changed? Did you realize I was getting bored there? You knew you needed to do something to keep me away from my life until my father figured out what he was going to do about the person who was leaking the letters. He told you to do what you had to do to keep me from digging and you found the only thing you knew would make me stay. You used my feelings against me."

He slammed his fist on the table, fed up with her accusations. She jumped and for a moment he felt guilty for scaring her, for losing his temper, but she was going too far. "I know you're upset with me, but if you ever think that I would reveal things to you that I have never told another soul just to keep you occupied, then you don't know me at all. Then you lied to me about loving me. I don't know much about love, but I didn't think you were supposed to turn your back at the first time things go wrong."

"You don't get to lecture me about love. My whole life is a lie. One that my parents created. I had to find out about it on the car radio. They won't even speak to me about it. They have made the decision that I don't need to know. That I'm not important enough to be let in on the plan. And then you do the same thing. You left me out. You treated me like a child. Like I wasn't important. Like it wasn't my life. I trusted you. With everything. You're the only one . . ." Her voice broke. Her eyes filled with tears. "You did to me what my parents did to me. I never expected that from you. And it makes me question everything." She paused for a moment. "If the people I love do this to me, then how can I trust anyone else?"

Realization washed over him. "I understand." He stepped forward and placed his hand on her cheek. "I'm sorry, love. I don't know what else to say besides that. I'm just . . . I'm sorry."

She turned away from his touch. "Can I have the information about my sister? I want to call her."

He nodded and went to his bag to pull the folder of information his friends had collected. They had been incredibly thorough. They had learned what he should have, but he had been too distracted, too wrapped up in her. This is why he had stayed away from love for so long. He knew he couldn't be good at his job and be there for someone else like he needed to be, like he wanted to be. But he had also never run into a person like Wynter before and he had hurt her. Unintentionally, but he had hurt her. Treated her like a child, protected her from the one thing that she didn't need to be protected from: Her life.

He handed her the folder and watched her as she walked to the couch. She sat down, placing the folder in her lap. She placed her hands on top of it, maybe to stop them from trembling. "You don't have to be here for this," she said, looking up at him.

"Are you telling me to go?"

She was quiet for a moment. "I'm telling you that your duty to me is over. I suppose I would have never found out anything without your friends and I am grateful for that, but you don't have to be here. You can go back to whatever life you had before this happened, or whatever life you had planned for after this came to an end."

"I'm not leaving." He sat in the armchair across from the couch.

She just looked at him for a long moment before she opened the folder. He didn't know what that meant, but he kept watching her, unable to take his eyes off her. "She was in foster care," she said, more to herself than to him. "Found locked in a closet. Never adopted." She choked on the words, her tears streaming down her cheeks. "Grace locked her in a closet? I don't think I can read anymore. How can someone do that to a child? How could my father fall for someone who would hurt a little child?"

"It's probably not as black-and-white as it seems. From what I understand, your sister seems very happy."

"On the surface, maybe. If I have learned anything these past few months, I have learned not to trust appearances. I need to speak to her. I hope she wants to speak to me."

Cullen pulled out his cell phone and gave it to her. "She will." Wynter took a deep breath before she began dialing the number at the top of the page.

She hit the speaker button and placed it on the table, her hands trembling too much to hold the phone. He wanted to go to her, wrap his arm around her, but he wasn't sure she would accept it, so he sat in his spot, waiting with bated breath for her sister to pick up.

She finally did. "Hello, Sunny. I'm sorry to bother you. My name is Wynter Bates —"

There was a sharp intake of breath. "My sister."

"You know?"

"I've been searching for you for a long time. Our private detective found you late last year, but then our son got sick and the scandal broke and I wasn't sure what to do anymore."

"I want to meet you. Is that okay with you?"

"Of course," Sunny answered quickly. "Where are you?"

"In D.C. But I'll come to wherever you are."

"You don't have to come to me. I'm in Maryland visiting my mother-in-law. I'll be there tomorrow morning."

Wynter gave her the address and disconnected. She sat back, placing her hands on her face. She was going through a tremendous amount and once again Cullen felt inadequate. He could physically protect her, but he could not stop her anguish.

"What can I do for you, Wynter?"

She removed her hands from her face and looked up at him. "My long-lost sister is coming. What does one serve a sister who was purposely kept from you for most of your life?"

"Cake?"

She smiled for the briefest of moments. It was gone too quickly, but he loved her smile. He knew he wouldn't be a whole man if he never got to see it again.

CHAPTER 19

Wynter had gone to bed early the night before. She was exhausted and thought she would be happy to be back in her own bed after all those months, but she didn't sleep at all. She was nervous about meeting her sister. She didn't read more than the first paragraph of the thick folder that Cullen's friends had put together for her. She didn't want to look at her picture or learn about her story by viewing words on a page. There were so many questions she had and they floated in her head all night. But she had one feeling that penetrated it all: Her bed was empty. Cullen wasn't there. He had been with her every night since his birthday. She had grown used to falling asleep after his lovemaking. She was used to waking up with his warm, hard body beside her. The bed, the pillow, the sheets had smelled like him, like his soap and his skin.

She missed him. Intensely. How could

she, when she was so upset with him?

She was angry that he didn't let her know his plans. She was annoyed that he had made her lie all those months for nothing. But she might have let it go easier if she knew he loved her. He never said it. She thought she felt it. Felt it in the way he looked at her, in the way he treated her, in the way he respected her. But she could have been swept away. In the romance of it all. In the setting of the islands. In the seclusion. She had no idea what was next for them. Even before this happened, she was questioning that. She wished she could be one of those people who could be calm and go with the flow, but she couldn't.

Her entire life had been knocked off-balance. Her past was a lie. She wanted to know the direction of her future. But the timing was off. He had worked for her father. He'd had such a difficult life. Maybe she was just meant to have those few months with him. Maybe it was time for her life to take a new direction. She had gotten that job offer. It wasn't the first time she had received it. It was in Charleston, heading up a small linguistics department that specialized in created languages for movies and television shows. It would be a change for her. She needed a change. She had promised herself she wasn't going to go back to the life she had before everything blew up.

She got dressed, not in the clothes she had worn on the island, but back into her normal clothing. It felt odd at first. No more brightly colored patterns. No skin showing. No sun streaming in through the windows or the faint smell of ocean water drifting through the air.

She went downstairs to see Cullen was there already. He had taken her to the store last night and it nearly felt that they had slipped back into the same pattern they had before they had gone to St. Thomas. He was her security once again. Silent. There to do as she asked, but there was a deeper layer to it. The knowledge that they had known each other's bodies, each other's secrets.

And now he was in her kitchen, standing there shirtless, boiling a pot of water for tea. She was surprised. She had thought he would have gone back to his apartment across the street last night, but she hadn't heard him leave.

"Good morning, love," he said softly. His deep, Irish-accented voice still made her heady. "How did you sleep?"

"I didn't."

"I know. You got up three times."

"Where did you sleep last night?"

"The guest room." His eyes passed her over. "Your hair is straight again."

"Yes." She self-consciously touched it. "It was a losing battle in all that humidity."

He nodded. "Your father is back in town. He called me this morning. He said he put a stop to the leak."

Her entire body snapped to attention. "Oh? Did he tell you anything else?"

"No. But I didn't tell him anything else either."

"He doesn't know I'm back?"

"He still thinks you're hidden away on an island. He's currently in his office, working to salvage his election campaign."

"Thank you."

"Don't thank me. I'm here for you. Not for him. Never for him."

He stepped forward and touched her cheek. This time she didn't turn away, but she didn't allow herself to lean into his touch like her body wanted her to.

"They'll be here soon. You probably shouldn't be shirtless in my kitchen."

"It doesn't take me that long to get ready. I was going to help you set up first."

"Having you shirtless in my kitchen will be more of a distraction than a help. I'm mad at you, but I still enjoy the sight of you."

He smiled, and she remembered how she had never seen him do so before all of this happened. He had been so quiet. He had changed so much in the past few months. It was unfair of her to accuse him of playing her. They might not want the same things, but it wasn't all a lie.

"I'll go get dressed."

She nodded as he walked away. Forty minutes later, her doorbell rang. Her sister had arrived.

Cullen watched as Wynter froze at the sound of her doorbell. Her breath caught. Her eyes went wide. The nerves had been vibrating off her all morning. He took the decision away from her. He opened the door to see a woman who looked remarkably like Wynter standing before him. Sunny was nervous too, but she was smiling and had beautiful wide eyes that seemed to smile too. Her hair was styled in short ringlets. She had chubby cheeks and a large, round belly. She was the personification of her name.

"Hello, I'm here to see Wynter."

"I'm here." Wynter walked forward and stepped around him.

The women silently stared at each other for a moment. "Hello, little sister. I'm so happy to meet you," Sunny said to her.

Wynter burst into tears and reached for her sister. The women held on to each other and just cried for a long time. Cullen almost turned away, feeling like he had been intruding on a private moment. He hadn't seen his sister for years, but he had known her. He had gotten to enjoy her. No one had hidden her existence from him. He couldn't imagine what it must have felt like for Wynter, but seeing her now, how she clung on to this woman, made the last few months of turmoil worth it. She had someone in her family that no one could take away.

"Come in," Wynter said, releasing her sister from the hug. "Excuse my manners. I should have let you come all the way in before I attacked you with a hug."

"Don't apologize." She turned back and looked at the man still in the doorway. "I have to thank you for reaching out to me. I'm sure I was driving my husband crazy talking about you. This is Julian, by the way."

A very large man walked through the door. He had green eyes and massive arms and it was then Cullen remembered that he had played professional football before he had become a lawyer.

"It's very nice to meet you, Julian," Wynter said.

"You as well. We've only seen your picture, but seeing you up close . . . It's remarkable how much you look alike."

"Thank you. Sunny is so beautiful. You both are. Your children must be gorgeous." She looked back at Cullen. He wondered how she was going to introduce him. What was he to her in that moment? "This is Cullen. If it weren't for him, I would have never found you."

"I'm glad you did," Sunny said, taking a seat on the couch and placing her hands on her pregnant belly. "I didn't want to intrude on your life. I didn't know how much you knew about our mother."

"I don't know anything about her. I was told I was an orphan adopted from South Africa. My father refuses to admit anything to me."

Sadness swept across Sunny's face. "Mama was not well. She was mentally ill. When I was five, she took me out of school and told me we were going on a trip. We ended up in New York and we spent the next year homeless and then moving from place to place. At first, I thought it was an adventure. I thought Mama was being a free spirit. My child's mind couldn't understand

366

what was wrong with her. But she got sicker and sicker as time went on. She was paranoid, especially after one of her boyfriends hurt me. She stopped allowing me to go outside. She would disappear for days and leave me in a closet to keep me safe until she got back. But one time she never came back, and a neighbor who I used to go to for food noticed that she hadn't seen me or Mama for a while sent the police to find me. I spent the rest of my childhood in foster care after that. Your father might have lied to you about who you came from, but Mama could have never taken care of you. She was too sick. He was right to take you away."

Cullen watched as Wynter sat heavily on the couch and processed the information that had been given to her. "He should have told me that. I would have understood." She looked up at Sunny. "She tried to take me from a horseback-riding lesson when I was ten. I could tell then that there was something wrong with her, but I had no idea who she was. I wish I had known."

"You don't know where she is now, do you? I have been searching for her for years, but everything comes up as a dead end. The last place we tracked her to was your father's office, but that was the year you were born."

"I don't know. I didn't know her name until Cullen's friends told me."

"Your friends?" Julian asked. "They must have powerful connections. It wasn't easy finding you."

"They are all former intelligence agents."

He nodded. "That's who I hired to be my private detective. Mr. Bates went through a lot of trouble to make sure no one ever learned of the connection."

"Yes." Wynter nodded. "He never expected his affair to be headline news this year either."

"Who do you think is behind it?" Sunny asked.

"I'm not sure," Cullen said. "But there's only one person who has the answer to all of your questions and I think it's time we start asking him."

CHAPTER 20

Wynter was having had a hard time believing that her sister was here. She kept staring at her, taking in her features. They had the same nose. The same chin. The same shaped face. She thought she was crazy to feel a connection to her, a stranger she hadn't even known a full two hours, but it was there. Sunny had known their mother. She lived with her, survived living with her. It pained her to know that she had to live with a mentally ill woman and then in foster care, bouncing from home to home with no real stability, no real family to love her.

Wynter had a lonely childhood, but her home was stable. The woman who raised her, the woman who she still called *Mother,* had loved her. That part wasn't a lie. There was love there and privilege. They had grown up so differently. Wynter had everything handed to her. Sunny had to work for everything. She had been a social worker, her degree paid for by scholarships. There was no studying abroad for her. No summering on Nantucket or on the Vineyard. Wynter felt guilty for having that kind of life when Sunny had to struggle all through hers, but she couldn't feel sorry for her sister. Sunny had happiness. It radiated through her. Her husband adored her. She had a big family that she created. There was so much love there. It was beautiful. It was the life Wynter had wanted for herself. She was almost jealous of her sister. The money meant absolutely nothing. Love was everything.

The car ride to her father's office was short. Cullen had called ahead to let her father's security team know that they were coming, but he had asked them not to warn him. They breezed through the entrance and through the hallways, no one stopping them. But there were looks. Wynter could feel them on her back as they made their way to his office. Who could miss the resemblance of the two women? Who could forget the content of those letters?

Cullen led the way. He walked into her father's office without knocking. He was dressed in all black again. His hair was tamed, still longer than it had ever been in the year that she knew him, but he looked every inch of the bodyguard that he was. Her father snapped to attention, his eyes widening with shock as he saw them all enter his office.

"What the hell are you doing here, Whelan? I just spoke to you this morning. You didn't tell me you were bringing her back."

"No, sir. I think it's time you speak to your daughter. I'm done being your middleman."

The rage that crept into her father's eyes was undeniable. He stood up, looking as if he wanted to wrap his fingers around Cullen's throat, but the one thing he wouldn't do was look at Wynter.

"No hello, Daddy? You haven't spoken to me in months and now that I'm before you, you won't even look at me. Are you that ashamed of me?"

"Ashamed?" He looked her in the eye for the first time in as long as she could remember. "How could I be ashamed of you? I love you. You are my only child."

"But not the child you saw in an orphanage, right? Mother always told me to be thankful that I had been rescued, but I wasn't rescued. You were taking care of your dirty little secret."

He said nothing, but his gaze traveled to Sunny and settled there. He looked back at

Wynter. There was no need for an explanation. There was no denying who Sunny was.

"You did this, didn't you?" He turned and started approaching Cullen. "You found Grace's daughter, when the only thing you had to do was mind your business and keep my daughter safe."

"You don't get to blame Cullen for this." She stood between Cullen and her father. "You need to talk to me! Why can't you admit to what you've done? Why did you have to put Cullen in this situation in the first place? That wasn't his job. You made me his problem instead of dealing with me yourself and it screwed up his life."

"His job is whatever I tell him to do. He was paid damn well to do it."

Cullen placed his hands on Wynter's shoulders. "Being with you has not screwed up my life, Wyn. It's only made it better."

She looked back at him, her heart giving a painful squeeze.

"You're sleeping with her, aren't you? I'll kill you." He lunged toward Cullen, but Wyn plastered her body against his. Sunny's husband grabbed Wynter's father and easily hauled him away.

"That's enough," Julian said firmly. "Only a guilty man passes blame to everyone else. You need to answer some questions. Your daughter deserves the truth, and so does my wife."

"What do you want me to say? You already know the truth. I am your birth father. You weren't adopted. Is that what you came here to learn?"

"There's more to the story and you know it. How could you do that to Mom?"

"I love your mother. She's brilliant. I wouldn't be who I am without her. She helped make me, but she's my partner, my strategist, the other half of my brain. There's a deep love, but there was no passion for a long time between us. Your mother wanted the lifestyle. The prestige that came with being married to a powerful man. We had an understanding."

"What about Grace?" Wynter asked. "Did she understand?"

"Grace worked for me. She had this kind of energy that was electrifying. She was adventurous and exciting. It wasn't supposed to be serious, but very soon into our affair, I learned she was pregnant. And then I learned she stopped taking her medication. I didn't realize she was sick when we first met, but she was very sick and she was dangerous. I caught her on the roof once, claiming people were after her. She would disappear for days at a time. I was scared. I went to your mother and asked her what we should do. She wanted you. We could never conceive together and we realized this was the only way we could raise a child. I had Grace quietly declared incompetent by a judge friend of mine and had her confined to a house in Virginia. She was under a doctor's care at all times when she was pregnant. The first three months, she couldn't take any medication at all, because there were potential birth defects. She was nearly out of control then. I had to hire more staff, more security to ensure you both were safe, but even after the first trimester when she could take her medication again, she often refused. I knew she could be no part of your life. Your safety had to come first. Especially, after she told me what happened to Sunny. I was terrified she would have hurt you."

"It's true," Sunny said, nodding her head. "There were times when she would be almost like a typical mother, when things were calm, and then she would go through these bad times and she became unbearable to live with." Sunny briefly shut her eyes as if trying to block out a memory. "I was older than you when she started to get bad. I could do some things for myself. I could take care of her. She couldn't have taken care of a baby."

"What was I supposed to do, Wynter?" her father asked. "I had to protect you."

"I understand the need to take me away from her. But you weren't just protecting me. You were protecting yourself. Your image. You could have hid Grace from the world, but you didn't have to hide her from me."

"Or me," Sunny said. "You're how she found me, aren't you? She wrote me two letters and I never understood how she could have tracked me down, but you must've helped."

"Yes." He nodded. "She loves you very much."

"She's still alive?" Wynter asked.

"Of course, she's still alive. What do you think I've done to her?"

"I don't know. You've gone through a lot of trouble to keep her a secret. No one has seen or heard from her since she tried to take me when I was ten."

"I couldn't allow that to happen again. She is in a very secure place now."

"What about the leak?" Cullen asked. "Who was it?"

"A former nurse. She had made copies of the letters Grace wrote to me. She was looking for a payday. I only hire former intelligence now."

"I want to meet her," Wynter demanded. "Today. You owe me that. Sunny deserves to see her mother again."

Her father nodded once. "It's a long drive. I'll lead the way."

They drove nearly three hours into Virginia, into the mountains. The ride was beautiful with all the deep greens and thickness of the trees they passed on the way. Wynter might have enjoyed the journey on another day. She was in the car with her sister and her brother-in-law and the man she loved, but it wasn't a joyful occasion. This was no fun family trip. Everyone was mostly silent on the ride up. She and Sunny just held hands in the backseat. She couldn't imagine what her sister was going through. The last time she had seen her mother was when she was locking her in a closet. And yet there was no anger there. She was a child. It must have been hard for her to understand why her mother was the way she was, but Sunny didn't hold a grudge. She didn't blame her mother for her illness.

Her mother. Wynter kept thinking of Grace as Sunny's mother, but she was their mother. Their birth mother. But Wynter had a mother already. There was a woman who had given her everything. There was a woman who readily agreed to raise the product of her husband's affair and never treated her any differently, never treated her less than.

She had spent her entire life wanting a connection to her roots, but now that she had finally learned the truth, she wasn't sure how she felt. They pulled up to what appeared to be a gated community. There was a booth there. An armed guard came out and approached her father's car in front of them. After a few words, they were allowed in. There were no other houses, just a long road, maybe two or three miles long, leading up to a large log cabin. It wasn't anything showy or overtly glamorous, but Wynter could tell this place had been designed as a retreat, with beautiful landscaping and a man-made lake to the side. It was calming and seeing it showed Wynter that her father had put some thought into where he hid the mother of his child.

"She's sitting on the patio," her father told them. "It doesn't matter what time of year it is, she likes to sit there and look outside at the trees. I had to enclose it and install a fireplace there."

"It's very nice here," Sunny said.

"Yes," Warren agreed. "I want her to be

comfortable." He walked into the house and led them directly to the back where Grace was. Warren motioned for them to stop.

It was a move he didn't have to make, because she and Sunny froze at exactly the same moment. She was sitting in a rocking chair, her hair long and light blond, with a just a few strands of silver weaved through it. She was wearing a thick cream-colored sweater over a long dress and in her hands was a crochet needle and the beginnings of what looked like a blanket. She was beautiful. The way she moved her hands, showed that she was as graceful as her name implied. Wynter had only seen her once and then she had been filled with panic and fear, but this woman wasn't the one she remembered. There had been no serenity floating around her.

She looked to Sunny, who had tears rolling down her cheeks. Wynter wondered if this was what she remembered of her mother at all or was it like she was seeing a new person.

Warren approached her. Very slowly. "Gracie?" He kept his voice gentle as not to startle her.

"Warren!" She smiled. "I didn't know you were coming to see me. You always call and tell me before you do. You call on Fridays.

It's not Friday."

Her voice was distinctly Southern. It was melodic, almost. She could see why her father was struck by her beauty. She was hard to look away from.

He knelt before her and took her hand. "I came because I brought you some visitors."

"Visitors?" She shook her head. "I can't have visitors. No one comes to see me. Only you and sometimes your wife. I like her. I do. How is she?"

That statement knocked Wynter sideways. Her mother had met Grace? More than met, it seemed. She had visited her.

"She's fine. She's been unhappy with me lately."

"You are a trying man," she said with a laugh. "What did you do?"

"I sent Wynter away. I didn't think she would be safe, but my wife is missing her."

"Mamas miss their babies." She nodded understandingly. "She's a good mama, right? You said she was."

"She is very good. Wynter came back home. She's grown up now. I can't tell her what to do anymore."

"No. I suppose not." Her eyes left Warren and looked at the group of them behind her. Her eyes passed over Wynter, Cullen, and Julian with mild curiosity. But they focused

379

on Sunny.

"Is that my Sunshine?" Grace got up out of her chair, her hands shaking excitedly. "That's her. That's my baby! You brought her to me."

"Hi, Mama," Sunny said with tears streaming down her cheeks. "I'm so happy to see you again."

Grace rushed over and cupped Sunny's face in her hands. She peppered it with kisses. It seemed natural and motherly, even though Sunny was over thirty with children of her own.

"You're so beautiful!" She stepped away and studied her. "Are you having a baby? I'm going to be a grandmama? I would like to be a grandmama. I always thought I would make a better grandmama than mama. I could just love and kiss the babies and then you can take them home because I don't like it when they cry."

"I have three babies already. Two girls and a boy. This is my fourth child."

"Are you married?"

"Yes, ma'am." She looked back at Julian and reached her hand out to him. "This is my husband Julian."

Wynter felt overwhelmed in that moment. She had to look away from them, from Sunny's moment with Grace. She was ashamed to admit that she felt disappointed that Grace didn't recognize her when she saw her. But she shouldn't have expected that.

Grace was clearly fragile. The last time she had seen Wynter was when she was ten. It made sense that she didn't recognize her, but there was still a little bit of hurt there.

A strong arm wrapped around her and then she was enveloped in Cullen's embrace. He kissed the side of her face and smoothed his hand down her back. "I wish I knew what to say to you, love. But I'm here. I just want you to know that I'm here."

She had missed him. It had barely been twenty-four hours, but she had missed his closeness. "I'm sorry, Cullen."

"For what?" He kissed her forehead. "For making me realize that things changed between us and I can't keep treating you like I work for your father?"

"I'm pretty sure you don't work for my father now. He's not happy about us."

"I knew that was going to happen. You make me do things I never thought I would do."

Wynter felt a hand on her back and turned to see Grace standing behind her. "You're my other baby, aren't you?" She looked into Wynter's eyes and studied her face.

"Yes."

"I tried to come get you once, but you didn't know about me. Warren said I scared you. I'm sorry I did that. I didn't mean to scare you."

Wynter nodded. "I'm sorry I didn't know who you were."

"I did it because I love you." She placed her warm hand on Wynter's cheek. "I couldn't take care of you. I have a hard time being a mama. Don't be mad at your father. He knew better."

"Can I hug you?"

"Yes." She smiled beautifully. "I would like that very much."

Wynter hugged Grace. Her mind went blank. She felt something settle inside her. She finally knew where she had come from. She didn't have to search anymore.

CHAPTER 21

They had spent the day with Grace at her mountainside retreat. They had lunch and they talked, Sunny leading the conversation with all the questions she had wanted answered her entire life. They were mostly about Grace's family. Where were they? How could they let her pull Sunny out of school and take her across the country? Grace's mother died in childbirth. Her father had died when she was twenty. There was an elderly aunt who was in her life, but she had passed away too. Grace had been alone.

There was a point in the day when she got overwhelmed and tired and abruptly got up and left the room. Wynter's father followed her, along with her two nurses and made sure she got in bed. He came back to tell them that they weren't allowed to talk to Grace anymore for that day. That it was all too much for her.

It really brought home the fact that her birth mother was sick. But it made her realize that her father truly did care for her. There was no romantic love when he looked at Grace, but there was love there and if it weren't for him, Grace would be alone. No one would care for her. It made her feelings for her father more complicated. He wasn't all good or all bad. He would forever be this giant gray area in her life.

"She was having a good day," he said to Wynter and Sunny as they were leaving the house. "They're not all good. We seemed to have finally gotten the right combination of medicine."

"I wish you would have told me," Wynter said. "I would have understood. I could have known her sooner."

He shook his head. "You don't know how long it took for us to get to this point. There were times when she wasn't safe. She would go into deep, dark places in her mind and it was impossible to pull her out. I don't know how Sunny survived and when I found out that Grace had left her, I knew that she couldn't be around you. I had to protect you. You are my greatest asset."

She went home, thinking about that conversation. Sunny and Julian checked into a hotel and she and Cullen returned to her home. Wynter was exhausted by the day. Meeting her birth mother and her sister in the same day was something she would have never thought would happen. She was still processing the enormity of it all. She was happy to have extended her family and yet the person she wanted to hear from the most was her mother. She called her that night as soon as she got home.

Her mother picked up on the first ring. "Hello, darling."

"Hello, Mom. I've missed you."

There was a pause. "I missed you too. I'm surprised that that is the first thing you said to me."

"What did you think I was going to say?"

"I thought you would be very angry with me."

"I'm not angry. I'm sad. I wish it didn't have to be like this."

"I wanted to tell you a thousand times. I begged him to tell you, but it was his story to tell. He was afraid to admit things to you, because he thought you would think less of him as a man."

"But finding out from the media was better?"

"We were both knocked backward by that one. He needed to protect you, but we also had to protect Grace. I'm not saying we handled things the right way, and I'm not saying I'm not extremely angry with your father for closing you out during this time, but Grace was a very large priority. We didn't want her identity exposed. We didn't want her mental illness to be splashed across the media and her to be painted as some crazy woman your father had an affair with. She's more than that."

"She said you visit her."

"I do. I like her. She's fragile. There's not good care in this country for people like her. The system is broken and institutions put bandages on these people's problems and kick them out on the street like they aren't human. I went with your father to pick her up from the hospital when she was taken there by the police for acting errati-cally. She called him because she had no one else. She had no shoes on and just a thin hospital gown and they were going to release her like that. It was disgusting. I knew we had to step in."

"You're the one who designed her house, aren't you?"

"Yes. I always want her to feel at peace there."

"You don't hate her at all? There's no anger there?"

"None. She gave me my baby. I never

thought I was going to be a mother, but because of her I got to be and it has brought me my greatest joy."

"I love you, Mom."

"I love you too. Now, what's this about your bodyguard I'm hearing?"

"Dad told you already?"

"Your father tells me everything. Believe it or not, there are no lies between us. It's not a relationship for everyone, but for us it works. We love each other. I don't expect you to understand it, but we do."

"I'm in love with Cullen," she admitted to her mother.

"I've always liked him. He was very attentive to you whenever I saw him. His gaze never left you, his hand lingered on your back just a moment longer than was necessary. I pushed your father to hire him. You needed a younger man in your life."

"What?"

"Wynter, my darling, you are a person who was in desperate need of some fun. Please tell me you have fun with him."

She thought back to their time on the island. To their skinny-dipping in the waterfall, to his birthday party, to their sightseeing in Europe, to those quiet nights they just sat around the table and played cards. She enjoyed him. His smile, his quiet presence, his strength. "We have fun."

"Good. You have my blessing. I'll work on your father."

"Thank you. Can I come see you soon?"

"Of course. Come tomorrow. Bring your sister. I would like to meet her."

They said their good-byes and disconnected. Wynter left her bedroom and walked down the hall to her guest room, where she found Cullen sitting on the bed with his packed bag beside him. She froze for a moment by the door.

He was leaving. Of course, he was. This was all over. There was no reason for him to stay. He had a home with his friends on an island and she knew as much as she enjoyed it, that that life just wasn't for her.

"Can I come in?"

"Please do." He patted the bed beside him. She sat next to him, close enough so that their arms were touching. "I didn't want to bother you while you were on the phone with your mum. Did you have a good chat?"

"Yes. She made things clearer for me. I wish my father was able to say things like she can."

"We men are not often good at that. There's a million things I want to say to you, but most of the time I can't find the right words. Or there are things that I think you already know, but you don't because but you can't read my mind."

She rested her head on his shoulder, holding back her tears. She had cried enough today, but it was hard to hear that the man you love was ready to walk out of your life. "What do you want to tell me? What do you think I should know?"

"I often think I'm not good enough for you. That I don't deserve to be with you."

"That's ridiculous."

"Don't interrupt me, love. I'm trying to tell you things."

"I'm sorry." She smiled. "Go ahead."

"You have a doctorate. I dropped out of school."

"But —"

"Hush. I don't need you to make me feel better. I need you to listen."

"Okay."

"I know you won't be happy living on the island. I know you need to work to be fulfilled. I know you want your own home and family. I know you want a normal life."

She opened her mouth to speak, but shut it when he looked at her.

"I don't know how normal life would be with me. What is an ex–intelligence agent supposed to do with his life? I have some money saved. Sometimes, I think I would like to go to university."

"I like that idea. What would you study?"

"English, I think. I would like to write my story down and I don't want it to be a jumbled mess."

"Would you publish it?"

"Maybe. You think anyone would want to read about me?"

"Yes. I find you fascinating."

"Would you be okay with a husband who went to school? I can work part-time as a consultant for security firms as well. I don't want you to think I won't be contributing."

She shook her head, not sure she heard him correctly. "What?"

"I've always turned down consulting jobs before, because I thought I would be better in the field, but I can work from home."

"Not that. The husband part."

"See? I keep forgetting you can't read my mind. I've loved you for a long time. I think it started happening the moment I shook your hand for the first time. I had gotten so used to loving you in silence, so used to hiding my love that I don't tell you I love you. But I do love you. I love you more than should be possible."

"Cullen . . ."

"I want to marry you. I want to be the

father of your children. I want to create a home with you." He pulled a ring out of his bag and went down on his knee before her. "That is, if you'll have me."

"I thought you were about to leave!"

He frowned. "Why?"

"You were sitting here with your bags packed."

"I was hoping to move into your room tonight. I missed you. I'm afraid you're stuck with me, love."

She grabbed him by the collar and pulled him in for a kiss. "I love you."

"I love you too. Now don't keep me hanging. Will you marry me?"

"Oh, I had forgotten you can't read my mind." She smiled. "The answer is yes."

"Thank God, because I wasn't taking *no* for an answer."

EPILOGUE

"I wasn't sure you would come," Wynter said to Jazz as they sat together on the porch swing at her sister's home a few months later. Sunny lived in a large, rambling oceanfront home on a little island in South Carolina. It turned out it was the perfect place to have a private beach ceremony.

"You asked me. I came," Jazz responded. "You make my friend happy. I owe you for that."

A lot had happened since Cullen had proposed to her. They had left her life in D.C. and they moved to Charleston. She had been open to moving anywhere, but she and Cullen had gone down for a visit to check out the university and he had fallen in love with the city. They had put an offer down on a house before the end of their trip. Wynter had already had a job lined up for her, but it was Cullen who went back to work first. Just part-time, but he was an instructor at a military school there and he loved working with the young men. He had already enrolled in his own college classes. He was happy. Wynter loved seeing him that way.

"You're not mad at me for keeping my identity from you?"

"No. I was miffed that you didn't tell me yourself, but I figured out who you were far before any of the men did."

"You knew?"

"Yes. That day we went for manicures, I saw your last name on your credit card and then it clicked. How many people are named Wynter Bates? I wanted to hate you, but your father was real shitty to you."

"So if my father hadn't been shitty, you would not be here now?"

"I would. I got to know you. You became my friend. I don't have very many of them. I can't afford to lose you."

"Thank you," she said, taking Jazz's hand. "You look very pretty."

She looked down at herself. "This bridesmaid dress is not my style, but it's all right."

"You're supposed to say *thank you* when someone gives you a compliment."

"Thank you. Why did you pick me to be your maid of honor? I was sure once you learned you had a sister that you would forget about me."

"Sunny is very special to me, but she just had a baby and she has three other kids."

"Are you saying you didn't want to burden her with this stupid job?"

"Precisely." She grinned. "Plus, I knew I could count on you to help me to throw together this wedding quickly. You are extremely resourceful."

"But your parents are billionaires. You could have had a huge wedding with a planner and a million guests."

"That's not what we wanted. You know us better. I knew I could trust you to make everything beautiful and you did. You got to work as soon as you landed and you've been a whirlwind ever since."

"I met your birth mother today," she said softly. "She was with your other mother. She was clinging onto her. Do you think she'll be all right?"

"I think so. We've been talking to her about it for two weeks now. That's why we chose to have the ceremony here at Sunny's. It was private enough and it was close enough to fly her home, just in case it's too much. She hasn't left her home in years. This is a lot for her, but I'm happy she's here."

"I'm happy things worked out for you, but

why did you have to throw this wedding together so fast? If you had given me more time, I could have made things even more beautiful."

"Cullen wanted to rush."

"Why?" Jazz looked over at her, puzzled.

Wynter took her hand and placed it on her belly. "You're going to be an aunt in six months."

"What!"

"Hush. You're the only one who knows, besides Cullen."

"Why are you telling me this?"

"Because . . . You're my best friend and I wanted you to know."

Jazz's eyes began to tear. "Thank you. I appreciate that."

"Love?" Cullen walked up to them. He was looking dashing in a blue chambray summer suit. "Everyone's here. And I'm growing impatient to call you my wife."

"I'm ready." She smiled up at him and reached for his hand as she stood.

"Isn't it bad luck for the bride and groom to see each other before the wedding?" Jazz asked.

Cullen laughed. It was hard to think that a year ago she had never heard him do that. She had never seen him smile, but now it was constant. Now she couldn't imagine a life where she didn't get to see his smile every day.

"I don't believe in bad luck, Jazz. How could I? My life has gotten better every day since I met Wyn."

"I feel the same way," Wyn said.

Cullen leaned down to kiss her, setting his hand on her belly. "Let's go, love. I can't wait to start my life with you."

ABOUT THE AUTHOR

Jamie Pope first fell in love with romance at thirteen when her mother placed a novel in her hands. She became addicted to love stories and has been writing them ever since. When she's not writing her next book, you can find her shopping for shoes or binge-watching shows. Visit her website at jamiepopebooks.com, find her on Facebook at www.facebook.com/sugarjamisonbooks, and follow her on Twitter @sugarjamison.

The employees of Thorndike Press hope you have enjoyed this Large Print book. All our Thorndike, Wheeler, and Kennebec Large Print titles are designed for easy reading, and all our books are made to last. Other Thorndike Press Large Print books are available at your library, through selected bookstores, or directly from us.

For information about titles, please call:
    (800) 223-1244

or visit our website at:
    gale.com/thorndike

To share your comments, please write:
    Publisher
    Thorndike Press
    10 Water St., Suite 310
    Waterville, ME 04901